MIST

A local grabbed [...] [...]rom the saddle. Frank ki[...] grab him from the other side and missed, [...] ny's hooves. The citizen yelled in pain and rolled away.

"What the hell's the matter with you people?" Frank yelled as dozens of hands attempted to drag him from the saddle.

There was no answer from the wild-eyed crowd as several men tore the reins from Frank's hand and brought Stormy to a halt. Dog was nowhere to be seen. He had ducked into an alley and disappeared.

Frank was dragged from the saddle and thrown to the ground.

"Somebody get a rope!" a man yelled.

"Yeah!" another hollered. "Hang the murdering scum! It's Val Dooley!"

"I don't care if it's Satan himself!" the sheriff said, pushing his way through the crowd. "He gets a trial." He looked down at Frank. "Get up slow, Dooley. And keep your hand away from your gun."

"I'm not Val Dooley!" Frank said, getting to his feet. "My name is Frank Morgan."

"You're goin' to have to do better than that, Val," Sheriff Davis said. Then he chuckled. "Frank Morgan? That's a good one, Val. You must not have heard the news. Frank Morgan's dead. He was killed last week in a gunfight over in Montana."

"Yeah," a deputy said. "It come over the telegraph wires just hours after it happened. It's true. Move, Val. You got a date with the hangman."

BOOK YOUR PLACE ON OUR WEBSITE AND MAKE THE READING CONNECTION!

We've created a customized website just for our very special readers, where you can get the inside scoop on everything that's going on with Zebra, Pinnacle and Kensington books.

When you come online, you'll have the exciting opportunity to:

- View covers of upcoming books
- Read sample chapters
- Learn about our future publishing schedule (listed by publication month *and author*)
- Find out when your favorite authors will be visiting a city near you
- Search for and order backlist books from our online catalog
- Check out author bios and background information
- Send e-mail to your favorite authors
- Meet the Kensington staff online
- Join us in weekly chats with authors, readers and other guests
- Get writing guidelines
- AND MUCH MORE!

**Visit our website at
http://www.kensingtonbooks.com**

THE LAST GUNFIGHTER #6: IMPOSTER

WILLIAM W. JOHNSTONE

PINNACLE BOOKS
Kensington Publishing Corp.

http://www.kensingtonbooks.com

PINNACLE BOOKS are published by

Kensington Publishing Corp.
850 Third Avenue
New York, NY 10022

All Kensington Titles, Imprints, and Distributed Lines are available at special quantity discounts for bulk purchases for sales promotions, premiums, fund-raising, and educational or institutional use. Special book excerpts or customized printings can also be created to fit specific needs. For details, write or phone the office of the Kensington special sales manager: Kensington Publishing Corp., 850 Third Avenue, New York, NY 10022, attn: Special Sales Department, Phone: 1-800-221-2647.

Pinnacle and the P logo Reg. U.S. Pat. & TM Off.

First Printing: October 2002
10 9 8 7 6 5 4 3 2 1

Printed in the United States of America

ONE

Frank Morgan reined up and called out to the lone figure sitting by the tiny campfire. "I'm friendly! You want some company?"

"Shore. Come on in and pull up a piece of ground and take a load off."

Frank walked Stormy, his big Appaloosa, into the clearing and swung down from the saddle. "That coffee sure smells good."

"Come on over and have a taste," the man said. "I got plenty."

Frank dug his cup from the packsaddle of his packhorse and poured a cup of the hot brew, squatting down by the fire. "Fire feels good too," he said. "It's turned chilly."

"For a fact," the man replied, his eyes narrowing suspiciously as he looked at Frank.

Frank wondered about that, but said nothing.

The man, a miner from the look of his clothing and lace-up boots, inched a bit closer to his shotgun.

"Finding any color around here?" Frank asked.

"Enough to get by." He looked hard at Frank for a few seconds. "Why, you figurin' on robbin' me?"

Frank returned the hard look. "Don't be stupid!" he snapped back at the man. "I'm no thief."

"Since when?" the miner came back at him.

Frank set his cup on the ground. "What the hell are you talking about?"

The miner moved a hand toward his shotgun. Frank leaned over the hat-sized fire and grabbed the scattergun.

"I knowed it!" the miner said. "You're gonna kill me, ain't you, Val?"

"Who the hell is Val?" Frank asked, breaking open the double barrel and tossing the shells to one side.

The miner blinked a couple of times. "You is."

Frank sighed and picked up his cup, taking a swig of the strong brew. Tasted good. "My name is Frank, not Val."

"Says you! I know who you is. You're Val Dooley."

Frank laid the scattergun to one side. "Friend . . . I never heard of anyone called Val Dooley. And personally, I don't give a tinker's damn if you believe that or not."

"Then he's your twin brother!"

"Nope. I don't have a twin brother." Frank took another gulp of coffee and held out the cup. "Fill it up, friend. That's good coffee."

The miner carefully picked up the battered old pot and filled Frank's cup, then his own cup. "Might as well have me one too. Be my last cup on earth. I ain't scared to die, Val."

"Damnit, man, I am not this Val person!"

The miner stared at Frank. "Shore look like him."

"Oh, hell, forget it," Frank said, disgust evident in his voice. "How far to the nearest town? I need supplies."

" 'Bout twenty miles southwest. But you'll get a rope if you go there, Mr. Whoever-in-the Hell-You-Is."

"A rope?"

"Val Dooley is wanted dead or alive, and you is the spittin' image of Val."

"If this Dooley person is so famous, how come I never heard of him?"

"He ain't been outlawin' long. But in the few months he's been rampagin', he's been a rapin' and a-killin' and a-stealin' to beat the band. And that ain't all he's been doin'."

Frank waited, then asked, "Well . . . what else has he been doing?"

"Liftin' the dress tails of a lot of good women. You're . . . I mean, *he's* a mighty handsome man, you is—ah, he is. Women get all flighty and stupid around you . . . *him.* You right shore you ain't Val Dooley?"

"I'm sure."

"I guess you ain't. But if you want some good advice, you'll get back on your horse and head east. Get the hell out of this part of California. 'Cause if you stick around here, you gonna be a shore-'nuff dead man."

"Mister, look hard at me. Think of a gunfighter. A very well-known gunfighter. Now, who am I?"

"Val Dooley. I done told you that 'bout a dozen damn times."

Frank shook his head. "I've got to get to the bottom of this." He drank the rest of his coffee and stood up. "I think I'll head for this town. What's the name of it?"

"Deweyville. The sheriff there is damn mean too. Name's Carl Davis. But you're a damn fool if you don't hightail it out of this state, Mr. Whoever-You-Are."

"I've been called a lot worse than a damn fool. Thanks for the coffee. Hey, how far's the road that'll take me to Deweyville?"

"Couple of miles." He jerked a thumb. "That way."

"Old coot," Frank muttered as he rode away from the miner. "Surely he's not right in the head."

He made camp with about an hour of daylight still left. He hobbled the horses so they could graze, and then fixed food for himself and Dog. While his bacon was sizzling in the pan and his bread baking in the small Dutch oven, he looked over at Dog and said, "If I tell you to get, boy, you get, you hear me?"

Dog looked at him and cocked his head to one side.

"That old rummy back there might have been about half right, and I don't want you to get shot. So if I tell you to get, you run."

Dog growled.

"I'll take that as a yes. You just do as I tell you."

Dog walked closer and licked Frank's hand.

"All right. Good boy."

After his meal, Frank sat by the fire, smoking and drinking coffee and thinking. "Maybe I'll get lucky this time, Dog. Maybe I can find me a little place where folks don't know me and I can buy me a little spread and we can stop this eternal wandering. Would you like that?"

Dog looked at him, unblinking.

Frank laughed. "It doesn't make a damn to you, does it, boy?"

Dog again cocked his head to one side.

Frank patted the animal's big head. "Well, I like to dream about having a place where I can settle down and live in peace. But I know it's just a dream."

Frank Morgan was a gunfighter, but it was a profession he did not choose. When he was in his mid-teens, working on a ranch in Texas, a bully pushed him into a gunfight. It was a fight the boy did not want. But the bully died from the bullet Frank fired into his chest. Frank drifted for a few months, then joined the Confederate army, and at war's end, he was a captain of Rebel cavalry. He headed back west, looking for work; that was when the brothers of the bully who had forced him into a fight caught up with Frank. One by one, they stalked him, forcing him into gunfights. Frank killed them all. His reputation spread.

Frank Morgan was just a shade over six feet tall. He was broad-shouldered and lean-hipped. His hair was dark brown, lightly peppered with gray. His eyes were a pale gray. Women considered him a very handsome man.

He wore a .45 Colt Peacemaker on his right side, low and tied down.

Frank had married once, right after the end of the War of Northern Aggression. That marriage produced a son; a son that Frank knew nothing about for many years. The woman's father had forced Frank to leave, and had had the marriage annulled, not knowing his daughter was with child. The woman, Vivian, had gone back East, married well, and built a new life for herself, becoming very wealthy. Vivian and Frank reunited briefly, Frank learning then he had a grown son. After Vivian's tragic and untimely death, Frank learned she had willed him a portion of her estate, making Frank a moderately wealthy man. But the son never really warmed to his father, and the two went their separate ways, seeing each other only occasionally.

Frank drifted aimlessly, looking for a quiet place where he could build a home and hang up his guns forever. But that was something he knew in his heart he would probably never find.

Frank had earned the nickname the Drifter. He was both feared and hated by many, idolized by some. There had been many newspaper articles written about him—most of them untrue—and a number of books, penny dreadfuls, published, supposedly chronicling his life. There was a stage play touring the country, a play about his exploits . . . most of those exploits pure fiction. Frank had had people who knew him tell him the production was awful.

Frank drifted, trying unsuccessfully to escape his reputation. And now he was in Northern California and had been told he looked just like a local desperado named Val Dooley.

"I'll get this straightened out and be on my way," Frank muttered. "The last thing I want is a bunch of locals taking potshots at me."

At midmorning, Frank rode slowly into the town of Deweyville. People began coming out of stores to line the boardwalks on both sides of the street, to stand silently and stare at him. Frank cut his eyes to Dog, padding along beside his horse. The big cur seemed tense, his ears laid back.

"Steady now, Dog," Frank whispered.

"You got your nerve, Val!" a woman called from the boardwalk.

"Somebody shoot that murderer!" a man yelled.

"Get him!" a man hollered. "Don't let him get away!"

Crowds from both sides of the street rushed toward Frank, yelling and calling him all sorts of names.

"Go, Dog!" Frank yelled. "Go!"

Dog took off running just as Frank put the spurs to Stormy. The big Ap leaped forward, the packhorse trailing at a run.

A local grabbed Frank's leg and tried to pull him from

the saddle. Frank kicked the man off. Another tried to grab him from the other side and missed, falling beneath Stormy's hooves. The citizen yelled in pain and rolled away.

"What the hell's the matter with you people?" Frank yelled as dozens of hands attempted to drag him from the saddle.

There was no answer from the wild-eyed crowd as several men torn the reins from Frank's hands and brought Stormy to a halt. Dog was nowhere to be seen. He had ducked into an alley and disappeared.

Frank was dragged from the saddle and thrown to the ground.

"Somebody get a rope!" a man yelled.

"Yeah!" another hollered. "Hang the murdering scum!"

A pistol boomed and the crowd suddenly fell silent. "That's it!" a man yelled. "I won't tolerate any lynch mob. Back off, all of you. Now, damnit. Get your hands off that man and stand away. Move!"

"But it's Val Dooley, Sheriff Davis!" a woman protested.

"I don't care if it's Satan himself!" the sheriff said, pushing his way through the crowd. "He gets a trial." He looked down at Frank. "Get up slow, Dooley. And keep your hand away from your gun."

"I'm not Val Dooley!" Frank said, getting to his feet. "My name is Frank Morgan."

"Bull!" Sheriff Davis said.

"Frank Morgan?" a women yelled. "The famous gunfighter? In a pig's eye you are. You're Val Dooley and now we've got you!"

"And now we get to see you hang, you murdering scum!" another woman yelled.

"You're goin' to have to do better than that, Val," Sheriff Davis said. Then he chuckled. "Frank Morgan? That's a good one, Val. You must not have heard the news."

"What news?" Frank asked.

"Frank Morgan's dead," the sheriff said. "He was killed last week in a gunfight over in Montana."

"Yeah," a deputy said. "It come over the telegraph wires just hours after it happened. It's true. Move, Val. You got a date with the hangman."

TWO

Frank sat on the narrow bunk in his cell and pondered his situation. He had to conclude it did not look good.

He wondered about Dog, but he did not dare ask about the big cur for fear one of the locals or deputies would find him and shoot him for sport.

The sheriff did tell him he had stabled Stormy and his packhorse. Frank had thanked the lawman for that. The sheriff had given Frank a very odd look.

Frank knew one thing for sure: He had to get out of jail and find this damn outlaw named Val Dooley.

And Frank wondered about this so-called Montana shootout where he had supposedly been killed. Another rumor about him, he thought, shaking his head in disgust. *It never stops; if anything, it's getting worse.*

Frank looked up at the sound of boots in the narrow corridor of the cell block.

Sheriff Davis stepped into view through the heavy bars and stared at Frank for a moment. "What the hell are you up to, Val?" he asked.

"My name is Frank Morgan, Sheriff. How many times do I have to tell you that?"

The sheriff shook his head and sighed. "Frank Morgan is dead, Val. It's been confirmed. Let me show you something." He took a dodger from his pocket and handed it to Frank. "Look at that and then tell me that isn't you."

Frank stared at the wanted poster in disbelief. The face on the dodger was his likeness, no question about it. It was like looking into a mirror. "I read somewhere that everybody on earth has a twin, Sheriff. I guess I've found mine."

"Oh, come on, Val!" the sheriff said, exasperation in his tone. "Give it up, man. You're caught and that's that."

"My name is Frank Morgan."

"Damn!" the sheriff said, then turned around and walked out of the cell block. He slammed the door behind him.

Frank sat down on the bunk and stared at the wall. *Now what?* he pondered. He stood up and hollered, "Hey, Sheriff! Sheriff!"

The door opened and Davis again stepped into the corridor. "Now what, Val?"

"Is there a lawyer in this town?"

"Sure. Charles Carter. Why?"

"I want to see him."

"I'll tell him. But it isn't goin' to do you any good."

"Why not?"

"Because you're goin' to hang, Val. Just as sure as the sun comes up in the east."

"You mean I'm not going to get a trial?"

"Of course you're goin' to get a trial. We're not a bunch

of savages. It'll all be legal and dignified. We'll hang you right after the trial.''

Frank stared at the man for a few seconds. "That's not very comforting. Are you going to get that lawyer for me?"

"Sure. But there's no hurry. Judge won't be through here for a couple of weeks. So just relax, Val. I'll talk to Lawyer Carter in a few days. One of the deputies will see about getting you something to eat in a little while. My sister, Alberta, cooks for the jail. It'll be a good meal. You can count on that."

"Sheriff, I can prove I'm Frank Morgan."

Sheriff Davis smiled. "No, you can't, Val. So stop harping on Frank Morgan, will you? It's gettin' tiresome."

"Not as tiresome as this is getting for me."

The sheriff smiled at him and walked away, out of the cell block area.

Frank cussed under his breath and stepped up on a small stool so he could look out of the barred window. Nothing to see. He carefully inspected the bars. They were set solid. Not a chance he could get out that way.

Frank sat back down on the bunk and looked at the picture of the outlaw, Val Dooley. The resemblance was uncanny. Startling. He could certainly understand why he had been mistaken for the outlaw. *But,* he thought as he folded the wanted dodger and put it in his shirt pocket, *that doesn't help me out of this fix.*

Frank knew one thing for a fact: No one was going to hang him. He certainly didn't relish the thought of killing some innocent person, but he had learned a long time back that if a man didn't look after himself, no one else would.

Frank stretched out on the bunk and went to sleep.

He was awakened by the slamming of the cell block's outer door. He sat on the edge of the bunk and listened to the soft scrape of footsteps. He could tell it wasn't a man.

"Mr. Dooley?" a woman's voice called.

"I'm not Val Dooley," Frank replied. "But everyone around here sure thinks I am."

The woman stepped into view, a tray in her hands. She was just about the homeliest woman Frank had ever seen. She was thin as a rail, her mouse-colored hair was unkempt, there was a big wart on her pointy chin, her long nose and her chin almost met, and if she had taken a bath in the past six months, she had forgotten the soap.

"Don't be silly, Val," she said. "Of course you're Val Dooley. I'd know you anywhere."

"Lady, I never saw you before in my entire life." *And if I had,* Frank thought, *you would have given me nightmares.*

"Oh, you're such a card, you are, Val. Look, I brought you a good supper of fried chicken and mashed potatoes and gravy." She set the tray down on the floor and pushed it under the bars with her foot. "Now, you eat that up."

"Alberta?" Frank asked.

"Silly!" she simpered. "Of course I'm Alberta."

"Ah . . . sure you are. The food looks good."

"I want you to enjoy it, Val. I'll bring you meals every day. I remember how you like your food prepared."

Frank picked up the tray and set it on the bunk. *How do I play this?* he wondered. *Good Lord, this situation is terrible.*

"Val?" the woman whispered softly.

Frank turned to look at her.

"Do you remember the times we used to have when we were children?"

"Ah . . . how could I ever forget them, Alberta?"

"Especially the times we used to go swimming down at the creek. I'll never forget those good times."

"Me either, Alberta. I sure won't."

"Do you ever think about the times we went swimming without clothes?"

Frank stared at the woman. *What a nightmare,* he thought. Then he forced a smile. "Yes, I think about those times often." *This woman just might be my ticket out of this mess,* he thought. *But I've got to play this close to the vest.*

"Me too, Val," she said with a giggle. "Sometimes I get . . . well . . . all gooey just remembering them. Do you?"

"Do I . . . get gooey? Ah, well, I guess you could call it that."

"Alberta?" Sheriff Davis called from outside the cell block. "You all right in there, sis?"

"Of course I'm all right!" she yelled. Frank winced at the sharpness in the woman's voice. "Why wouldn't I be all right, you ninny?"

"Just checking, sis."

"He doesn't understand," Alberta whispered. "He doesn't realize that you would never hurt me, Val. We have too many good memories to share, don't we?"

"We sure do, Alberta."

"Well, I must be going for now, darling. But I'll be back later with a pot of coffee just for you and then we'll talk some more."

"I can hardly wait."

"Ooh . . . me either." She giggled as she walked out of the cell block.

Frank sat down on the bunk. Talking with Alberta had cut his appetite down to nothing. Just thinking about the woman prompted him to think that he might never eat again. Frank sighed and pushed those thoughts away. He had to eat. He picked up a chicken leg and took a bite. It was delicious. The woman might look like something the cat dragged in, but she could cook, no doubt about that.

The sheriff stepped into the corridor, walking up to Frank's cell. He stood silent for a moment.

"Something on your mind?" Frank asked.

"My sister," the sheriff said.

"What about her?"

"I don't want you messin' with her, Val. I know you and her was close when you were kids, but that was a long time ago. So leave her alone."

"Well, Sheriff, just how in the hell do you think I'm going to mess with your sister if I'm locked up in your damn jail?"

"You been warned, Val. Just leave her alone." Sheriff Davis wheeled about and stalked out of the cell block.

"Idiot," Frank muttered as he sat down on his bunk and resumed eating. "Whole damn town is loony as a tree full of monkeys."

Frank ate his fried chicken, potatoes, and bread and drank the single cup of coffee, then stretched out on the bunk. When he awakened, he could tell by the sun it was late afternoon. He longed for a cup of coffee. He called out for Sheriff Davis, but received no response.

"Hey, Val." The voice came from outside the stone jail, drifting in through the single barred window.

Frank stood up on the stool and looked out. A small boy was standing in the alley. "Miss Alberta said to tell you she's takin' care of your dog and that she'd be around about dark to bring you a tray of food."

"Thank her for me, will you, boy? And ask her if she'll bring me a pot of coffee."

"Shore 'nuff, I will. See you, Val."

The boy started to leave, then stopped and looked up at Frank. "The men in the town are talkin' 'bout hangin' you, Val. Sheriff Davis is leavin' tomorrow afternoon for a couple of days. I heard the men sayin' that tomorrow night would be a real good time to come get you and string you up."

Frank had been expecting some talk along those lines. So the news came as no surprise. "Thanks for warning me, boy."

The boy disappeared.

Frank sat back down on the bunk and rolled a cigarette. "Time to start making some plans," Frank muttered. "Before time runs out."

THREE

"Hello, my secret love," Alberta whispered from outside Frank's cell.

Frank suppressed a shudder as he rose from the bunk.

"I brought your evening meal," she said. "Even though I'm not supposed to."

"That's, ah, very nice of you, Alberta."

"It's roast beef, with gravy and potatoes. I know you like that."

"Yes, I sure do," Frank said as she passed the tray to him. "Alberta, where is the sheriff? I need to speak to him."

"Oh, he's out of town for a few days. But Deputy Tucker is in charge. He's sort of new at the job, but my brother has faith in his ability."

"That's, ah, nice, Alberta. I'm sure glad to hear that.

Alberta, can we trust each other? Really, really trust each other?''

"Of course we can," she replied, smiling at him, adding, "darling."

Frank could feel his stomach churn at that, and he almost puked. He fought that back and said, "Alberta . . . ah, dear, I've got to get out of this jail."

"I know, darling. I'll do anything I can to help."

"You will?"

"Certainly. Then we'll be free, and together forever."

Frank thought about that for a few seconds as he stared at the woman. Just for a few seconds, the gallows seemed awfully appealing. "I need a pistol, darling. Preferably my pistol. I give you my word, I won't hurt anyone."

"You promise?"

"Cross my heart and hope to die."

"Spit in your hand to seal the pact."

Good God! Frank thought. Then he spat in his hand. "All right?"

She pulled his Peacemaker out of the folds of her dress and smiled. "This pistol, Val?" she said impishly.

"That's the one." Frank took the .45 and checked the cylinder. Full up. "You get out of here, Alberta. I want you clear when I make my move."

"I brought your horses around a few minutes before I got your food. They're around back. In that stand of trees behind by the creek. Your dog is there too."

"You go back to your house and wait for me. Pack a few things. I'll be over to get you at eight o'clock this evening. All right?"

"Oh, yes. I'll be waiting impatiently for you."

You'll wait a long time, Frank thought. *By eight o'clock, I plan on being about ten miles from this crazy town.*

Frank sat down on the bunk, his Peacemaker beside him.

He wondered for a few seconds if this was all a nightmare, a really bad dream. Was he really asleep back on the trail, and would he wake up in a little while and have a good laugh about it?

"No," he whispered. "I'm not asleep. But it is a nightmare. A real, living nightmare."

And, he silently added, *that noose waiting for me is damn sure real.*

And, he added with a frown, *so is Alberta.*

With that, Frank experienced a slight pang of conscience about the way he was manipulating the woman. He wondered how, once he was free, he could possibly make it up to her.

He shook that away. He would think of something ... once he was out of this lockup and far away from this town.

Frank looked up as Deputy Tucker walked into the cell block. He walked to Frank's cell and stood staring in.

"You want something?" Frank asked.

"The great Val Dooley," the deputy said, a sneering tone to his words. "You don't look so damn tough to me."

"I'm not Val Dooley. I keep telling you people that. My name is Frank Morgan."

"You're a liar. Frank Morgan is dead."

Frank sighed and shook his head. He cut his eyes to the single window of his cell. It was dusk. Time to make a move. He looked back at the deputy. The jail keys were hanging from his belt.

"I'm surprised the sheriff would leave an idiot like you in charge," Frank said. "You don't appear to have sense enough to come in out of the rain."

"What!" Deputy Tucker blurted out. "What the hell did you say?"

"I said you're a fool. You want me to repeat it?"

Deputy Tucker cussed Frank as his face reddened. He

sputtered and spat the obscenities while Frank sat on the bunk and smiled at him.

"Why don't you go somewhere and play with dolls, Tucker," Frank suggested. "You're not man enough to take charge of me."

"I'll stomp you flat, Dooley!" Tucker hollered.

Frank yawned at him. "Not a chance, little boy. Or are you a girl all dressed up in man's clothes?"

Tucker reached for the keys hanging from his belt. "By God, I'll teach you a hard lesson, Dooley. I'll show you a thing or two, I sure will."

Frank showed his contempt by spitting on the floor and then making a very obscene hand gesture toward the deputy.

Deputy Tucker's face flushed even deeper as he jerked the keys from his belt and opened the cell door, stepping inside.

When he drew close, Frank stood up and cringed, "Oh, please don't hurt me, Deputy," he whimpered. "I was only funning with you."

"You yellow skunk!" Deputy Tucker said with a laugh. Then he slapped Frank across the face.

Frank suddenly drove his left hand into the deputy's belly and followed that with a right fist to the man's jaw. Deputy Tucker folded like a house of cards and hit the hard floor, unconscious. Frank quickly handcuffed and gagged the man and shoved him under the bunk. He locked the cell door and pocketed the keys, then walked out of the cell block into the main office.

Frank retrieved his gunbelt and pocket watch, and then locked the front door from the inside and pulled down the blinds. Then he walked out the back door and locked it, using a key he found on the key ring taken from Deputy Tucker.

Frank ambled along nonchalantly, looking like a man just

out for an evening stroll. Stormy, his packhorse, and Dog were waiting for him in the stand of timber by the little creek. Frank petted Dog for a few seconds, then swung into the saddle and lifted the reins.

"Let's get out of here," Frank said. "I think we've overstayed our welcome in this part of California."

Frank headed south for a few miles, then cut due west, riding deeper into the Sierra Nevada range. He had no particular destination in mind . . . just getting away. But he had a plan: He was going to find this damn Val Dooley, hand him over to the authorities, and clear his name. But first he had to contact his attorneys in Denver and establish his own true identity. He could do that with a bank code that only he, his attorney, and the bank knew.

However . . . that would have to be done in a town that was a bit more friendly than Deweyville. Frank had never been that close to a rope before, and didn't ever want to experience that sensation again.

He rode for several hours, rested his horses for a few hours, then headed out again, carefully avoiding roads. A couple of hours before dawn, Frank made a cold camp and slept for a time. He was awakened by Dog's soft growling. Frank opened his eyes as he closed his right hand around the butt of his Peacemaker.

As soon as Dog saw that Frank was awake, he ceased his growling and was silent, lying a few feet away from Frank.

Frank hoped this was not a posse after him; he did not want to kill anyone who was chasing him under the mistaken idea that he was this Val Dooley. But he also knew he was not going to be taken prisoner and face a hangman's rope.

"Ride on, boys," he muttered. "Just ride on and live a long and happy life."

The group of riders drew closer and slowly passed Frank's location in the timber without stopping. Frank breathed a bit easier as he holstered his .45

He longed for a cup of hot, strong coffee but knew that even a small hat-sized fire would be a danger now. He would stop after a few miles on the trail and make some coffee. He saddled up and rode on, constantly keeping a wary eye out for riders. He skirted a small community in a green valley, keeping to the timber. Frank knew he should turn around and head back east, get the hell out of California, but running away had never appealed to him, and damned if he was going to start now.

Frank rode on, heading west. Dog stayed close, never more than a few yards away on either side of the trail. It was as if the big cur sensed his master was in a great deal of danger. And if Frank was in danger, so was he. About midmorning, Frank stopped by a small creek and built a fire, boiling some water for coffee and for a skillet of salt pork. He drank his coffee and ate the last of his bread with the bacon, sopping up the grease with the last chunk. He rested for about an hour, then rode on.

Just as the sun was slowly sliding into afternoon, Frank came to a crossroads and had to make a decision. He was slap out of supplies—everything. He was down to just enough tobacco to maybe very carefully roll a couple of cigarettes. That was it. He had to buy some supplies. He lifted the reins and rode out onto the road, following the westward telegraph wires. He then thought of a plan, realizing immediately it was a chancy one. But if he was going to clear his name, it was a chance he had to take. He came to a road sign: CHANCE, 1 MILE.

"A very fitting name," Frank muttered. "I'm taking a chance with my life." He headed for the town of Chance.

About a quarter of a mile outside of Chance, Frank spotted

a young boy, maybe eight years old, walking along the side of the road. Frank reined up. "Howdy, boy," he greeted the lad.

"Howdy, mister." The boy smiled up at him.

"You know if there is a lawyer in town, son?"

"Sure is, mister. One. My daddy. Lawyer Whitter."

"Well, how about that. You reckon he's in his office?"

"Should be. You want to see him?"

"I sure do. Say . . . is there a bank in Chance?"

"Sure is. Can you give me a ride into town?"

Frank smiled and held out his right hand, and the boy grabbed hold, Frank swinging him up behind him.

"That's a mean-looking dog you have, mister," the boy said, looking down at Dog, who was looking up at him.

"Not really. He's just suspicious of strangers, that's all. You look after him while I see your daddy, all right?"

"He won't bite me?"

"No. Just let him make the first move toward being friends."

As Frank rode into Chance, he attracted little attention at first. Then someone hollered out, "It's Val Dooley! He's got Lawyer Whitter's boy!"

A woman yelled, "Get the marshal! It's Val Dooley!"

"Are you really Val Dooley?" the boy asked.

"No, son. I'm not Val Dooley. I'm Frank Morgan."

"The gunslinger?"

"Yes."

"Creepers! You wouldn't tell me a fib, would you?"

"No, son. I wouldn't. I'm Frank Morgan. Now where is your daddy's office?"

"Right down there on the right," the boy said, pointing. "That's his buggy in front of the office."

A crowd was rapidly gathering on both sides of the street,

the men armed with rifles and shotguns. And it was a very unfriendly crowd.

"Don't shoot yet!" a man called. "You might hit the boy."

"Halt that animal and dismount with your hands in the air," a fat man with a large silver badge pinned to his vest yelled, stepping into the street.

"I'm not Val Dooley," Frank said, walking Stormy past the marshal. "I'm Frank Morgan and I can prove it. Give me a minute or so with Lawyer Whitter and some time at the telegraph office and you'll see I'm telling the truth."

"You're Val Dooley!" the marshal yelled. "I know who you are."

"You're wrong," Frank called over his shoulder as he reined up and he and the young boy dismounted. Frank tied the reins to a hitch rail and stepped up onto the boardwalk, turning to face the marshal and the crowd. "I'm Frank Morgan," he called. "Just give me a few minutes and I'll prove it to you all."

"Frank Morgan!" a citizen yelled. "The gunfighter?"

"Yes," Frank said calmly.

"Thirty years ago, I lived down in Texas with my brother," said the citizen, "That's 'fore I got smartened up and moved out here. You was just a snot-nosed kid then. 'Bout fourteen or fifteen."

"That's right, I was. I was working for the Phillips spread."

"That's right, you sure was. You killed a man and had to take off."

"Yes. His name was Luther Biggs."

"You're Frank Morgan, all right. He's who he says he is, folks," the citizen shouted. "That's Frank Morgan."

"Well, he shore looks like Val Dooley to me," a woman yelled.

"He's Frank Morgan," another man yelled. "Here's a book that'll show his picture. Look at it."

The crowd of locals gathered around the older man and stared at the penny dreadful, passing it around until everyone had an opportunity to look at the picture, then glance up at Frank, standing on the boardwalk, visually comparing the two.

"I reckon you're who you say you are, Frank," the town marshal said, holstering his pistol. "But you and Val Dooley shore resemble."

"What's going on out here?" a man asked, stepping out of the office behind Frank and the boy. "Johnny? What have you been up to now?" he asked the boy.

"Nothing, Pa," the boy replied. "This here is Frank Morgan, the gunslinger." He jerked a thumb toward Frank.

"You look like Val Dooley," the lawyer said, peering closely at Frank. "But I can see a subtle difference."

"Thank you," Frank said. "I'd like to have a few moments of your time, if I may."

"Certainly," Lawyer Whitter said. "Come into my office."

"Johnny," Frank said to the boy, "would you take my horses down to the livery and tell the man to take care of them?"

"Sure will, Mr. Morgan."

"Dog will go with you. Don't worry, he won't bite you."

The boy led the horses away, Dog following, staying a few yards back.

"Just calm down everyone," Lawyer Whitter told the crowd. "This man is not Val Dooley. Although the resemblance is uncanny. Come on into my office, Mr. Morgan. Let's get this mess straightened out."

Frank sighed. "I sure as hell hope we do."

FOUR

"Val Dooley or Frank Morgan," a man yelled. "It don't make a tinker's damn to me. Turn around and face me!"

Frank turned to once again face the crowd of citizens. A young man stepped out of the knot of people. He wore a tied-down pistol, left side. "I'm facing you," Frank said. "What do you want?"

"If you're Dooley, they's reward money for you, dead or alive. If you're Morgan, folks back East will pay to see you dead. Money for me whoever you are."

"But first you have to kill me, boy," Frank quietly reminded him.

"I ain't no boy, damn you!"

"Ed Simpson," the town marshal hollered, shoving his way through the crowd. "You take that gun off and git on back to your daddy's spread, you hear me?"

"Shut up, Tom," the would-be gunhand said. "You bes' carry your fat ass back to your office and stay out of my way."

"Why . . . you young pup!" the marshal said. "You can't talk to me like that." He took a couple of steps toward the young man.

Ed turned to face the marshal, his hand dropping to the butt of his pistol. The marshal stopped, his face flushing with anger. "Back off, Tubby," Ed warned. "This is between me and what's-his-name here."

"Let them have at it, Tom," a citizen told the marshal. "This ain't worth you gettin' shot."

Ed again turned to face Frank, standing patiently on the boardwalk. "How about it, gunfighter?"

"How about what, son?" Frank asked.

"You and me, that's what!"

"I don't have any quarrel with you."

"The hell you say!" Ed almost shouted the words. "I'm callin' you out. Right now. You and me."

"Calling me what, boy?"

A few people in the crowd chuckled at that.

"Don't laugh at me!" Ed yelled, whirling around to face the locals for a few seconds. "Don't you dare laugh at me."

The crowd fell silent.

Ed again faced Frank. "Pull iron, gunfighter!"

"I'd really rather have a good meal and a pot of coffee, boy."

"I ain't no boy, damn you!"

"All right. If you're a man, then act like one."

"What do you mean by that?"

"Let's talk about this. There is no need for gunplay."

"Listen to him, Ed," the marshal urged.

"You shut your fat mouth, Tubby!" Ed yelled.

The marshal shrugged his shoulders. "It's your funeral."

Ed shook his head. "No. No, it ain't my funeral. It's *his* funeral!" He glared at Frank. "You gonna die, gunfighter!"

"We're all going to die, boy," Frank told him. "When the Lord decides to call us home, nothing can change that."

"Amen," a woman spoke softly.

"I'm tired of this," Ed said. "Drag iron, gunfighter."

"I don't think so," Frank said calmly. "It's too pretty a day for a gunfight."

"What?" Ed shouted. "What the hell has the weather got to do with anything?"

"Everything," Frank told him.

"I think you're crazy!" the young man said.

"Could be," Frank agreed. "I've sure been called worse. How about you?"

"How 'bout me what?"

"Are you crazy?"

"Hell, no, I ain't crazy!"

"Are you sure? You seem sort of crazy to me."

"Are you callin' me crazy?"

"Maybe a little."

Many in the still-growing crowd began to smile; still others began to chuckle as they sensed what Frank was doing. Frank Morgan didn't want to shoot the young man; he was turning the townspeople against Ed Simpson. And it was working.

"Aw, go on, Ed," a man hollered. "Get on back home and act your age."

"You shut up, George!" Ed yelled. "This is none of your business."

"And this isn't Dodge City, Kansas," a woman shouted. "We're a law-abiding community here. So just go on home, Ed."

"Not until I do what I come here to do!" Ed yelled. "And I come here to face Frank Morgan and collect the bounty that's on his head. And by God, that's what I aim to do.''

Ed had turned away from Frank as he talked to the crowd. He did not see Frank move swiftly off the boardwalk and come up behind him. He felt someone tap him on the shoulder, and turned around just in time to catch Frank's hard right fist on the side of his jaw. Ed Simpson collapsed onto the dirt of the street, out cold.

Frank reached down, jerked Ed's pistol from leather, and handed it to the marshal. "Keep this, will you, Marshal? Until someone can talk some sense into this boy's head.''

"You could have shot him, Morgan,'' a man stated.

"I didn't want to shoot him,'' Frank replied. "He'll have a headache and a sore jaw when he wakes up, but he'll be alive.''

"And he'll be comin' for you,'' another local said. "He'll be mad as a hornet.''

"He won't come after Morgan if he's in jail,'' the marshal said. "Some of you boys carry him over to the jail, will you? We'll let him cool off in a cell for a few hours. Matthew, will you ride out to the Simpson spread and tell his daddy what happened here? Tell him to come in and fetch his boy.''

"Sure thing, Marshal.''

Ed Simpson was toted off to the jail and the crowd began to drift away. Frank stepped back up on the boardwalk to stand by Lawyer Whitter.

"You saved Ed's life, Mr. Morgan,'' the attorney said. "Most men would have just shot him and been done with it.''

"It would suit me if I never had to shoot another man,'' Frank replied. "Hell, I really didn't want to shoot the first one . . . and that was many years ago. After it was over, I got sick and puked all over the place.''

"Wow!" Johnny Whitter said. He had stopped to watch the action on his way to stable the horses. "Frank Morgan right here in town. I can't hardly believe it. How come you didn't hook and draw and shoot Ed Simpson, Mr. Morgan? I would have liked to seen that."

"No, you wouldn't, Johnny," Frank told him. "There is nothing pleasant about seeing a gunfight."

"I wouldn't know," the boy replied. "I ain't never seen one."

"Ain't?" his father said sharply.

"I mean, I've never seen one," Johnny quickly said.

"That's better, son. Now go tend to Mr. Morgan's horses."

"Yes, sir. I'm going."

Frank smiled. "Good boy there."

"Thanks. But he's a handful, I assure you."

"I 'spect he is." Frank cut his eyes as a woman walked up to stand by Lawyer Whitter. And what a woman! She was surely one of the most beautiful women Frank had ever seen. Blond hair and blue eyes. Frank immediately took off his hat.

"Mr. Morgan," the lawyer said, "this is my wife, Lara. Lara, Frank Morgan."

Lara smiled and held out a hand. Frank gently took the softness in his hard and calloused hand. "A pleasure, Mrs. Whitter."

"Mr. Morgan," Lara said softly. "The famous pistol shooter?"

Frank smiled. "I reckon, ma'am."

"My word!" She fanned herself with a gloved hand. "What in the world brings you to our little town?"

"Just passing through, ma'am."

"Please call me Lara, Mr. Morgan."

"As you wish, Lara."

"May we speak for a moment, John?" Lara asked her husband. "It's rather important."

"Do you mind, Mr. Morgan?" the attorney asked.

"Not at all. Take your time. I'll just sit down out here and have me a smoke."

The lawyer and his wife stepped into the office. Frank sat down on a bench on the boardwalk and rolled a smoke. Before he had finished his cigarette, half a dozen locals appeared, each carrying a penny dreadful, asking that Frank sign their copy.

"Be glad to," Frank told them. "Just don't believe all that's written on the pages. Most of it is nonsense."

"You mean these writers are telling lies about you?" a woman asked.

"Well," Frank said with a smile, "let's just say they're stretching the truth a mite."

"You don't look like a depraved killer," a man stated.

Frank glanced at the man. "What does a depraved killer look like?"

The local grinned sheepishly. "Good point, Mr. Morgan."

Just as the autograph seekers were leaving, the marshal huffed up and sat down on the bench beside Frank. He mopped his sweaty face with a bandanna and said, "You always create this much of a stir when you hit town?"

"Not usually, Marshal. How's the young gunhand?"

"He has a sore jaw and a big mouth. But I keep reminding him that he's still alive. You would have been justified in killing him, Morgan."

"I know. But it all worked out my way."

"Until I turn him loose."

"Maybe he'll cool down by then."

"Where's Lawyer John?"

"With his wife in the office. Beautiful woman, that Lara."

"You'll get no argument from me about that. She's a big-city woman. From somewheres back East."

"She like it out here?"

"Not much," the marshal said. "Place ain't refined enough for her tastes. She told one woman here in town that she missed the opera and the symphony and high-toned e-vents like that. Ballet too, I think she said."

"I guess moving out here would be quite a letdown."

"I reckon. You gonna be in town long, Morgan?"

"Day or two, I reckon. I want to get this mess about who I am straightened out, and get some supplies and a couple of meals I don't have to cook myself. Don't worry, Marshal. I'm not planning on starting any trouble."

"Oh, I wasn't thinkin' you would, Morgan. Nothin' like that."

"What is it, Marshal? Something is gnawing on you."

The marshal sighed. "Val Dooley is in this area, Morgan. I was warned by telegraph 'bout it. He's got him a big gang and the sheriffs all around in a five-county area is sendin' out warnin's 'bout the gang hittin' the towns."

Frank nodded his head in understanding. He waited.

"This is a rich town, Morgan. I mean *rich!* The bank is fairly bulgin' at the seams. I'm tellin' you this 'cause I know now you ain't Val Dooley. I went back to the office and took me a peek at some new dodgers on Dooley. I figure you're maybe five or six years older than Val. But the resemblance is really spooky."

"And you think you night need some help?"

Once again, the marshal sighed. "That's it, Morgan. I ain't no young squirt no more. I took this job 'cause I'm too damn lazy to farm or log." He smiled. "But oddly 'nuff, I've turned into a pretty fair lawman."

"I'm sure you are, Marshal."

"How 'bout it, Morgan. Want to help out an old fat man?"

Frank smiled. "I'll stick around for a time, Marshal. Things might prove real interesting here in Chance."

"Boy, that's a relief to my mind, Morgan."

"Call me Frank, please."

"Frank, it is. I'm Tom." He stood up and stuck out his hand. "I'm right proud you're gonna be helpin' out."

The office door opened and Lara stepped out to stand close to the bench. Frank could smell the heady fragrance of her perfume. He looked up; her blue eyes locked with his. Frank knew right then he was in trouble. Silent messages passed between the gunfighter and the lady. Totally inappropriate missives.

Frank stood up and removed his hat. "Ma'am," he said.

"My husband will see you now, Mr. Morgan," Lara replied.

"Thank you."

Lara glanced at the marshal. "Marshal," she said, acknowledging his presence.

"Mrs. Whitter," Tom said. "You're looking well."

She nodded and stepped closer to Frank. *Any closer,* Frank thought, *and we would be subject to a lot of gossip.*

"Good day, gentlemen," Lara said. She brushed against Frank as she walked away. The scent of her lingered.

"That there is one helluva woman," the marshal said softly. "Too much for any one man to handle."

"You're probably right about that, Tom."

"I been told that she and her husband are havin' a mite of trouble. I also been told that John is a man that's prone to hittin'."

"He hits her?" Frank asked.

"That's the word around town."

"Has she been unfaithful to him?"

"Lara? Oh, no. And believe me, in a town this size, I would know."

"Hard to believe a man would strike something that beautiful."

"He does, though," the marshal said. "Dr. Evans has ... well ..." He paused for a few seconds. "I'm talkin' too much. When you get your business done with John, come see me, Frank."

"I will."

The marshal walked away, and Frank stepped into the lawyer's office. The scent of Lara lingered in the hallway.

It was very disconcerting.

FIVE

John Whitter and Frank went over to the bank, met with the bank president, and began the process of verifying Frank's identity. It didn't take long. By closing time, Frank's bankers in both Denver and San Francisco, and his attorney, working with John Whitter, had established who he was beyond any shadow of a doubt.

Frank walked over to the marshal's office, and Tom smiled when Frank opened the door. "Coffee's hot and fresh," he said. "Cups hanging on hooks on the wall." He pointed. "Help yourself, Frank."

Coffee poured, Frank sat down and rolled a smoke. "I've decided to take you up on your offer, Tom. Who swears me in?"

"I do. Stand up and raise your right hand."

The quick ceremony over, Frank pinned on the star and sat back down to enjoy his coffee and smoke.

"You speak to the town council about this?" Frank asked.

"Yes. While you were meeting at the bank. They were all in favor of it."

"That's very interesting, Tom."

"How so?"

"I'm a gunfighter, Tom. Not exactly what many would consider a model citizen. And I've only been in town a few hours."

"You've worn a badge before," the marshal countered. "Several times. And you've always done right by the job. The mayor says you were pushed into being a gunfighter."

"I had some help, sure. In the beginning. But in the end it was my decision. I've learned to accept that."

Tom drummed his thick fingertips on his desktop as he stared at Frank. "Maybe this will be the town that settles you down."

Frank smiled. "Doubtful."

"You might meet that special lady here. There are some fine-lookin' widder women around here."

Lara suddenly popped into Frank's head. He could smell her perfume. He pushed that image away. *Dangerous,* he thought. *Besides, she's a married woman, and it isn't right to steal another man's wife.* "Maybe so, Tom. But I'm not looking for a marriage partner. Especially a grass widow."

The marshal smiled. "Oh, you'd probably be good with kids."

Frank's only reply to that was a smile. "What shift do you want me to work, Tom?"

"Same as mine," the marshal replied. "We're both on call twenty-four hours a day. But not much happens here in Chance. The occasional drunk, a fight now and then, kids acting up, getting into some harmless mischief."

"Sounds exciting."

"Exciting enough for an old fat man," Tom replied with a laugh, heaving himself out of the chair. "You got a room at the hotel yet?"

"Yes, I'm all set up."

"Well, I'm goin' home then. I live on Walnut Street. Everybody knows where. Just ask. I done give Smart-Aleck Ed his supper. Soon as his pa shows up, you can cut him loose."

"Will do, Tom. See you in the morning."

Tom waved and left the offce. Frank walked into the cell block area to check on Ed Simpson.

"I'm gonna kill you, Morgan!" the young man said as soon as he spotted Frank. "Just as soon as I get out of here."

"Don't be a fool, boy. I don't think that bounty on my head is anything but a rumor. Where would you go to and who would you ask to collect it?"

"I'm still gonna make you pull on me."

"You're gonna have a long wait for that, boy. Why don't you just settle down?"

"I'm faster than you, Morgan. And I'm gonna prove it."

"You want some coffee, Ed?"

"You go to hell, Morgan! I don't want nothin' from you."

"Suit yourself. I didn't want to make any for you anyway." Frank walked into the office, found a ring of keys, and stepped out onto the boardwalk, locking the office door. He walked to the Blue Bird Café and got a plate of scraps for Dog, then strolled down to the livery. He fed Dog, made sure he had a bucket of water, and then walked the main street of town, both sides, greeting people as they passed. Almost all were friendly, some stopping to chat for a moment. A few had disapproval in their eyes as they curtly nodded at Frank's greeting. Frank didn't blame them a bit.

His reputation had labeled him a killer, and he had killed. He had killed a lot of men. But what people, some people, failed to understand was that the men he had killed had been trying to kill *him*.

Frank stopped in every store and introduced himself. Most people seemed genuinely glad to see him, greeting him warmly. Frank bought a sack of tobacco and some rolling papers at O'Malley's General Store and chatted for a few minutes with the owner, Jack O'Malley, and his wife, Ginny. They had moved west right after the War of Northern Aggression and settled there in Chance. They had two kids still living at home, a boy, Jackie, seventeen years old, and a girl, Amy, fifteen. Frank bought some new clothes, and Jack said he'd take them over to the laundry and have them pressed.

Frank walked across the wide street to the barbershop and got a shave and his hair trimmed, arranging for the barber to have a bath ready for him first thing in the morning. Frank then walked across the street to the Blue Bird Café for some supper.

Just as he was finishing his apple pie and coffee, the waitress said, "Eddie Simpson's father is riding in, Mr. Morgan. And he looks angry."

Frank looked out the window into the street as four men came riding in, reining up in front of the marshal's office. The bigger of the four men stepped down and said something to the other men.

"Is that Simpson?" Frank asked the waitress.

"That's Big Ed Simpson," she replied. "Mr. Bull of the Woods himself."

"Sounds like you don't like him," Frank said with a smile.

"I don't. He thinks he's better than everybody else. He's

got money and a big spread and wants to boss everybody in town.''

"One of those types.''

"Yes.''

"He's a big one,'' Frank said, watching Big Ed try the door to the marshal's office, rattling the doorknob impatiently, then turning to his men in frustration.

"He's a bully too,'' the waitress said. "He's almost killed several men with his fists. He's crippled one that I know of.''

"I can see how that might happen. He's sure a bull of a man. How old is he, would you say?''

"Oh, early to mid-fifties, I'd guess.''

"Good with a gun?''

"I don't know about that. I did hear someone say once that they thought he used to be a gunfighter years back. Right after the war, I think it was.''

If he was, it was under a different name, Frank thought. *I never heard of any Ed Simpson. And if he was any good, I would have.*

"You going to go let him in the office, Mr. Morgan?'' the waitress asked.

Frank looked up at her and smiled. "I'll just let him find me. The exercise will do him good. What do you think?''

She returned his smile, then giggled. "I think I like you, Frank Morgan.'' She hottened up his coffee, then walked away, laughing.

Five minutes later, Big Ed Simpson and his men stomped into the café. Big Ed immediately started hollering for service.

"Calm down,'' Frank told him. "The waitress will be out in a minute.''

Four pairs of eyes cut to Frank, sitting alone at a corner

table, his back to a wall. "Who the hell are you to talk to me that way?" Big Ed demanded.

Frank smiled. "Frank Morgan. And who the hell are you to come in here yelling?"

"That's Val Dooley," one of the Simpson hands said.

"No," Big Ed said, staring intently at Frank. "That's Frank Morgan. Man they call the Drifter." His eyes shifted to the star on Frank's chest. "You a lawman now, Morgan?"

"Brand-spanking-new deputy for this town, Simpson. Just sworn in a few hours ago. You have a problem with that?"

"Since when does this town hire gunslingers as the law?" Big Ed asked.

"Oh," Frank said, after taking a sip of coffee, "I reckon they figured if a former hired killer can become a respectable rancher, they could hire me as a deputy."

That remark got to Big Ed. His face flushed a deep red and he balled his big hands into fists. "Who the hell are you talkin' about, Morgan?"

"I'll give you three guesses, Simpson. Now why don't you shut up, sit down, and let me enjoy my coffee in peace? Then we'll go over to the office and get your loudmouthed son out of jail."

Standing by the counter, the waitress smiled at that. The men with Big Ed tensed at Frank's comments. Nobody, but *nobody,* ever spoke to Big Ed in such a manner. Not unless they were looking for a good butt-kicking.

Big Ed stared at Frank for a few seconds, disbelief in his eyes. "What the hell did you just say to me, Drifter?"

Frank repeated it, word for word, speaking slowly and clearly. "You understand that now, Ed?"

"I think I'll just rip that tin star off you and kick your butt!" Ed replied.

"I wouldn't try that, Ed," Frank warned him.

"Oh, I'm not gonna try it, Drifter. I'm gonna do it."

Frank smiled and again took a sip from his coffee. "You must be really anxious to see your loudmouthed son, Ed."

"What do you mean by that?"

"I'm gonna try to explain it real simple, Ed. I want you to understand. If you take a swing at me, you're going to jail. Is that understood?"

Ed smiled and unbuckled his gunbelt, handing his rig to a cowboy. "You're headin' for the graveyard, Drifter. Nobody talks to me like that and lives. I'm gonna beat you to death with my fists. And I'm gonna enjoy doin' it."

"You're going to pay for any damage caused to this café, Simpson. You understand that?"

"The only damage is gonna be to you, Drifter!" Ed took a step toward the table where Frank was sitting.

Frank stood up and unbuckled his gunbelt, placing it on the table. "Then come on, you loudmouthed ape. Let's get this over with."

With a roar of anger and defiance, Big Ed charged Frank. Frank braced himself.

SIX

Big Ed tried to ram Frank with his considerable bulk. Frank stepped out of the way and stuck out a boot, tripping the much bigger man. Big Ed slammed into a wall with enough force to shake the building. Frank was all over him, hitting the man on the kidneys with lefts and rights and just before backing off, slugging the rancher on the side of the head with a fist, connecting directly on the man's ear. The head blow staggered Big Ed and his ear immediately began to swell. Frank backed off a step and waited.

Big Ed cussed Frank and slowly turned around. Frank hit him a straight shot to the nose. Blood and snot flew as Big Ed's nose was flattened all over his face. Before he could even begin to recover, Frank hit him four more times: twice to the face with a left and a right, and twice to the belly. Big Ed backed up against the wall, hurt. Frank kept pressing while he had the fight going his way. He pounded Ed's face with lefts and rights, bloodying the man's mouth and nearly closing one eye. Still the big man would not fall. Ed was tough as an oak tree.

Frank bored in, slamming his fists into the man's belly with sledgehammer blows. Big Ed's one good eye was beginning to glaze over, and Frank was panting from the exertion. Frank stepped back, giving himself just enough room, and swung a right, putting everything he had behind it. The fist connected against the side of Big Ed's jaw. Big Ed slowly sank, sliding down the wall, coming to rest on his butt on the café floor.

"Gawddamn," one of the hands said, his voice low with awe at what he had just witnessed. "Big Ed didn't even hit the man oncet."

Frank picked up his gunbelt and buckled it, tying down the holster. "You boy . . . pick up . . . your boss." He panted the words. "Carry him . . . over to the jail. Move, damnit!"

"You gonna throw Big Ed in jail?" one of the hands asked, a note of incredulousness in his tone.

"I sure am. Now pick him up and carry him over to the jail."

"Big Ed's gonna kill you for sure," another hand said.

"I doubt it," Frank replied, quickly getting his wind back. He motioned for the Simpson hands to pick up Big Ed. When they hesitated, Frank dropped his right hand to the butt of his Peacemaker.

"Whoa!" one of them said, seeing the movement. "Take it easy, Mr. Morgan. We'll carry him across to the jail. Don't do nothing hasty now. Come on, boys. It'll take all three of us to tote Big Ed. Let's get to it."

The three hands managed to get Big Ed Simpson up on

his feet. He was only half conscious and not able to help much, but he did manage to put one boot in front of the other and stagger out onto the boardwalk. Then he fell down and rolled off the high boardwalk, landing half in and half out of a horse trough, taking one of his hands with him.

"Oh, Lord!" the hand hollered. "I done sat down in a pile of horse crap! And it's fresh too."

"Come on, Jimmy," one of the other hands told his partner. "Let's get the boss out of the trough. He's gonna be plenty pissed enough without gettin' half drowned."

The third Simpson hand was trying to get the horse crap off his britches. He succeeded only in spreading it all over him.

"You stink, Pete," Jimmy told the man.

"Yeah," the second hand said. "Git away from us. Go wash, or something'."

"Oh, go to hell, Claude," Pete said.

"What happened?" Big Ed muttered through smashed, swollen, and bloody lips. "Where am I?"

"On your way to jail," Frank told him. "Now shut up and walk."

"What's that smell?" Ed mumbled.

"That's Pete, Boss," Jimmy said. "He sat down in a pile of crap."

"What the hell'd he do that for?" Big Ed asked, looking around him, trying to get his eyes to focus. "Jail! What'd I do?"

"Assaulted a deputy," Frank told him. "Now, move, you big ox."

"Big ox!" the rancher yelled. "You can't talk to me like that."

"I just did," Frank said. "Now move your big butt."

"Get your hands off me!" Ed yelled to his men. He shook

off the hands that were holding him up, and promptly fell down in the street. Big Ed began crawling around in the dirt, trying to get up, mumbling and cussing all the while.

By this time, a large crowd had gathered on both sides of the street, lining the boardwalks. The locals seemed to take a great deal of pleasure in watching Big Ed Simpson get what many felt was his long-overdue comeuppance. Frank would soon learn that Big Ed was not the best-liked person in the area.

"I'll kill you, Morgan," Big Ed mumbled. "No man does this to me and lives."

"What in the hell is going on here!" Marshal Tom Wright hollered, shoving his way through the crowds. "Get out of the way." He stepped into the street and stopped, staring in total disbelief at the sight before him.

"This man assaulted me, Tom," Frank explained. "I subdued him."

"You sure did," Tom agreed, a smile playing on his lips. "Yep, I'd say you done a right good job of subduin' the prisoner."

"Get him on his feet," Frank told the Simpson hands. "And get him over to the jail."

"We'll have to drag him," Pete said.

"Then drag him."

The three cowboys lifted Big Ed to his feet and began dragging the cussing rancher toward the jail.

"I'll fire you all!" Big Ed hollered.

"All right," Jimmy said. "If that's the way you want it." He turned his boss loose, and Claude and Pete did the same.

Big Ed hit the dirt of the street face-first.

"Now that's plumb disgustin'," Marshal Wright observed. "A man of your position eatin' dirt and horse crap."

"Shut up, you big fat tub of lard!" Big Ed mumbled, his face in the dirt.

"Stand aside, people," a local said. "Here comes Doc Evans. Let him through."

"What in the world is going on here?" a man asked, stepping through the crowd. He stopped when he saw Ed Simpson, finally getting to his hands and knees in the dirt. "You testing the soil for something, Ed?"

"Go to hell, Doc!" Big Ed told him.

"All in due time, Ed." Doc Evans looked at Frank. "You would be the famous Mr. Morgan, right?"

"I'm Frank Morgan, yes."

The doctor pointed to Big Ed. "Did you do this to Ed?"

"I sure did."

"Then you are some man, Mr. Morgan. I don't think Ed Simpson has ever been bested in a fistfight. At least, not since I've known him."

"He got lucky," Ed mumbled.

"Somehow, I doubt that, Ed." Doc glanced at Frank. "You object if I get him over to my office and check him, Deputy?"

"Not at all. But if he can't walk, he'll have to crawl. He just fired the three hands who came in with him."

"I was only funnin' with them," Ed muttered. "I didn't mean nothing by it." Big Ed coughed and spat out blood and a piece of a tooth. "I swear I'm gonna get you, Morgan."

"Oh, shut up, Ed," Doc Evans told him. "Take your whipping like a man and forget it. I'm sure you started it."

"I don't take no lip from any man, Doc, you know that," Ed said, struggling to get to his feet. He made it, only to fall down again.

"You men get him up and over to my office," Doc Evans told the three hands. "Go on, hell, he didn't mean it when he fired you."

Pete, Jimmy, and Claude got Big Ed to his feet and half carried, half dragged him out of the street.

Doc Evans walked over to Frank. "Are you hurt?"

"Not a scratch, Doc."

"You *were* lucky, Morgan. I hope you know that. Big Ed is pure hell in a fight."

"He's also overconfident and careless, Doc."

Doc Evans nodded his head. "I sure can't argue that. Morgan, get some hot water and soak your hands for a few minutes. Help keep down the swelling. I'll see you later." The doctor walked off to tend to Big Ed.

Marshal Wright made his way to Frank's side. "What happened, Frank?"

Before Frank could reply, his eyes touched those of Lara Whitter, standing alone on the boardwalk, staring at him. She smiled and turned away.

"Frank?" Tom pressed.

"What? Oh . . ." Frank briefly explained.

"You've made a bad enemy, Frank," the marshal cautioned. "Big Ed will never forget or forgive."

"Where'd he come from, Tom?"

The marshal shrugged his shoulders. "Drove a herd of cattle in here about twenty years ago. Right after the war, I'm told. I wasn't here. I come in in seventy. Why?"

"Just curious."

"There was some talk about him once bein' a gunfighter. You ever heard of him?"

"Not under the name he's now using."

Tom looked at him, questions in his eyes. "You got suspicions, Frank?"

"Not really. But if Big Ed gets up in my face again, there'll probably be a killing. I won't take a lot of crap from his type."

"He's a pushy one, for a fact. Used to gettin' his way.

And he's got some randy ol' boys workin' for him. Real hardcases, I'd say."

"Is he married?"

"To a woman that's just as mean as he is . . . maybe more so. Elsie's her name." Tom shuddered. "Don't nobody like that woman, and I mean *nobody*. She's stuck up and got a dirty mouth on her. Pretty woman, until she opens her mouth."

"Sounds like she and Ed were made for each other."

"I reckon that's one way of lookin' at it."

"I'm going to toss his big butt in jail, Tom."

"Might do him some good. But I doubt it."

"You don't have any objections to my doing that?"

Tom shook his head. "Nope. You're the law. You're wearin' a badge and people have to respect that. If they don't, well, then, we've got a breakdown in the system, don't we?"

"Yes."

"Toss his butt in jail."

"Has he ever bowed up on you, Tom?"

"Once. I told him if he ever done it again, I'd go back to my office, get a Greener, and spread his guts all over the street. He don't like me, I don't like him. But he's polite around me since that happened."

There was some real sand in the fat man's craw, Frank thought. When push came to shove, Tom would stand.

Frank looked around in the waning light of late afternoon. It would be dark soon and he still had not checked out the town's two saloons.

"What's worryin' you, Frank?" Tom asked.

"Nothing, really. Just thinking about the two saloons in town, that's all."

"The Gold Nugget and the Purple Lily. The Lily is the

tough one. Sorry 'bout that, Frank. I should have told you. You kinda got that badge shoved on you real quick.''

"No problem, Tom."

"You want some backup?"

Frank shook his head. "No. I'm just going to walk in, look around, and walk out." He smiled. "I hope."

"Shouldn't be any trouble in the middle of the week. On Friday and Saturday nights it's mostly drunks who act up a little."

"I'll see you in the morning, Tom. Have yourself a nice quiet evening."

"Take care, Frank." The marshal walked slowly away, blending quickly into the gathering dusk of fast-approaching night.

Frank flexed his hands a couple of times. They didn't hurt and did not appear to be stiffening up. A few hours might make a difference, but for now they were all right. He crossed the street and walked down to the Purple Lily Saloon. A piano player was hammering out a fast tune, and there were several tables of cardplayers and a half dozen or so men dressed in rough range clothing standing at the bar.

Frank pushed open the batwings and stepped inside. The piano player spotted him and stopped playing. The men at the bar turned to stare at him. The cardplayers stopped their games and stared.

"Don't let me interrupt, boys," Frank told the group. "I'm just looking around and getting acquainted."

"Don't bother in here, Morgan," a man standing at the bar said. "Don't nobody here want to meet you."

Frank looked at him for a moment, recognition slowly lighting in his eyes. "Hello, Slick. It's been a long time."

"Not long enough, Morgan. I heard you got killed over in Montana. I celebrated that news for two days. Now you come show up and spoil everything."

"Sorry to spoil your celebration, Slick."

"Not as sorry as I am. My shoulder still bothers me where that doc dug out the lead you put in me."

"I had to hurry that shot, Slick. It was my intention to kill you."

Slick turned back to the bar and picked up his drink.

Frank walked to the end of the bar closest to the batwings and signaled to the bartender. "Coffee, please."

"My, my," a man said from a card table. "Ain't he the po-lite one?"

"Hello, Curly," Frank said. "You didn't think I recognized you, did you?"

"Hell with you, Morgan!" Curly replied.

"You're a long way from Wyoming," Frank said.

"Free country."

"Yes, it is. You working around here, Curly?"

"I might be."

"How about you, Slick?"

"I been thinkin' 'bout signin' on with the ES spread."

"Ed Simpson's brand?"

"Yeah. You got a problem with that?"

"You real sure you remember how to rope and brand?"

Slick did not reply, just stared at Frank with open, unbridled hate in his eyes.

The bartender put Frank's cup of coffee on the bar in front of him and then carefully backed away.

The piano player began playing a slow, quiet song.

A bar girl walked up to Frank, her face heavily rouged. "Buy a lady a drink, Deputy?" she asked, her voice whiskey soft.

Frank motioned to the barkeep to pour the woman a drink.

She sipped her drink and whispered, "I'm available for a poke, Deputy."

"I'm sure you are," Frank said coldly. "Now back away and find someone else to proposition."

"Never hurts to ask," she replied, winking at him before picking up her drink and walking away.

"What do you want in here, Morgan?" Curly asked.

"Some friendly conversation maybe," Frank said with a smile.

"You won't find that in here," another voice added.

Frank recognized the voice, and he could feel the hairs on the back of his neck tingle. He turned slowly to look toward the rear of the saloon. Johnny Vargas sat alone at a table, staring at him.

"It's been a while, Johnny," Frank said. "I figured you'd be long dead by now."

"A few have tried, Morgan. They didn't make it."

"Same here, Johnny."

Johnny Vargas was perhaps the most dangerous gunslick in the entire West—incredibly fast. Frank would be the first to admit that Johnny was swifter in pulling iron than he was, but Johnny was not the most accurate shot, oftentimes missing that most important first shot. Frank, on the other hand, almost never missed.

"What brings you to this peaceful town, Johnny?"

"Just passin' through. I been here a few days. I like it. Hell, I might just stick around."

"You do that, Johnny. As long as you obey the law."

"And if I don't?"

"Then you'll have me to deal with."

Johnny laughed at that. "You couldn't beat me on your best day, Drifter."

"Are you that anxious to back up that statement, Johnny?"

Johnny Vargas pushed back his chair and stood up.

Frank stepped away from the bar.

"Oh, hell!" a cowboy said, as the piano player stopped playing and the saloon grew deathly silent.

SEVEN

For several slow heartbeats the two men faced each other in silence. Then Johnny began to smile.

"Something funny, Johnny?" Frank asked.

"You might say that. Killin' a lawdog is somethin' I ain't never done . . . least I ain't never been convicted of doin' so. I ain't gonna start now and spend the rest of my life on the run. So just stand easy and finish your coffee. You ain't gonna make me pull on you." Johnny Vargas slowly held his hands out in front of him and then sat back down in his chair. "I'm done for this time, Morgan."

"Suits me, Johnny." Frank turned back to the bar and picked up his coffee cup . . . with his left hand.

The piano player resumed his playing and the cardplayers turned their attention back to the games.

Frank walked back to Johnny's table and sat down, placing the coffee cup on the table.

"Have a seat, Morgan," Johnny said, a smile playing on his lips.

"Thanks. Believe I will."

"Something on your mind?"

"You."

Johnny cocked an eyebrow in a questioning gesture.

"This saloon is more than half filled with thieves and gunslicks, Johnny."

"I noticed. So?"

"Why?"

Johnny shrugged his shoulders. "That I don't know, Morgan. The word went up and down the line to gather here. That's all I know about it."

"Val Dooley maybe."

"Val Dooley is a piker, Morgan. He's crazy to boot. There ain't nothin' he's doin' that interests me."

"What do you know about him?"

"Why should I tell you, Morgan? Hell, I don't even *like* you."

Frank smiled. "Want me to get up and leave?"

Johnny chuckled. "Naw. I reckon not. What do I know about Dooley? Well, not much, really. He's younger than us. You and him resemble a whole lot. I know he's a woman-abuser. I don't much hold with that."

Like many fast guns, Johnny Vargus operated under an odd moral code: It was perfectly acceptable to kill a man, but against the code to be disrespectful to a good woman.

"What else, Johnny?"

"Nothin,' I reckon. Well . . . nothin' 'ceptin' I don't much like a lot of these men that's come driftin' into town. They're worthless trash."

"Yes. Thieves and murderers."

"And worser, Morgan. A lot worser."

"Johnny, I don't expect you to turn on your friends, but if you hear of anything that these men are up to that turns your stomach, will you let me know?"

Johnny Vargas stared at Frank for a moment, then slowly nodded his head. "I reckon I could do that, Morgan. Yeah, I will."

"Good enough, Johnny. Thanks."

"But I'm still gonna kill you, Morgan. Someday."

"Let me know when you're going to try."

"Oh, you'll know, Morgan."

Frank pushed back his chair and walked away, out of the Purple Lily Saloon. He stood on the boardwalk for a moment, breathing the cool air, then walked across the street to the town's other saloon, the Gold Nugget . . . the Nugget as the locals called it. It was the middle of the week and unlike the Purple Lily, the Nugget was nearly empty. Frank looked in over the batwings, then walked on up the boardwalk. He shook his head as he thought of Johnny Vargas.

"Strange man," Frank muttered.

The town was shutting down for the evening, most of the stores already dark. Only O'Malley's General Store was still open and doing business. Frank stepped inside, bought another sack of tobacco, and looked at the selection of men's clothing for a few minutes. A suit caught his eye and he fingered the material. Nice.

"That's a new style, Mr. Morgan," O'Malley said, walking up behind Frank. "Got that in just the other day from Kansas City. I bet that's your size too."

"It's nice. I'll come in tomorrow and try it on."

"I'll put it up for you."

"Thanks."

Frank stepped back onto the boardwalk and stood in the shadows, watching as several men slowly walked their horses up the street. They stopped in front of the Nugget and dismounted, slowly looking all around them.

They're up to no good, Frank thought. *And judging by their outfits, they aren't working ranch hands.* When the trio stepped up to stand in front of the windows of the saloon, letting the light bathe them, Frank could see the men wore their guns tied down.

"Hired guns," he muttered. "Or outlaws. Going to be interesting here in Chance before long, I'll bet. Real interesting." Frank walked down to Doc Evans's office and opened the door.

"I put Big Ed to sleep with laudanum," the doctor said. "He's got some cracked ribs. Don't worry about him escaping from this office. He'll be out until midmorning. I assure you of that."

"Good enough, Doc. I'll see you in the morning."

Frank went back to the hotel and went to bed.

Frank was up early the next morning, as was his habit. The Blue Bird Café had not yet opened when he walked down to the livery to check on his horses and Dog. He had bought several cans of bully beef and some bread the day before, and he fed Dog some beef and bread and filled up his water bucket. After Dog had eaten, Frank played with him for a time, and then walked up to the Blue Bird Café and had breakfast. He had the waitress fix a breakfast plate, and took the food over to the jail.

"Where's my pa?" Little Ed yelled from his cell.

"At the doctor's office," Frank told him, placing the tray of food in the cell.

"What's he doin' over there when I'm in here?"

"He's resting after getting his butt kicked."

"My pa got his butt kicked? By a horse?"

"No. By me."

"I don't believe that!"

"Believe what you want to believe, boy. But for now, eat your breakfast and shut up."

"I'll kill you, Morgan!"

"I've heard that a few times in my life."

"I mean it!"

"Yeah, yeah!" Frank said, waving off the threat. He walked back into the main office and began making a pot of coffee, leaving Little Ed Simpson yelling and cussing.

Marshal Tom Wright walked in just as the coffee was ready to pour. "Smells good," Tom said, grabbing a cup from a hook on the wall. "I just come from the doc's. Big Ed is sleeping like a baby. Doc said you stopped by."

"Yes. Big Ed's got some stove-up ribs. He'll be out of commission for a time."

"When he gets on his feet, he'll be comin' for you, Frank."

"I'll be here."

"He don't worry you?"

"Not a bit."

Tom sat down at his desk and sipped his coffee, his eyes on Frank.

"Something on your mind, Tom?" Frank asked, pouring a cup of coffee and taking a seat.

"I don't like the idea of all these strangers in town. They look like a rough bunch."

"They are." He told the marshal what Vargas had relayed to him.

"What do you think it is, Frank?"

"I think Val Dooley has put out the word he's hiring guns."

"Then my hunch was right. They're plannin' on hittin' this town."

"That would be my guess."

"Oh, hell!" The marshal heaved himself out of the chair and stalked around the room. "That damn Val Dooley."

"It's a good-sized town, Tom. With lots of capable-appearing men in it. Just pass the word and tell the men to go armed."

Tom shook his head. "Val's not a stupid person, Frank. He wouldn't hit this town head-on. He knows him and his gang would be shot to pieces. No ... he's got something else in mind."

"I can't imagine what."

"Val's sly like a fox, Frank. Not brilliant, just sly. He's got something up his sleeve. Bet on that."

"Then we'll just have to get ready and stay ready. Not every man in town. Just a dozen that you know will stand when it gets rough."

"Good idea." Tom was thoughtful for a moment, then added, "And can keep their mouths shut. I don't want to throw this town into a panic."

"Yes. That too."

Tom finished his coffee as he stood by the front window, gazing out into the broad street. He turned to look at Frank. "You're damn calm about this, Frank."

"Nothing has happened yet. I've been a hunted man, in one way or another, most of my life. I don't panic easily."

"This has been a peaceful town for years, Frank. Very little trouble. The town has a lot of women and kids in it." He paused and shook his head. "I don't want to see any of them get hurt."

"Then we'll just have to make sure that doesn't happen." Frank's thoughts immediately leaped to Lara Whitter. He tried to push them away. He could not. She stayed in his mind, smiling at him.

"You have a funny look on your face, Frank," Tom remarked. "What are you thinking about?"

"This town and the people in it." Not really a lie.

Tom gave him an odd look, then plopped his hat on his head and headed for the door. "I'm goin' to start talkin' to a few people. It's time to get the home militia set up."

"I'll be around," Frank said.

Little Ed Simpson had thrown his breakfast all over his cell and out into the corridor. He sat on his bunk and stared defiantly at Frank.

"Clean it up," Frank told him.

"Go to hell!"

Frank shrugged that off. "Then it can stay there and rot and stink. I don't care."

"Fine with me," Little Ed replied. "My pa's gonna kill you anyways."

"Doubtful, boy. Real doubtful."

"Nobody shoves my pa around and gets away with it."

"I didn't shove him around, boy. I *knocked* him around."

"You say!" Little Ed sneered.

Frank turned away and walked out of the cell block.

"You're a dead man, Morgan!" Little Ed shouted. "I'll spit on your grave!"

Frank closed the door behind him and stepped out onto the boardwalk, looking up and down the street. Foot traffic was picking up in the town, men going to work, women going shopping, kids playing. A peaceful scene in a nice town.

"Morning, Deputy Morgan." The voice came from Frank's left.

He turned to gaze into the blue eyes of Lara Whittier. "Morning, ma'am." Frank took off his hat and stared at her. A vison of loveliness, for sure.

"It's a beautiful morning, isn't it, Deputy?"

"It sure is, ma'am. And would you please call me Frank?"

"Only if you call me Lara."

"That would be my pleasure, Ma' . . . ah, Lara."

"Thank you, Frank."

"How's that boy of yours?"

"Which one?" she asked, her eyes clouding somewhat.

"Beg pardon?"

The clouds drifted away and she smiled. "Forgive me. But sometimes my husband behaves like a little boy." The clouds blew back in, darkening the blue. "A mean, spiteful little boy."

"I'm . . . sorry to hear that."

She lifted a dainty, gloved hand. Unusual gloves, Frank noticed. The fingers were exposed. *Dumb gloves,* Frank thought. *What the hell good are they?*

"Oh, I shouldn't burden you with my problems," she said.

"I don't mind a bit, Lara."

She locked her cool blue eyes onto his pale gray eyes. "You're entirely too easy to talk to, Frank."

Frank smiled. "Big Ed Simpson might not agree with you about that."

She returned his smile. "That man is a pig. I despise him. And his wife is so foul-mouthed, few women in town will have anything to do with her."

"So I heard."

Lara arched an eyebrow. "Oh?"

"Tom told me."

"Tom is a fine man. He's a good marshal. People didn't think so until the day he stood up to Ed Simpson. Feelings changed after that."

"I heard he backed him down."

"He sure did! It was a pleasure to see."

"You saw it?"

"Yes. Much of the town did. It was a sight to behold, and that is a fact. Big Ed facing Marshal Tom with a shotgun in his hands. Ed swore he'd kill him for that. But obviously, that didn't happen."

Frank wondered why Lara Whitter was out walking about so early in the day. And dressed to the nines as well.

Lara swirled her little parasol and looked at Frank. "My husband says you are a vicious killer, Frank. Is he correct in that assumption?"

"I certainly don't think so."

"But you have killed men?"

"Yes. Of course. But they were trying to kill me."

"Umm. Well . . . you were defending yourself then?"

"Yes."

"Were you ever married, Frank?"

"Once. My wife is dead."

"Yes. I read about that in some magazine. Tragic. And you have a son."

"Who doesn't want anything to do with me."

"I read that as well. That's so sad."

Frank shrugged that off. "I don't give it much thought anymore. He's a man grown now. It's his decision to make."

"Umm. Yes. Well . . . would you walk me back to my house, Frank?"

"Of course. It would be my pleasure."

Frank took Lara's arm and they began strolling up the boardwalk. The gunfighter and the lady.

They were greeted by merchants and customers alike as they walked slowly up the town's main street . . . and received many curious looks.

"People are going to talk about this, Lara," Frank cautioned her.

"Let them. I'm used to people talking about me."

"Oh?"

"We'll discuss that some other time."

"As you wish."

"What the hell is that?" a man shouted, pointing down the main street.

Frank and Lara turned to look. Frank sighed.

"Is that a woman riding that mule astride?" Lara asked.

"Yes," Frank replied. "And she's carrying a shotgun."

"She looks like a . . . well . . . a witch."

"Close enough," Frank said. "That's Alberta Davis. From a little town called Deweyville."

"What in the world is she doing here?"

Alberta was drawing closer.

"Looking for Val Dooley, I imagine."

"Why?"

"She's sweet on him."

"Val Dooley is sweet on that . . . pathetic-looking person?" Lara asked. "You can't be serious!"

"No, Lara. *She* is sweet on *him.*"

"How do you know all that?"

"It's a long story, believe me."

Lara stepped closer to him. "You simply must tell me all about it sometime."

Before Frank could reply, Alberta yelled. "I see you, Val Dooley!"

"She thinks I'm Val Dooley," Frank said.

"Oh?"

"Val Dooley, you whoor-chasing no-good!"

"Did that woman just call me a whore?" Lara asked. "The nerve of her! How dare she!"

"I don't believe she was specifically referring to you, Lara."

"I'll give that skinny trollop a piece of my mind!"

Alberta leveled the old repeat shotgun and yelled, "You'll pay for toying with my affections, Val Dooley!"

"I'm not Val Dooley, damnit!" Frank hollered.

"How dare you curse me!" Alberta yelled.

"I believe that woman is going to fire that weapon," Lara said.

"I hope not," Frank replied.

"I waited for you, Val!" Alberta yelled. "I waited and waited and you left me in the lurch, you sorry piece of white trash!"

"Now you hold on, Alberta," Frank yelled. "I tell you I am not Val Dooley. I just look a lot like him."

"Liar, liar, pants on fire!" Alberta hollered. She put her heels to the mule and the mule started running.

"Oh, hell!" Frank said.

Just an instant before the shotgun boomed, Frank grabbed Lara and jumped into the door of the barbershop.

Lara screamed, Alberta cussed, the shotgun boomed, and the barber hollered and hit the floor as the shop window was shattered by buckshot.

EIGHT

Alberta whooped and hollered and put the mule into a run. She galloped past the barbershop and the shotgun boomed again. The buckshot hit the striped barber pole and started it spinning and squeaking.

"What the hell is going on?" the barber yelled from his position on the floor. "Who is that crazy woman?"

"Alberta Davis," Frank told him, speaking from his position on the floor. "Her brother is the sheriff over in Deweyville."

"Woman called me a whore," Lara said, pressing against Frank.

Frank was having a difficult time concentrating with Lara close against him and the scent of her perfume in his head.

"Well, her brother damn sure better come get her before somebody puts some lead in her!" the barber said.

The shotgun boomed again just as Frank was getting to his knees to look out the window. The buckshot tore off the hanging sign in front of the Boots and Saddle Shop and sent the owner scrambling for cover.

"Good Jesus Christ!" the saddle maker hollered. "What's the matter with that woman?"

Marshal Tom Wright came running out of O'Malley's General Store, and Alberta spotted him and swung the shotgun to bear.

"Now you see here, lady!" Tom called from the edge of the boardwalk. "We'll have none of that in this town. I won't tolerate such nonsense. Now, you put down that shotgun and dismount that animal."

Alberta pulled the trigger. The shot whistled past Tom and blew out one of O'Malley's storefront windows.

"Whooo! Whoooo!" Tom did a pretty fair imitation of a train whistle and took off. For a fat man, he could move along very well. Smartly, as the British would say. Tom hauled his butt back into O'Malley's. "You're a menace, woman!" Tom shouted from the doorway.

Alberta said a few very profane words to Tom, about where he could shove his remarks . . . sideways, and then turned her mule toward the barbershop.

"Is that crazy female coming over here?" the barber asked.

"Looks like it," Frank told him.

"Well, do something, Deputy!"

"You want me to shoot her?"

"Well . . . no, not really. But can't you talk to her?"

"I'll try." Frank stood up. "Alberta. It's me, Frank Morgan."

"Liar, liar, pants on fire!" Alberta shrieked. "You're my Val, that's who you are."

"I am not Val Dooley, Alberta," Frank called. "And I can prove it."

"Never! Never! You're my Val, and if I can't have you, no one will." Alberta put her heels to the mule's side and loped away. She was out of sight a moment later.

The people on Main Street who had taken cover when Alberta opened fire slowly made their way out of stores and alleys onto the boardwalk, shaken but unhurt.

Marshal Wright stepped out of O'Malley's and cautiously looked all around him, just as Frank and Lara came out of the barbershop. "Frank, do you know that woman?" Tom called.

"Her brother is the sheriff over at Deweyville," Frank called across the street. "Davis is his name."

Tom nodded his head. "That's Val Dooley's hometown."

Frank turned to Lara. "Are you all right?"

"I'm fine," she replied, brushing at her fashionable dress. Then she smiled. "That was quite an experience, Frank."

"Do you want me to see you home?"

She shook her head. "I've changed my mind. I believe I'll do some shopping. But thank you for saving my life. I'll think of some way to repay you."

"No need for that."

She touched his arm. "Oh, but I insist. I'll give it some thought."

Frank walked her slowly sashay away. Quite a woman, he thought. He pulled his eyes from Lara's retreating figure as Tom stepped up onto the boardwalk.

"I'm going to get a posse together and try to catch that crazy woman, Frank. Take care of things here in town."

"All right, Tom. Be careful. Alberta is . . . unbalanced."

"That ain't exactly the word I'd use, but I reckon it'll do." The marshal walked away, heading for the livery.

Frank walked to the Blue Bird Café for a cup of coffee.

The place was filled with locals and there was no place to sit. He strolled over to the jail, stoked up the stove, and made a pot. While the water was boiling, he checked on Little Ed.

"What the hell was all that shooting?" Little Ed asked.

"A crazy woman. You want a cup of coffee?"

"I want to get out of here!"

"I'll cut you loose as soon as your father shows up and posts bail for both of you."

Little Ed cussed him. "You're a dead man, Morgan. I'm gonna spit on your grave. My pa will kill you for this."

"I'll ask again. Do you want a cup of coffee?"

"Hell with you!"

"Suit yourself."

Frank walked out and closed the door. He had a cup of coffee and a smoke, and then stood by the window and watched as Marshal Wright rode out with the hastily formed posse. He doubted they would find Alberta, for the area around the town was hilly and thickly wooded. Her behavior notwithstanding, Alberta was no fool ... except when it came to Val Dooley, that is. And Frank didn't know what in the world he was going to do about that mix-up.

Frank loafed around the office for an hour, looking at old wanted dodgers, studying the town's list of fines for various offenses, straightening up the place, and drinking coffee.

Then Frank walked over to Doc Evans to check on Big Ed. Doc Evans waved him in and said, "I've got Ed up and walking. He's all yours, if you want him."

"I'll walk him over to the jail and he can pay his fine and get out of this town."

"You've made a really bad enemy, Frank. I hope you know that."

"I've got more enemies than I have friends, Doc. Don't worry about it."

"I watched that shotgun-toting crazy woman on the mule." He smiled. "Friend of yours, Frank?"

Frank returned the smile. "Not hardly. She thinks I'm Val Dooley and she's in love with him."

The doctor frowned. "I can't imagine why. If there ever was a man who needed hanging, it's Val."

"So I'm told. He's done some despicable things, the way I hear it."

"Well . . . raping, looting, killing. Genghis Khan didn't have a thing on Val."

"I've read about that Khan fellow. He was a bad one for a fact."

Doc Evans looked surprised. "You've read about the Mongol conqueror? That's very interesting, Frank. You like to read?"

"Oh, yes. I always carry books with me."

"Interesting," the doctor replied, looking at Frank. "Certainly changes my perception of you, Frank."

"Oh?"

The doctor waved a hand. "It isn't important." He pushed back his swivel office chair. "You ready for Big Ed?"

"Let's do it."

Big Ed was sitting on the side of the bed. He glared at Frank but kept his mouth shut . . . at least for the moment.

Frank waved him to his feet. "Let's go, Ed. You can pay your fine and the one for your boy and be on your way."

"I ain't paying no damn fine, Morgan."

"Then you can post a bond and still be on your way. When the judge gets here, you can settle up with him."

"All right. I can do that." Big Ed got slowly to his feet. "You banged me up pretty good, Morgan. I won't forget it."

"That's up to you."

"We'll even up matters, you can count on that."

"Keep running that mouth, Ed. You're talking yourself right into a jail cell."

Big Ed opened his mouth to speak, and Doc Evans shushed him. "You're only making matters worse, Ed. So shut up, will you?"

Ed gave the doctor a dirty look, but closed his mouth.

"Let's go, Ed," Frank told him.

Ed nodded his head and opened the door, stepping out onto the boardwalk, Frank right behind him.

"How is my boy, Morgan?"

"Just like you, Ed."

"Huh? What'd you mean by that?"

"He's got a big mouth and thinks he's tough."

Ed cussed Frank

"Move!" Frank said.

Frank let Little Ed out of his cell and handed him a mop and a broom. "What the hell's that for?" Little Ed asked.

"For you to clean up the mess you made of your breakfast."

"I ain't mopping no damn floor! Hell with you, Morgan!"

Frank pushed him back into his cell and slammed the barred cell door. "Then you'll stay in there until you decide to clean it up."

"Pa!" Little Ed hollered.

"Clean it up, boy," Big Ed said sourly.

"You mean that, Pa?"

"I said it, didn't I? Now damnit, clean the mess up and let's get out of here."

Frank unlocked the cell door and pointed to a bucket of water in the runaround area. "Get busy, boy."

"I'm gonna get you for this, Morgan!" Little Ed said.

"I keep hearing that. Over and over. Can't you two think of anything else to say?"

Big Ed and Little Ed glowered at him and remained silent.

Frank motioned Big Ed into the office and told him how much the bond would be. The rancher tossed some money on the desk and Frank wrote him out a receipt.

"Are we free to go, *Deputy?*" Big Ed sneered the words at him.

Frank smiled at him. "Any more grease on those words and you'd have to get a bucket for the overflow."

"A lousy damn gunslick totin' a badge," Big Ed said. "I never heard of such."

"*You* were a fast gun, Ed," Frank said softly.

Big Ed clenched his teeth and balled his fists. "Prove it!" he growled.

Frank shrugged his shoulders. "It's nothing to me. As a matter of fact, I envy you for walking away from it. I'm not going to tell anyone."

"You can't prove a damn thing, Morgan. It's dead and buried."

"Good. I'm glad for you. And I mean that."

Big Ed stared at him for a moment; then his expression softened and he sat down in a chair beside the desk. "I got out in time, Morgan." He spoke the words quietly, so his son could not hear. "You never will. It's too late for you."

"I know it."

"Someday somebody will come along that's faster than you, and it'll be over."

"I know that too."

"That someone just might be me."

"I doubt it, Ed."

"Johnny Vargas might be the man."

"He's fast, for a fact."

"I'm ready, Pa," Little Ed shouted from the runaround. "I done cleaned up this crap."

Big Ed stood up. "Come on," he called. Then he looked down at Frank. "You and me, Drifter. We'll meet again."

"Probably. But the next time, only one of us will walk away from it."

Big Ed snorted his contempt and he and his son stalked out the front door.

NINE

Marshal Wright and the posse rode back into town about midafternoon, without Alberta.

"Lost her trail," Tom said, dismounting wearily. "That woman is tricky."

"She is that," Frank agreed. "And crazy as a lizard in a locoweed patch."

"You know her better than me, Frank. Big Ed and son?"

"Paid their bond and gone."

"Big Ed give you any trouble?"

"Just a lot of mouth."

"That's normal for him. But you be careful, Frank. Big Ed is a dangerous man, and you made a fool out of him. He won't forget."

Frank nodded his understanding, and Tom led his tired horse to the livery, leaving Frank standing alone on the boardwalk. *Quite an eventful past few days,* Frank thought as he rolled a cigarette. *From facing a hangman's noose to being a deputy marshal. Life sure takes some strange twists and turns.*

"Deep in thought, Frank?" The woman's voice jarred him out of his musings.

Frank turned around and gazed into the eyes of Lara Whitter. She had changed from the outfit she'd been wearing that morning. Now it was a high-collar, very form-fitting pink dress.

"I reckon I was, Lara. I do that occasionally."

"Care to share your thoughts?"

"They might not be anything suitable for a lady to hear," he replied with a smile.

"Oh, I'm not so prudish, Frank. I don't shock very easily." She smiled at him. "You might find that out someday."

Frank didn't know quite how to respond to that, so he simply returned the smile and remained silent.

"Did Marshal Tom apprehend that dreadful woman?"

"No. And I have a strong suspicion Alberta will be caught only when she wants to be."

"You may be correct in thinking that. I have heard that many deranged people are actually quite sly about certain matters."

Frank nodded his head at that as his eyes locked on to two riders drifting into town. His eyes narrowed as he recognized the pair. Idaho Red Reeves and Jim "King" Burke. A pair of really bad ones. Frank knew they were wanted in several states, but obviously not in California.

"You know those two men, don't you, Frank?" Lara asked as she followed his eyes.

"Yes. Gunslicks, both of them."

"There certainly seems to be quite a number of rowdies gathering in this town."

"Yes, there sure are." Frank watched as the pair of gunhands dismounted. Idaho Red spotted him and said something to King Burke. Together, the men stood by their horses and stared at Frank.

Frank stared back, silent, unblinking, unmoving.

"Are those two ruffians laying down unspoken challenges directed at you, Frank?" Lara asked softly.

"You might say that."

"And you're picking up on that challenge, aren't you?"

"I'm not backing down from it."

"It must be a male sort of thing."

"Oh, it is, Lara."

"Will there be shooting?"

"Not now. But it will come . . . in time."

"Why?"

"Because I'm me."

"Frank . . . that makes absolutely no sense to me."

Frank chuckled. "I'll try to explain it sometime."

"Promise?"

He turned to look at her. Her expression was very serious. "Of course, if it's important to you."

"It is."

Frank did not immediately pursue why his feelings were important to the woman. He thought he knew, and if he was correct in his assumptions, he was, at least so far, an unwilling participant in a very dangerous man-woman game.

"Those men are walking over here, Frank," Lara said.

Idaho Red and King Burke were walking across the street. Frank slipped the hammer thong off his Peacemaker and waited.

Idaho Red caught the movement and said, "Whoa, Morgan! We ain't lookin' for no trouble here. Just some conversation."

"Conversation is free, Red," Frank told him. "What's on your mind?"

"A bath, something to eat, and a bed, for starters," King said.

Frank nodded his head and waited.

"Mighty pretty lady with you, Morgan," Red remarked, his eyes mentally undressing Lara. "Yours?"

"No. Her husband is a local attorney. What are you boys doing here?"

"I don't figure that's any of your affair, Morgan," King said. "Far as I know, it's still a free country."

"I can make it my business."

Red held up a hand. "Easy, Morgan. We're just passin' through."

"Plan on staying long?"

"Maybe. All depends."

"On what?"

Before either of the gunslicks could reply, a drunk staggered out of the Purple Lily and began cussing loudly.

"How vile," a local woman said, stepping up onto the boardwalk. "Deputy, I demand you do something about that miscreant."

"Certainly, ma'am," Frank said, touching the brim of his hat.

Before Frank could make a move toward the drunk, a friend of the man came out and led him back into the saloon.

"Problem solved, ma'am," Frank said with a smile.

The woman gave Frank a dirty look, gave Lara an even dirtier one, harrumphed loudly, and walked on.

"Mrs. Hockstedler," Lara said when the woman had walked beyond earshot. "One of the town's most active busybodies."

"See you around, Morgan," Idaho Red said. He and King

Burke walked back across the street and entered the Purple Lily.

"I think there will soon be talk about us," Frank said.

"There already is," Lara replied. "The town's gossip machine has been very busy."

"I'm sorry about that."

"I'm not," Lara replied. "I'm not a bit sorry." She smiled at him, twirled her little parasol, and strolled on up the boardwalk.

Frank watched her move away, and it was quite a sight. He reluctantly pulled his gaze away from her departing figure and took off his Stetson, scratching his head at her final remark. He concluded that he would never be able to figure out women, and the best thing for him to do would be to stop trying.

Frank walked over to the Purple Lilly and stood at the end of the bar. When he caught the bartender's eyes, he ordered coffee. The bartender very reluctantly poured him a cup and set it down in front of him.

"I hope you won't be staying long, Morgan."

"Are you trying to hurt my feelings?" Frank asked with a smile.

The bartender gave him a dirty look and moved away.

"Morgan!" His name was harshly called out from the rear of the saloon.

Frank slowly turned. A man was standing in the shadows. "Do I know you?"

"Yeah, you do, Morgan. You killed my partner, Bud Jenkins, a few years back. Remember him?"

"As a matter of fact, I do. He was a back-shooting, woman-molesting piece of crap, as I recall."

"Damn you!" the man shouted. "He was my pard."

"He was a sorry piece of trash. What's your name?"

"Lon. Lon Bailey."

"Ah, yes. I remember you. A horse thief and back-shooter. You're wanted for murder in Texas, right?"

"Goddamn you!" Lon yelled.

"What do you want, Bailey?"

"You, Morgan!"

Frank laughed, picked up his mug of coffee with his left hand, and took a sip. "What do you think you're going to do with me, Lon?"

"I'm goin' to kill you."

"Doubtful, Lon. Real doubtful."

"I'm ready to do it, Morgan. How 'bout you?"

"Naw. I think I'll finish my coffee. This is really good coffee. You should try some, Lon. It might calm you down."

"I don't want no damn coffee!"

"That's a shame. I would think you might want to live a bit longer. But"—Frank shrugged his shoulders—"I guess not."

"I ain't gonna die, Morgan!" Lon shouted. "You gonna be the one who dies! And I'm gonna be the one who kills you. What do you think about that?"

"Nothing."

"Nothing?"

"That's what I said, Lon. Is something wrong with your hearing?"

"Huh?"

"Must be," Frank said after taking another sip of coffee.

"There ain't nothin' wrong with my hearin', Morgan!"

"Good, Lon. Not that it matters much to me."

Lon cussed for a moment, then said, "Are you gonna put that damn coffee cup down and face me, Morgan?"

"As soon as I finish it, Lon. Don't be in such a hurry to die."

"I ain't gonna die, Morgan!"

"Are you trying to convince me, or yourself?"

"Huh?"

Frank sighed.

"I don't need no convincin', Morgan," Lon said defiantly. "I'm better than you and I know it."

"A lot of men have said that, Lon. I'm still here. I'd give that a lot of thought if I was you. A lot of thought."

"I don't need to ponder nothin' neither, Morgan. I know what you're doin'. You're tryin' to confuse me, ain't you?"

"I'm trying to save your life."

"Bull!"

With that comment still hanging in the air, Frank set his coffee cup on the bar and turned to face Lon Bailey. "You ready, Lon?" Frank asked softly.

Lon paled and took a step backward. Reality had suddenly slapped him in the face and uncertainty now gripped him in a trembling hand. "I . . . reckon I am, Morgan. Make your play, Drifter."

"This is your show, Lon. You wanted this. Not me. You want a gunfight, you start it."

Those seated close to Lon and those standing close to Frank began edging away, out of the line of fire.

"You killed my pard, Morgan," Lon said.

"So you said."

"He was a friend of mine."

"You said that too."

"I got to even things up for him. I think that's my sworn duty."

"You need to do some more thinking about that, Lon."

"Huh?"

The man is not a mental giant, Frank thought. "Your friend braced me, Lon. I didn't start it."

"You still killed him."

"No doubt about that."

"I reckon I'm ready, Morgan."

"Then drag iron, Lon. Let's get this over with. I'm tired of waiting. I want another cup of that good coffee."

"What you done drunk's gonna be leakin' out of your belly, Morgan!"

Frank waited in silence.

"Pull on me, Morgan!" Lon shouted.

"Sorry, Lon. You wanted this, you start it."

"Damn you, Morgan! You're yellow."

Frank only smiled at that.

"Now, Morgan!" Lon's hand snaked for his six-gun.

TEN

Lon had just cleared leather when Frank's bullet tore into his lower chest. Lon stumbled backward, fell against a table, then slid to the floor. He tried to raise his six-gun, tried to cock it, but could do neither. He seemed to have no strength left in his right arm and hand.

"You bastard!" he weakly cursed Morgan.

"It was your game, Lon," Frank told him. "You wanted to play."

"It wasn't 'posed to be me on the floor, Morgan."

Frank said nothing in reply.

"Damn you!" Lon said as he dropped his pistol.

"There's Doc Evans!" a local called from the batwings. "I'm wavin' him over here."

"Maybe I won't die," Lon said.

"And maybe pigs fly," a hardcase said after looking down at Lon's wound. "You're hard hit, Lon."

"Well, that's a hell of a thing to tell a man, Orvis!"

Orvis Handy, Frank thought. *From down in the Cherokee Strip. I thought he looked familiar.*

"It's the truth, Lonnie," Orvis said.

"Kill Morgan for me, Orvis," Lon said.

"That's a hell of a thing to ask me to do."

Before Lon could reply, Doc Evans pushed his way through the swinging batwings and looked at Frank.

Frank shrugged his shoulders. "No way out of it, Doc. And I did try."

"I'm sure you did, Frank." He walked over to where Lon lay and squatted down, placing his medical bag on the floor.

"Can I have a drink, Doc?" Lon asked. "I feel sorta weak all over more than anything else."

"It won't hurt you," the doctor said. "You're bad hit, mister. I have to tell you that."

"Am I gonna die, Doc?"

"I wouldn't be at all surprised."

"Oh, my Lord!" Lon hollered.

"You want me to call for the preacher, Doc?" the bartender asked.

"Don't ask me," Doc Evans said. "Ask this poor fellow on the floor."

"How about it, Lon? You want a gospel shouter to look on you?"

"Oh, hell, yes, I does!" Lon said.

"Somebody go fetch Preacher Bankson," the bartender called. "You, Ned. You ain't doin' nothin'. Go get him."

"You reckon he'll come into a saloon?"

"Hell, I don't know. Ask him. Go on with you."

The shock of the bullet wound wore off and Lon began

groaning as the sudden pain hit him hard. "Gimme somethin' for the pain, Doc!" he hollered. "I can't stand it."

Frank motioned for the bartender to refill his coffee cup.

"You're a cold one, Morgan," the bartender remarked as he poured the coffee. "I never in my borned days seen anyone so cold."

"What do you want me to do?" Frank asked. "Lead a prayer service?"

The bartender gave him a dirty look and walked away.

Frank sipped his coffee and waited.

"Oh, my!" a man uttered as he entered the saloon. He carried a Bible in one hand. "Lead me to the poor unfortunate wretch so I can pray him into heaven."

"Heaven!" Lon hollered. "Hell with that. I want someone to patch me up. I ain't ready to go to heaven!"

"Here, now," Preacher Bankson said. "Everyone wants to go to heaven."

"But don't nobody want to die," Orvis added.

"I shore as hell don't!" Lon said.

Doc Evans stood up. "I can't do a thing for you," he told the wounded man. "The bullet tore you up real bad. Make your peace with God."

"Oh, Lord!" Lon hollered.

"He hears you, son," Preacher Bankson said, squatting down beside Lon. "I'll pray for you."

"Thank you, Parson," Lon said. "But could you get me some laudanum too?"

Doc Evans dug in his bag and handed Orvis a bottle of painkiller. "Let him sip this. It'll ease the pain some."

Preacher Bankson began praying and Lon took a swig of laudanum. Doc Evans joined Frank at the bar.

"Good coffee, Morgan?"

"It'll do."

Doc Evans motioned for the bartender to bring him a cup.

Coffee poured and sugared, Doc Evans said, "What brought on this shooting, Morgan?"

"Lon did. Too many hired guns in this little town, Doc. Something is definitely in the wind. And it stinks."

"It's a rich town, Morgan. And Val Dooley knows it. I've thought for some time it would be a prize for him."

"Could be. Something is sure building up to pop."

"I'm fadin'!" Lon shouted as another wave of pain hit him hard. "Bury me deep so's the coyotes can't git at me."

Doc Evans glanced over at the dying man. "Your bullet tore up his innards, Morgan. He won't last long."

"He brought this on himself, Doc. I can't work up much sympathy for him."

Marshal Wright walked into the saloon, rubbing his face. He walked over to Frank and Doc Evans. "I was taking a nap before supper," he admitted without a hint of guilt in his voice. "Damn good nap too. What brought all this on, Frank?"

"Lon Bailey wanted to kill me. He didn't make it."

"I can see that," Tom replied. "Why'd he want to kill you?"

"I shot a friend of his a few years back."

Tom looked longingly at the cups of coffee on the bar. "That coffee smells good."

Frank waved at the bartender and he brought the pot and a cup. "Afternoon, Clarence," Tom said to the man as his cup was filled.

"Marshal. Did you just have to hire this man as a deputy?" He cut his eyes to Frank.

"Seemed like a wise thing to do, Clarence. You have a problem with Frank?"

The bartender looked at Frank for a second, then dropped his gaze and mumbled, "I reckon not." He moved away.

"You're not very popular in here, Frank," the marshal said, sugaring his coffee.

"I'm all broken up about that, Tom," Frank replied. "I'll probably go back to the hotel and cry myself to sleep."

"I'm sure," Tom said dryly.

"The angels is a-comin' to carry me home!" Lon yelled.

"That's the spirit, son," Preacher Bankson said.

"That's the laudanum I gave him," Doc Evans said. "He's already drank the whole damn bottle."

"He's bleedin' all over my floor," the bartender said. "Cain't y'all tote him out of here?"

"Oh, shut your blow-hole!" Orvis told him. "Let the man croak in peace."

Clarence shrugged his shoulders and went back to polishing glasses.

"Croak?" Lon asked. "I really am dyin'?"

"Yes," Orvis said. "Can I have your horse, Lonnie?"

"What a terrible thing to ask of a dying man!" Preacher Bankson shouted. "You're a heartless heathen!"

"I ain't neither!" Orvis said. "Lonnie'd want me to have his horse. It's a damn fine horse and I'll take care of it."

"I'd like to have his guns," another man said. "Them's Colts and I could use 'em."

"Another heathen!" Bankson said. "Is there no compassion in any of you?"

"I'll take his boots," yet another gunslick said. "They look like they'd fit me and mine's 'bout all wore out."

"Oh, my Lord, spare me this!" Bankson intoned.

"Does that leave anything for me?" another gun-for-hire asked, walking closer to the dying man.

"Y'all can take anything you want," Lon said, his voice growing weaker. "I shore as hell won't have no use for none of it."

"You're a good man, Lonnie," Orvis said.

"The shame of it all," Bankson said, shaking his head. "Lord, forgive them, for they know not what they do."

"I does too," the gunslick who wanted Lon's Colts protested. "You don't bury a man with his guns. That ain't decent."

"How long is this going to go on?" Marshal Wright asked the doctor.

Doc Evans shook his head and took a sip of coffee. "Might go on for hours. But I rather doubt it."

"My wife's 'bout got supper ready," Tom replied. "Beefsteak and mashed potatoes and gravy. I don't want that to get cold."

"Go on home, Tom," Frank told him. "I'll do the paperwork after Lon expires."

"Thanks, Frank. I'll take you up on that. See you, Doc." Tom swallowed the last of his coffee and walked out of the Purple Lily.

"Git over and do something, Doc," Lon said. "You can beat back these angels, can't you? I don't want to die."

"You should have thought about that before you braced Frank Morgan," Doc Evans replied. "There is nothing I can do for you now."

"Oh, Lord!" Lon said. "Them angels is gettin' closer."

"I wish they'd hurry up," Clarence muttered. "This is bad for business."

"And you called me cold?" Frank questioned the barkeep.

"Well, I didn't kill him, Morgan. You did!"

"Them's dark angels," Lon hollered. "I don't like them angels. I don't think thems angels a-tall."

"Fight the demons, boy!" Preacher Bankson thundered. "Fight them. The devil's sent his minions to get you! I'm praying for you . . ." He looked down at Lon. "What's your name anyway?"

"Lon Bailey."

"Thank you."

"The devil's done sent his what?" Orvis asked.

"Don't interrupt me whilst I'm talking to the Lord."

"Excuse me," Orvis said.

"That's all right. You get down here on your knees beside me and start praying, you heathen. Your soul is in danger too."

"You mean them dark minnows is comin' after me too?"

"Minions, not minnows! Yes. That's a possibility."

"Oh, Lord!" Orvis hollered, and fell down to his knees. "Save me!"

"Beg for forgiveness, you heathen!" Bankson yelled. "Your soul is in dire need of spiritual help."

"Don't I know it," Orvis said.

"I thought this was *my* death," Lon said. "Who the hell invited Orvis?"

"Will you hurry up and die!" a gunhand said. "I want to try out them Colts."

"Good Lord!" Doc Evans mumbled. "I don't believe I'm hearing this."

"Wahooo!" Lon yelled. "I'm cold. Them dark things is puttin' their icy hands on me. I'm a-feared!"

"Don't be afraid, Don . . ."

"Lon."

"Whatever. I'm with you all the way."

"Are you gonna die with him?" Orvis asked.

"Don't be an idiot!" Bankson snapped. "I am with him in spirit. You too."

"I don't know about that. I ain't ready to go."

"Them dark things is gettin' closer!" Lon yelled. "I'm freezin', I tell you. And I cain't hep it, I'm a-feared."

"Do you believe in whatever Bailey is seeing, Frank?" Doc Evans asked.

"He's sure seeing and feeling something."

"Hang on, Von!" Bankson hollered.

"Lon."

"I knew that. Hang on, Lon. The Lord is with you."

"How come I cain't see him?" Lon questioned.

"That's not his style."

"Oh, Jesus!" Lon screamed.

"That's the ticket, boy!" Bankson said.

Lon drummed his boot heels on the floor and stiffened.

"Good God!" Orvis said, jumping to his feet. "I'm freezin'."

"It did get about ten degrees cooler in here," Doc Evans said. "I sure felt it."

"Drink some coffee," Frank suggested.

"I thank he's done passed away," a gunslick said, peering over the preacher's shoulder.

Doc Evans moved quickly to Lon's side and tried for a pulse. He could find none. He sighed and stood up. "Better get hold of Pennybaker. Tell him we've got a body for him."

"I got first dibs on Lon's boots!" a gunslick said.

ELEVEN

After Lon's body was carried off to the undertaker's, the patrons in the Purple Lilly quickly settled down, returning to their drinking and gambling. Frank stepped outside for a breath of fresh air, away from the ever-lingering smell of stale cigar and cigarette smoke and cheap beer and whiskey. He decided to stroll down to the livery to check on Stormy and feed Dog. After doing that, he returned to the office and prepared to shut it down for the evening.

When he stepped into the office, there was a sealed envelope on the floor; someone had shoved it under the front door. Frank sat down at the desk, tore open the envelope, and read the brief message: *Frank, please meet me behind the church at six.* It was signed, *Lara*.

Frank looked at the note, suspicion in his eyes. He really wanted no part of some illicit affair with a married woman, no matter how beautiful the lady might be. It was emotionally and physically dangerous, for if the husband found out and put a bullet in Frank, the townspeople would have no pity for Frank, figuring he got only what he deserved for messing around with a married woman.

But deep down, Frank knew he would meet the woman, for the physical pull of the blue-eyed Lara was strong.

He glanced at the wall clock. Five o'clock. He leaned back in the chair and rolled himself a smoke. "I ought to saddle up and get the hell out of here," he muttered. "Leave this mess behind me."

But he knew he wouldn't do that.

"And I certainly shouldn't meet Lara."

But he knew he would.

A few minutes before six, Frank was waiting behind the church, located just off Main Street. The church was surrounded by trees, and it was a beautiful, quite serene setting. Frank felt guilty just being there.

"Hello, Frank," Lara said, stepping out from the back door of the church.

Frank removed his hat. "Lara. This is dangerous, you know."

"I know. But this is a very isolated spot and we aren't likely to be seen here. Besides, what difference does it make if we are seen? We aren't doing anything. Just talking."

Frank said nothing.

"I want you to take me away from here, Frank."

"I beg your pardon?"

"Blunt, aren't I?" she asked with a smile.

"I would certainly say so. You're married, Lara. I can't just ride out of town with you. Husbands have been known to object to that sort of thing. Usually violently."

"My husband is only violent toward women, Frank."

"He hits you?"

"He beats me. Sometimes with his fists, sometimes with a belt. He beats me into submission."

Frank did not ask into submission to *what*.

"Why don't you leave him, Lara?"

"He won't let me. He threatens me every time I bring it up. I finally stopped doing that. Let me show you something, Frank."

Before Frank could say a word, Lara was opening the front of her dress. She was amply endowed and the sight was very disconcerting to Frank . . . to say the least. There was a large bruise on her neck and bruises on her arms, both old and new. There was no doubt she had been beaten and probably choked.

"All right, Lara," Frank said. "Button up your dress."

"You doubt me now?"

"I never doubted you, Lara. I just don't know how to help you. Does he hit the boy?"

"Occasionally. Even though I know he loves Johnny. But I'm very tired of him hitting me."

"Move out and get a room in the hotel."

"I have no funds to do that, Frank. John controls the purse strings in our . . . home." She said *home* with a bitter note in her voice.

Frank was thoughtful for a few seconds, then said, "I have an idea, Lara. If you're willing."

"I'll do almost anything to get away from him."

"Let's go see Doc Evans."

"What good would that do?"

"It would get another person on your side. A person whose word carries a lot of weight in this town."

"I . . ." She hesitated. "All right, Frank. I'm willing."

Frank took her arm. "Come on. I'll walk you to the doctor's office."

"People will see us."

"You care?"

She smiled. "No. I really don't. Not at this point in my life."

The gunfighter and the lady walked out of the grove of trees at the rear of the church and strolled up to the boardwalk on the main street of town. There were only a few people on the street, and they all stopped what they were doing to stand and stare at the unlikely couple. Frank opened the door to Doctor Evans's office and they stepped in. The door to the examining room was open and Doc Evans looked up from his desk, surprise on his face.

"Frank, Mrs. Whitter. Is something the matter?"

"There sure is, Doc," Frank said. "Lara needs to talk to you."

"She has a medical problem and she came to you with it?"

"She has a problem, for sure. I'll just step out of here for a moment and she can show you, Doc."

"She showed you?" Doc Evans asked. "If she's already shown you, why are you stepping outside?"

"Doc . . ."

Doc Evans held up a hand. "All right, Frank. All right. Have it your way."

"I'll be outside having a smoke."

Five minutes later, just as Frank was stubbing out his cigarette, Doc Evans stepped out of his office. His hands were clenched into fists and his face was tight with barely controlled rage. "I need a drink," he said, anger thickening his voice. "But it will have to wait. I saw what John Whitter did to Lara."

"Fine man, isn't he?"

"The bastard needs to be horsewhipped."

"I will certainly go along with that. Did she tell you what she wants to do?"

"Leave him? Yes. Where do you come into this . . . mess?"

"I'll put her in the hotel. I'll pick up the tab for it. I can afford it."

"I'm sure of that. She needs clothing and other women's things."

"Then we'll go to her house and get them."

"Now?"

"Yes."

"The town's wagging tongues will love this."

"Hell with them."

Doc Evans stood beside Frank for a moment, neither man speaking. The doctor finally broke the silence. "You want me to go with you, Frank?"

"I would appreciate it. That would sure still a lot of the town's gossips."

"All right. Let me get my coat."

At the Whitter house, at the end of a quiet street, the trio halted. Lara said, "I saw the curtains move. John always sits by the front window. He knows we're out here."

"You want to wait until he steps out onto the porch?" Frank asked.

"No. Because he won't. He'll wait to see if you and Dr. Evans go away."

"Then he suspects you've told someone about his beating you?" Doc Evans asked.

"Probably. I wasn't home to fix his supper, so he knows something is wrong. I'm sure he was all set to beat me for not being home when he got here."

Doc Evans muttered some very uncomplimentary things under his breath about men who beat women.

"He wants his supper on the table when he gets home," Lara continued. "And he gets upset when it isn't."

"Your boy?" Doc Evans asked.

"He asked my permission to spend the night with the Carter boy. I told him he could. But if he didn't get out of the house before John got home . . ." She shrugged. "He's probably in the house."

"I hate that," Frank said.

"He's seen his father beat me before," Lara admitted. "I'm afraid he thinks that's what all men do."

"I hate that even worse," Doc Evans said. "For what you said, Lara, is probably true concerning the boy."

"Let's do it," Frank said, stepping ahead of Lara and the doctor and walking up to the porch. He knocked on the front door.

John Whitter jerked opened the door and stepped out onto the porch, his face dark with anger. He glared at his wife. "What is the meaning of this, Lara?"

"I'm come to get some clothes, John. Kindly step out of the way and let me pass, please."

"Some clothes? What on earth are you talking about?"

"I'm moving into the hotel for a time, John."

"The devil you are! I forbid it!"

"You have nothing to say about it." Lara stood her ground. "I'm leaving you. Now be a gentleman about this matter and get out of the way."

"*Leaving me?* You're leaving *me?*"

"Yes."

"That is absurd, Lara. Have you taken leave of your senses? What on earth brought all this on?"

"You've beaten me for the last time, John," Lara stated quietly but firmly.

"Beaten you? You're accusing me of *beating* you?" The lawyer laughed at that. "I have never beaten you."

"Then explain the bruises on her shoulders, arms, back, and stomach, John," Doc Evans said. "And the marks on her neck and throat."

"Why . . ." The lawyer flushed, deepening the red already on his face. "She's a very clumsy person, Doctor. She falls a lot."

"John," Lara said. "You'll have to do better than that. People in this town have seen me dance at social functions. They know I am anything but clumsy."

"Damn you!" John Whitter yelled. "You've been sleeping around with some lowlife!"

"I have not, John. I have never been unfaithful to you."

There was a note to her voice that convinced both Frank and the doctor that she was telling the truth, and the gossips in the town be damned with their wagging tongues.

"You whore!" John shouted, and lunged at Lara, his right hand balled into a fist.

Frank stepped between them and shoved John back into the house. John stumbled and landed on his butt in the foyer.

"Damn you, Morgan!" John shouted. "Are you sleeping with my whore of a wife?"

"I'm not sleeping with your wife, John, and your wife is not a whore."

"I say she is!"

"Then you're wrong, John Whitter. In addition to being a wife-beater."

"If I have struck her, rarely at best, she provoked me."

"I'm sure she did, John," Frank said very dryly. "You're about a foot taller and a hundred pounds heavier than your wife, and yet *she* provoked *you.*"

"What damn business is this of yours, gunfighter?" John yelled.

"She came to me, asking for help."

"And what favors did she bestow upon you for your help?" the lawyer asked, using a very sneering tone as he rose from the floor with as much dignity as he could.

"You're about to let your butt overload your mouth, Whitter," Frank warned the man.

"Get out!" Whitter screamed. "Doctor, Morgan, you both get out of my house. You, Lara, you stay. Get in here and forget all this foolishness."

"I want my clothes, John," Lara told her husband. "Kindly step out of the way."

"You go to hell!" John yelled at her.

"Where is Johnny?" Lara asked.

"Spending the night at the Carters'. Thank God he isn't here to witness this."

"I will certainly agree with you about that. Now, get out of my way, John."

"No!"

"Step out of the way, John," Doc Evans told the man. "It's a free country and Lara has the right to come and go as she pleases. Either step out of the way or I'll ask Deputy Morgan to forcibly remove you."

John struggled with his emotions for a few seconds, his face clearly mirroring his inner fight. Then he waved a hand. "Oh, go get your things. I'm glad to be rid of you." He stepped out of the way.

Lara looked at Frank and the doctor. "Will you help me with my trunks? And how will I get them to the hotel?"

"Certainly, Lara," Doc Evans said. "Frank, will you arrange for a buggy?"

"Right now." Frank stepped out of the house and pushed through the crowd of neighbors that had gathered in the street in front of the Whitter house. He walked to the livery and hitched up a team, then went to the hotel and arranged for a room for Lara. The desk clerk looked at him with a number of questions in his eyes. Frank ignored the look and drove to the Whitter house. The crowd of neighbors had increased.

"What's going on here, Deputy?" a woman asked.

"Mrs. Whitter is taking a short vacation. That's all."

"You mean she's leaving that bastard?" a man asked. "Good for her. She should have done that a long time ago."

"Now, Cecil," the woman beside him cautioned.

Frank ignored the couple and walked on into the house. A pile of luggage was stacked by the front door, and he began loading the trunks onto the buggy.

"You'll be sorry you had a hand in this, gunfighter," John told him as Frank once more entered the house. "I have friends in very high places."

"I'm sure you do," Frank replied. "Now get the hell out of the way."

"No!" John yelled, and took a wild swing at Frank.

Frank sidestepped, and John lost his balance and went stumbling out onto the porch, almost knocking down Doc Evans.

"Good God!" the doctor yelled as John went rolling off the porch, to land in a sprawl of arms and legs on the front yard.

Several neighbors standing outside the white picket fence started applauding at the sight.

"Goddamn you all!" John hollered, sitting on his butt on the ground. "Goddamn you all to hell!"

"Pitiful," Frank said, picking up a trunk. "Just plain pitiful."

TWELVE

It was well after dark when Frank stepped out of the hotel and rolled a smoke. He had gotten Lara settled in and all her luggage toted up to her room. John had cussed and threatened while they were at the Whitter house, but had not thrown any more punches at Frank. The lawyer was still cussing and yelling as they drove away in the buggy.

Frank walked over to the café for supper, then lingered over a last cup of coffee while the waitress fixed a bag of scraps for Dog. With Dog fed and Stormy looked after, Frank went back to the office, sitting down at the desk, wondering if anything else was going to happen this day.

"Lord, I hope not," he muttered.

No sooner had the words left his mouth than he heard a shot, then another. Frank took a Greener from the gun rack, stuck a handful of shells into his jacket pocket, checked to see if the double-barreled sawed-off was loaded, and stepped outside.

"It come from down that alley 'crost the street, Deputy," a local told him, pointing.

"Obliged," Frank said, and stepped off the boardwalk.

"I seen some Simpson hands ride into town a few minutes ago," the local called.

"Thanks," Frank called over his shoulder, and walked on into the night.

When Frank approached the dark mouth of the alley, he moved swiftly and unexpectedly to his right, quickly stepping out of any line of fire. It was a good move, for the night was suddenly alive with gunfire, all of it coming from the darkness of the alley.

Frank dived behind a water trough as other guns in the darkness of the alley joined in the barrage, the lead whining all around him. Frank rolled away from the trough and crawled under the raised boardwalk, crawling as fast as he could to his right, all the while staying under the protection of the boardwalk. The boardwalk narrowed down to the point where he could no longer stay under it. He rolled out just as a man stepped out of the alley, both hands filled with six-guns.

Frank cut loose with both barrels, the buckshot catching the gunman in the belly, lifting him off his feet, and flinging him backward, almost torn in half.

"Good God!" a man in the alley yelled as the wall of the building was splattered with blood.

"I'm gone!" another gunslick said.

"You wait just a damn minute, Shorty!" another man said. "You ain't goin' nowheres. You know what the boss said."

"Hell with you and the boss!" Shorty said. "I ain't goin' up against no Greener at close range. Look what happened to Carl layin' over yonder. He's blowed nearly in two. I think I'm gonna puke."

"Well, don't puke on me."

"Shut up, both of you," a third voice was added. "Shorty, you and Ned circle around the buildin' and see if you can get a shot at Morgan. Move!"

"What the hell are *you* gonna be doin', Cal?" The question was thrown out of the darkness.

"Holdin' down this position," Cal said, his voice calm. "Now you and Ned move out and let's settle this mess."

Frank crawled to the edge of the building and looked into the darkness, waiting for someone to show himself in the narrow space between the two businesses. The locals had quickly vacated the street after the first few shots. The boardwalk on both sides of the street was empty of foot traffic.

Someone kicked a tin can at the rear of the building and cussed. Frank waited, the Greener cocked and ready.

"Damnit, Ned." Frank heard the hoarse whisper. "Watch where you stick your big feet, will you?"

Ned cussed his friend. Then . . . silence.

Frank caught movement from the mouth of the alley and flattened out on the dirt, trying to see under the boardwalk. He caught a glint of light off a spur and pulled the Greener to his shoulder. Another flash of light off the spur and Frank pulled the trigger. The sawed-off roared in the night, the muzzle blast kicking up dust in the confined space under the boardwalk. The dust was enough to severely limit Frank's vision for a few seconds and cause him to cough.

Cal screamed as his body jerked on the ground in the alley. "My foot!" he yelled. "The bastard blowed my foot off. Oh, God, it hurts. Kill him for me, boys. Kill that damn Drifter. Oh, Christ, I can't stand the pain.''

"Where's your foot, Cal?'' Ned hollered.

"Blowed off, you idiot!'' Cal hollered, his voice tight with pain. "I ain't got no foot no more. Kill that bastard for me. Kill him, I say.''

"I will, Cal,'' Shorty yelled. "Right now!'' Shorty came running through the night.

Frank turned and leveled the Greener under the boardwalk. He saw the glint of light off of spurs and squeezed the trigger. Again the sawed-off roared, and Shorty was suddenly facedown on the littered ground, screaming out in pain.

"I'm gone,'' Ned said. "Hell with this.''

"Don't leave me, you yeller coyote!'' Shorty hollered. "You got to hep me. My leg is all tore up. I cain't git up.''

"Hell with you,'' Ned called. "I'm gone.''

"I'll kill you, Ned!'' Cal yelled. "I'll skin you alive, you yeller bastard!''

"Hell with you too,'' Ned yelled.

"Frank!'' Doc Evans yelled from the darkness of an office window. "Are you all right?''

"I'm all right, Doc,'' Frank called. "But I've got two wounded here.''

"Hep us, Doc!'' Shorty yelled. "We give up. My legs is tore up and Cal ain't got no foot. Hep us.''

"Throw your guns out, boys,'' Frank called as he reloaded the Greener. "Do it right now. Doc? Stay where you are until I get this area safe.''

Two six-shooters were tossed out from the darkness. "We ain't gonna cause no more trouble,'' Cal said. "We just want some hep.''

Several locals carrying lanterns walked up, casting light on the blood-soaked ground. Marshal Wright strolled up, carrying a shotgun. He stood in the street as Doc Evans appeared on the scene, carrying his medical bag.

"Look at me first, Doc," Cal called, his voice weak. "I'm bleedin' bad."

Frank gathered up the weapons and put them in a gunnysack provided by Jack O'Malley from his general store.

"Some of you men carry the wounded over to my office," Doc Evans said. "I'm going to have to do some sawing on this man's leg. The bone's sticking out."

"Oh, Lord!" Cal hollered. "Get me some whiskey for the pain."

"You know these men, Tom?" Frank asked the marshal.

"They work for Big Ed," Tom replied tightly. "Some of the gunhands he's hired over the past few months." He pointed to what was left of Carl in the alley. "He come in here from Arizona, I think." Tom looked around him. "You men over there!" he shouted. "Get some shovels and bags. Help Pennybaker gather up what's left of Carl. Toss some dirt over the blood." He looked back at Frank. "Big Ed will deny any part in this, you know that, don't you?"

Frank nodded his head. "Sure."

"Soon as he's on his feet, Big Ed will come lookin' for you, Frank."

"I'm not hard to find."

"Want some help makin' out the reports on this?"

"No. I'll go do it now. Go on back home and relax."

The marshal thanked Frank and began slowly walking back to his house. Before he could go half a block, four men rode in, walking their horses slowly up the street. Marshal Wright stopped and walked back to Frank. "Trouble, Frank?" he asked.

"Might be. That's Sheriff Davis from Deweyville. One of the men I recognize as his deputy. He's the one I smacked on the jaw getting away. Deputy Tucker. I don't know the others.''

Sheriff Davis rode up to Frank and Marshal Wright. Without dismounting, he said, "I'm lookin' for my sister. You seen her?"

"Get off that horse before I jerk you off and stomp your butt!" Frank told him.

"We all make mistakes, Morgan," Davis said. "I made a mistake in thinkin' you were Val Dooley."

"When did you change your mind?"

"The day you busted out I got word that Dooley had robbed a bank fifty miles north of my town. You couldn't hardly be in two places at once. Sorry about the trouble." Sheriff Davis swung from the saddle.

"All right." Frank told him about Alberta riding into town and shooting up the place.

Davis sighed. "My sister is"—he sighed—"not quite right in the head, Morgan."

"You'll certainly get no arguments from me about that," Frank replied.

Sheriff Davis looked uncomfortable for a few seconds, then said, "Anyway, no hard feelings, Morgan. I am glad to see you're totin' that badge. You've had more than a peck of trouble here, I see."

"A mite, for sure. Big Ed Simpson's boys. Ed and me had a ruckus a couple of days ago. He came out on the losing end."

"I've heard of Ed Simpson. Thinks he's the he-bull around these parts, don't he?"

"That's him."

Sheriff Davis took Frank away from the crowd of locals and said, "I think Big Ed used to be a hired gun. That's the word I get."

"I heard the same. But he must have changed his name. I never heard of any gunslick named Ed Simpson."

Davis nodded his head in agreement. "Morgan, do you have any idea where my sister is hiding?"

"No. She got away from the posse. She needs help, Davis."

"I know. But getting any sort of real help is damn near impossible. The doctors I've taken her to all want to put her in some sort of asylum."

Flank offered no reply to that, but silently thought that the idea had some real merit. "If she comes into town again shooting up the place, someone is likely to put lead in her."

"I understand."

"But I'll do my best to keep that from happening, Davis."

"Thanks, Morgan. She's ... well, she's my sister, you know."

"Yes. That's a nice hotel over yonder." He pointed. "You boys look like you could use some rest."

"For a fact. We've been pushing it hard. We'll go get rooms and I'll see you later."

Watching the sheriff walk away, Frank thought: *Davis might turn out to be a decent sort after all.*

"Cal just died," Doc Evans said, walking up to Frank. "Shock, loss of blood."

"How's the other one?"

"He'll probably live. But I'm not giving any guarantees about that. A shotgun is a nasty weapon."

"It does the trick, for a fact."

Doc Evans cut his eyes upward, toward the hotel. "Mrs. Whitter is watching you, Frank. Not us, *you.*"

Frank turned and looked at the second floor of the hotel. Lara was standing at the window, looking at him. She lifted a hand in greeting, and Frank returned the gesture.

"You two have something going on between you, Frank?" the doctor asked.

"Not yet," Frank answered truthfully. "But there is sure something in the air that keeps circling around us."

"So I noticed," the doctor replied dryly.

"I haven't done anything to encourage it, Doc." He hesitated. "At least not much."

"Uh-huh," the doctor replied dubiously.

"I swear to you, Doc."

"Okay, Frank. Whatever. Let me go see about the one who lived through this shootout. Talk to you later."

As Doc Evans walked away, Johnny Vargas walked up to Frank. "I see your luck's still holding, Drifter."

"Looks that way, Johnny."

"Carl and Ned was riding pards, Drifter. Ned will get his nerve back and come looking for you."

"Not if he's smart."

"I never said he was smart."

"I'll be here for him, if that's the way he wants it."

"So will I, Drifter."

"What's that mean, Johnny?"

The gunslinger shrugged his shoulders. "Just that, Drifter. It might be a good show and I wouldn't want to miss it."

Frank looked at him and said nothing.

"See you around, Drifter," Johnny said with a smile. He lifted a hand and turned away, walking back to the saloon.

Frank stood in the street for a few moments, watching as a group of locals gathered up bits and pieces of Carl and then scrubbed down the side of the building and shoveled dirt over the blood spots.

"Hell of a way to die," one said.

"Name me a good way," another challenged.

The locals walked away, and Frank turned to go back to

the office. He looked up at Lara's room in the hotel. She was still standing there, staring at him.

Frank lifted a hand in greeting and turned away. He was getting himself into a real bad situation, and he realized it.

Trouble was, he was sort of looking forward to it.

THIRTEEN

After Frank had breakfast, he took a sack of scraps down to the livery for Dog and filled up the big cur's water bucket.

"You're getting fat, boy," Frank said, smiling at the animal as he ate. "All this inactivity is making you lazy."

Dog looked at him for a few seconds, then resumed his eating. After taking a long lap at the water bucket, Dog lay down in the stall and promptly went to sleep.

Frank stepped out into the growing light of early morning and looked around. Both saloons were still closed; the swampers had not yet arrived for work. He walked to the office and unlocked the door. Frank built a fire in the potbelly, put on water to boil for coffee, then sat down at the desk and began writing up the report about the shooting of the previous night. That done, he fixed a cup of coffee, rolled a smoke, and sat back down behind the desk. Lara

Whitter came sashaying into his thoughts, all bright and blond and smiling . . . very inviting.

Frank quickly got up, deciding to take a stroll around town. He wasn't going to sit in the office and entertain thoughts about Lara . . . as pleasing as they were.

He had walked only a few steps from the office when Doc Evans hailed him from across the street. Frank waited for the town's doctor to join him.

"Had breakfast yet, Frank?"

" 'Bout a hour ago, Doc. How's the patient?"

"He'll live. But he'll probably have a limp for the rest of his life. The buckshot broke his leg in several places."

Frank said nothing. He wasn't exactly overcome with grief concerning the health of the man who'd tried to kill him.

"Seen Mrs. Whitter this morning?" the doctor asked.

"No. She's probably still asleep."

"The town is, as the saying goes, buzzing with gossip about you and Lara."

"Let them buzz. There is nothing going on with us."

"Yet."

Frank smiled at that. The doctor was a very astute man. "If you say so, Doc."

Doc Evans took his arm. "Come on. I'll buy you a cup of coffee."

Seated at the Blue Bird Café, the doctor said, "John Whitter came to see me last evening. He admitted to striking Lara, but says he loves her and wants my help in persuading her to come back home. He thinks they can work it out."

"And?"

"I told him to forget it. Personally, and I'm not telling you anything I didn't tell him, I think the beatings have been going on since the beginning and he's not going to change."

"What was his reply to that?"

"He didn't deny it."

"How could he? Some of the bruises we both saw were days or even weeks old. Bruises on top of bruises. The son of a . . ." Frank bit the last word back.

Doc Evans smiled at the expression on Frank's face and the heat in his voice. "And there is no attraction between the two of you at all . . . right?"

Frank sipped his coffee and said nothing.

Doc's breakfast platter came, and Frank ordered more coffee while the doctor ate. The place was filling up with hungry locals, and both the cook and the waitress were busy. Frank received a few curious looks and a lot of greetings of "How do" and "Good mornin'." It was while he was drinking coffee that something he had *not* noticed at the livery finally dawned on him: The stable was practically empty of horses. All the hired guns that had been drifting into town were gone.

Frank set his coffee mug down on the table hard and Doc Evans looked up. "What is it, Frank?"

Frank told him.

"Good riddance," the doc said.

"Maybe not for long."

"What do you mean?"

"They might be gathering somewhere to plan out a raid."

"Against this town?"

"Yes."

Doc Evans laid down his knife and fork. "I don't like the sound of that, Frank. Not one little bit."

"Marshal Tom and I discussed it. I told you, didn't I?"

"If you did, I forgot."

"So much has happened the past few days, I probably forgot to mention it." He told the doctor about Tom organizing the town's men in case they were needed.

"Good idea. And did he?" Doc Evans asked, buttering a biscuit.

"He said they were ready to go."

"There are some good men in this town. And they won't hesitate to protect what they've worked for."

Frank waited until the waitress had hottened his coffee and moved away. "I wonder if Ed Simpson is involved in this."

Doc Evans quickly shook his head. "No. I'd bet my poke on that. Why would he steal his own money? He's a major depositor in our bank."

"That answers my question then. How about the new hands he's hired? Many of them are hardcases. Why did he do that?"

"That is something I can't answer, unless . . ." Doc Evans paused.

"What is it, Doc?"

"A rumor, Frank. Just a rumor, that's all."

"About what?"

"Big Ed wanting to take over this entire area. That's a rumor that's been floating around for about a year."

"What would he do with it, Doc? From what I've seen, much of this area is not suitable for running cattle."

"I understand he wants the area that is suitable."

"Same old story, Doc. Greed."

"That's about it, Frank. Ed has more money than he could spend now. But he's a man who is power-hungry. He wants to be king and everyone else to be his serfs."

Frank smiled at that. "From what I've seen of the people in this town, I don't think Ed will get his wish."

"Oh, he won't try to gain control of the town. But he has tried to run off some of the small farmers."

"Tried or succeeded?"

"He's intimidated a few of them. They pulled out."

"The rest of them?"

"They've resisted . . . so far."

"Big Ed Simpson, King of the County," Frank said with a smile. "Has quite a ring to it, doesn't it?"

"It's nauseating . . . don't even think it. Oh, something else you need to know about, since you have no interest in Lara Simpson . . ." The doctor paused to chuckle.

"Very funny, Doc. See me laughing? What is it I need to know?"

"Big Ed Simpson wants Lara Whitter."

"He *wants* her?"

"Yes, he . . . ah . . . well, lusts for her. You get the picture now?"

"I get it. Talk about laughable. Beauty and the Beast."

Doc Evans almost choked on his sip of coffee. He coughed for a moment, then said, "That, Frank, is a very apt description. Yes indeed."

"Does Lara know about Ed's, ah, lusting after her?"

"Oh, yes. He acts like a lovesick boy whenever he gets around her. Or, as Marshal Tom put it, like a lost calf in a hailstorm."

Frank got a laugh out of that. "That must be a sight to see. Not that I care to see it. What about Ed's wife?"

"Elsie? That foul-mouthed female scorpion. She doesn't care. She has her own lovers. Doesn't bother to hide it from Ed. He doesn't care. Hell, he whores around. I don't think they've slept in the same room for fifteen years . . . or longer."

"What a wonderful couple."

"Oh, yes. The picture of marital bliss." Doc cut his eyes to the street. "Here comes Mrs. Whitter now. My, my, doesn't she look nice this morning?"

Frank looked. "Yes, she does. But then, I've never seen her when she didn't look nice."

"I do believe she's coming in here, Frank. Yes, she is." As soon as the door opened, Doc Evans waved Lara over to their table, and Frank held the chair for her.

"Good morning, gentlemen," Lara said. "I hope I'm not disturbing you."

"Not at all, Lara," Doc Evans assured her. "Would you care for some breakfast?"

"Yes. I am hungry."

The waitress was hailed and poured Lara some coffee, then left to put in her order. Doc stood up. "I must go and see to my patient. Nice to see you, Lara. Frank will sit with you during breakfast, won't you, Frank?" The doctor's eyes twinkled with mischief.

"Ah . . . sure. Of course. See you, Doc." As soon as the doctor had left the café, Frank leaned close and said in low tones, "This will really get tongues wagging, Lara."

"I don't care. Do you, Frank?"

"No. Not a bit, Lara."

"Good. Pass the cream pitcher, please."

For a lady her size, Lara had a hearty appetite. She cleaned her plate and the waitress filled her coffee cup. Frank asked, "So what do you have to do today, Lara?"

"Avoid my husband mostly," she said with a smile. "But I do want to see Johnny and try to explain to him what happened."

"He's seen your husband strike you?"

"Many times."

"I hate to hear that."

"He tried to come to my defense several times, and John knocked him to the floor. Not even Dr. Evans knows that."

"Then I suggest you tell him."

"All right. I will."

Frank fiddled with his coffee cup for a few seconds.

"What's the matter, Frank?"

He looked up, meeting her eyes. "Lara, are you aware about Ed Simpson's feelings toward you?"

She grimaced. "Oh, God, yes! That man is a pig! He's getting bolder and bolder every time I let him get near me . . . which isn't often. He scares me, Frank. I'm afraid he's going to do something really rash."

"Like what, Lara?"

"Oh, I don't know. Kidnap me, or something equally awful." She smiled and shook her head. "I'm being silly and I know it. But he really frightens me."

"More than your husband?"

"Much more. John is out of my life now, and I intend to keep him out. I shall file for a divorce as soon as possible."

"Is there another attorney in town?"

"No. But I can go over to another town and file. Perhaps you could escort me, Frank. Would you do that?"

"Sure. If you don't mind getting the town's gossips really going."

"I don't care. A lot of them already think of me as a scarlet woman."

"I'm sure they're wrong."

"Are you, Frank?"

"Yes."

"You've known me only a few days, Frank. Which means you don't know me at all. How can you be so sure?"

"I trust my instincts."

"And what do your instincts tell you about . . . well, us?" Her eyes were unblinking as they met his.

"I honestly don't know how to answer that, Lara. Not yet."

"You'll tell me when you have a clear answer?"

"Oh, yes, Lara. You may be assured of that."

She dabbed at her lips with a napkin and reached for her purse.

"Your meals are on me, Lara. I've arranged for the waitress to put them on my tab. She likes you a lot."

"Clemmie is a nice person. We've been friends since the first day I arrived in town."

"Morgan!" The shout came from the street. *"Morgan! Get out here."*

"Who is that?" Lara asked, looking at the man standing in the middle of Main Street.

"I don't know," Frank said. "Never saw him before."

"I know you're in there, Morgan," the man yelled. "Come out here and face me."

Frank pushed back his chair and stood up. "I'd better go see what he wants, as if I didn't know."

"What do you mean?" Lara asked.

"He's a gunslick. Or he thinks he is. He wants a reputation, or he thinks he does."

"I don't understand, Frank."

"He wants to kill me."

Every man in the café was silent, listening to Frank, watching him, wondering what Frank would do.

Frank turned to the café patrons. "Anybody know that fellow?"

"I never saw him before, Mr. Morgan," the waitress, Clemmie, said. "He's not from around here."

"Stay inside, Lara," Frank said. "This won't take long."

Before Lara could respond, Frank was walking out the door. He walked to the edge of the boardwalk and looked out at the man standing in the street. Mid-twenties, Frank figured. Tied-down gun. Looking for trouble.

"I'm Morgan," Frank said. "What do you want?"

"You!" the young man yelled.

"Why?"

"To kill you!"

Frank shook his head at that. "I don't know you, boy. Why do you want to kill me?"

" 'Cause you're Frank Morgan, that's why."

"You have something against my name, boy?"

That seemed to confuse the young man. He frowned for a few seconds. "You know what I mean, Morgan."

"I really don't, boy. Perhaps you might explain it."

"I heard from the stage driver you was here in town. I come lookin' for you. Does that make it clear?"

"No."

"Well, what the hell else do you want me to say?" the young man hollered. "Damn, are you dumb or somethin'?"

"I'm a deputy marshal, boy. Not an outlaw. Even if you did succeed in killing me—which you won't do, I can assure you of that—it would only bring you grief. Why don't you get back on your horse and ride out of here?"

"Step out into the street, Morgan!"

"I don't have the time nor the inclination to mess around with you, boy. Now, go away and leave me alone."

"Why would killin' you bring me grief, Morgan?" Before Frank could reply, the would-be gunhawk said, "I think it would bring me lots of fame and glory. That's what I think. And women too."

Frank laughed at him.

"Don't you laugh at me, Morgan. Don't you do it. I won't stand for that. No, sir, I won't tolerate none of that."

"Well, now, boy, I sure wouldn't want to do anything to make you angry."

"Are you funnin' with me, Morgan?"

"You might call it that."

A crowd had gathered on both sides of the street, staying well out of the line of fire if gunplay should occur.

"I'm ready to kill you, Morgan!"

"What's your name, boy?"

"Ben Hampton. Why?"

"As I have said so many times, Ben, to so many men just like you, a man should have his headstone marked."

"Huh? The headstone is gonna have *your* name on it, Morgan. And I'm gonna have the fame and glory of bein' the man who killed Frank Morgan." He paused for a second or two. "What happened to them other men you just mentioned?"

"They're dead, Ben," Frank said softly.

"Well, you ain't gonna kill me, Morgan. I'm sure of that."

Frank said nothing in reply.

"Is there a newspaper in this town, Morgan?"

"A small weekly, yes."

"I want this wrote up so everybody can read about it."

"I'm sure it will be, Ben."

"You ready, Morgan?"

"No. But it's your play, Ben."

"Now!" the young man shouted, and reached for his six-gun.

FOURTEEN

Just as Ben's hand curled around the butt of his pistol, Frank's .45 boomed. The slug slammed into the young man's right shoulder and he staggered back. He stumbled and fell to the street, landing on his butt. He had pulled his six-gun from leather on the way down. The pistol cracked and Ben shot himself in the right foot, blowing off several toes.

"Oh, God!" he hollered, dropping his pistol to the dirt of the street. "I done shot myself! Oh, Lord. I blowed my own foot off!" He reached for his six-gun again just as Frank approached and kicked the pistol away, out of Ben's reach.

"You've had enough, boy," Frank told him.

Ben fell over in the dirt and cussed.

Sheriff Davis and his deputies had walked out of the hotel to stand on the boardwalk and witness the entire affair.

Doc Evans came out of his office, carrying his medical bag. He walked out into the street. The doctor knelt down beside the wounded young man, took one look, and called to a group of men standing on the boardwalk in front of the Bluebird Café. "Some of you boys carry this man over to my office, please. Hurry. He's bleeding badly."

"I ain't got no foot, Doc!" Ben cried.

"Oh, your foot's still there," Doc Evans told him. "But you're going to be minus several toes, for sure."

"I'm a cripple!" Ben hollered.

"But you're alive, son," Doc Evans said. "That's more than most men who braced Frank Morgan can say."

"It's all your fault," Ben yelled, looking at Frank. "You're the cause of this."

Frank said nothing. He ejected the empty brass and slipped in a fresh round.

"Odd way to look at it, boy," Doc Evans said. "You braced Frank and he tried to talk you out of it."

Ben yelled in pain as the men picked him up and toted him away to the doctor's office. "Take him to the examining room," Doc Evans said. "And pull what's left of that boot off his foot, please."

"This is gonna hurt somethin' awful, ain't it, Doc?" Ben yelled.

"It isn't going to be a lot of fun."

"Oh, God!" Ben moaned.

"That was good shooting, Frank," Doc said. "You could have killed him."

"I didn't want to kill him, Doc."

The doctor nodded his understanding. "Well, let me go wash up. I've got some cutting and sawing to do."

"Sounds like a wonderful way to start the day."

"This is a cakewalk compared to my time in the Army during the Civil War."

"I imagine so."

"Did you see a lot of action, Frank?"

"I was at Gettysburg and Antietam, to name only a couple of battles."

"Enough said. See you, Frank."

Frank turned just as Sheriff Davis walked out to meet him. "We'll be heading out after breakfast, Frank. My men are provisioning up now."

"Good luck in finding your sister, Sheriff."

Sheriff Davis nodded and turned away, then paused and looked back at Frank. "I think you're the fastest gunhand I've ever seen, Frank. And I've seen some of the best. Did you deliberately place that shoulder shot?"

"Yes."

Davis arched an eyebrow. "Incredible shooting." He touched the brim of his hat. "See you in a few days."

"Luck to you, Sheriff."

Frank walked back to the Blue Bird Café. Lara was waiting on the boardwalk. "Are you all right?"

"I'm fine."

"You might have been hurt."

"I wasn't."

"He could have killed you!"

"He didn't."

She stamped her foot. "Frank, are you always this matter-of-fact after a life-and-death situation?"

"Lara, I've been in a hundred gunfights over the years." Probably more than that, he thought. A lot more. "I haven't come out of all of them unscathed. But I'm still alive."

"Unscathed," she whispered. "Frank, you don't talk like a gunfighter."

"How does a gunfighter speak, Lara? I've known gun-slicks who were illiterate, and I've known some who were educated men. John Holliday, for one. He was called Doc.

Then were was Cold Chuck Johnny, Black Jack Bill, Dynamite Sam, Dark Alley Jim, Six-Toed Pete. There are dozens of gunfighters still around, Lara. Some can't read or write. Others have fine educations.''

"And the young man who confronted you just a few minutes ago?"

"I don't know, Lara. I never saw him before today."

"Yet he wanted to kill you. Why?"

"For a reputation, Lara. He wanted to be known as the man who killed Frank Morgan."

Both of them watched as a local shoveled dirt over the bloodstains in the street.

"I would love to go back East, Frank. Back to civilization. Would you like to go back East?"

"Not particularly, Lara. I'm a Western man. Born and bred out here. I would be as out of place in the East as a fish out of water."

"You could change your life."

Frank shook his head. "No, I couldn't. But don't think I haven't thought about it. I have. I'm a known gunfighter, Lara. The genteel folks would look at me like a scientist looks at a bug. I wouldn't feel right without a gun. Folks don't carry guns in the East. Not legally anyway. You've got uniformed police officers on every corner in New York City, but yet from what I read, New York City still has lots of crime. I think every place that has disarmed the citizens has seen a rise in crime. That's not for me. I don't want to be dependent on someone to protect me—because they usually don't. I can protect myself."

"You might change your mind, Frank."

"Don't count on it."

Lara smiled and stepped off the boardwalk, heading back to the hotel.

Frank went to the livery and saddled Stormy. He swung

into the saddle. "Come on, Dog. You need some exercise. Let's hit the trail for an hour or so."

On the way out of town, Frank saw Marshal Wright walking toward the café. "I'm going for a ride, Tom. I'll be back in a couple of hours. Unless I come up on something I think I need to check out."

"Be careful, Frank. The Simpson spread damn near circles the town. Get on that range and you'll be a target."

"I'll keep that in mind."

Tom didn't know it, but Frank had carefully studied maps of the country around the town and knew very well the boundaries of the Simpson range. He would avoid the Simpson range if possible, but if he needed to cross any part of that range, he would do so, and if Big Ed Simpson didn't like it, he could go to hell.

Another reason for Frank's wanting to get out of town for a time was that he needed to be alone to think. About Lara. She was in his thoughts much of the time and that bothered Frank. He didn't need a woman in his life at this time. Didn't want a woman in his life.

So what should he do about Lara?

Frank immediately pushed Lara out of his mind as he spotted the approach of several riders, heading straight toward him. He reined up and waited, his right hand near the butt of his Peacemaker.

Frank had seen the men in town and had had them pointed out to him. Three Simpson hands, and Frank sensed them to be primed and cocked for trouble.

"Morning, boys," Frank said, greeting the trio.

"Morgan," one of the men said. "You're a little out of your territory, ain't you?"

"What do you mean?"

"You ain't got no authority outside of town," another said.

"Wrong," Frank replied. "Since the county sheriff's office is a hard two-day ride from town, Marshal Tom is a county deputy, and so am I."

"Well, that don't spell horse crap to us," the third one said. "What are you doin' out here?"

"What I'm doing is none of your damned business," Frank told him.

"Watch that dog," the first one said. "If he makes a jump, shoot him."

"And one second later, the shooter will be dead," Frank said, considerable heat in his voice. "And two seconds after that, the other two will be dead."

"Huh?" the Simpson hand blurted out. "You'd kill a man over a damn dog?"

"You'd hang a man for rustling one of your herd of cattle or stealing a horse, wouldn't you?" Frank challenged.

The trio of hands shifted in the saddle. "I reckon so," one reluctantly admitted.

"You boys go on about your business and I'll go on with mine. Have a nice day." Frank lifted the reins and rode on without looking back. Dog silently padded along beside him. At a curve in the wagon road, Frank reined up and looked back. The trio of Simpson hands were heading into town. None of them looked back at Frank.

"Some folks just don't seem to like you, Dog," Frank said to the big cur.

Dog bared his teeth at that.

"Might be your general attitude," Frank said. "You'll have to work on that some, I reckon. What do you say about it?"

Dog walked over to a bush and relieved himself.

Frank laughed. "My sentiments exactly."

Frank rode on, deliberately cutting onto Simpson land. He rode for a couple of miles, enjoying the peace and quiet of the morning. Cattle grazed all around him, fat and sleek on the grass. Dog suddenly broke into a short run, getting a few yards in front of Stormy and stopping. Frank quickly reined up, knowing that the big cur had sensed danger. He looked all around him, but could see nothing.

"All right, Dog," Frank said. "We'll play it your way." Frank headed into the thick timber and swung down, ground-reining Stormy. He pulled his rifle from the scabbard and knelt down behind a tree, waiting.

Dog came to his side and bellied down. He had done his job.

Frank heard the riders before he saw them. The one in the lead was Little Ed Simpson. Directly behind him was a man with his hands tied behind his back. Behind him rode three Simpson hands.

Little Ed reined up not far from where Frank was kneeling down. "This tree will do," he said, his voice carrying to Frank. "We'll hang the sodbuster right here."

Frank stepped out from behind the tree. "No, you won't, Ed."

FIFTEEN

Little Ed and the hands from the Simpson ranch froze in their saddles as they looked at Frank standing with his .44-40 rifle pointed at them. Little Ed was the first to speak.

"You don't have no authority out here, Morgan."

"Wrong, Ed," Frank told him. "I've got authority anywhere in this county. Now cut that man loose."

"You go to hell, Morgan!" Little Ed snapped.

Frank jacked back the hammer on his rifle, the sound carrying clearly in the cool morning air. "Any of you start trouble, you get the first bullet, Ed. Now cut that man loose!"

One of the Simpson hands swiftly released the bound man.

"Ride over here to me," Frank told the man. "But don't get between us. Come on."

"My pa will kill you for this!" Little Ed shouted.

"I doubt it," Frank replied. He cut his eyes to the just-released man. "Who are you and what brought all this on?"

"I was sitting on my front porch having a cup of coffee with my wife," the farmer said, stepping down from the saddle. "These men come up, slapped my wife around, and tied me up like a hog for slaughter. Said they was gonna hang me for stealing cattle. Deputy, I ain't never stole nothing in my life. This has all got to do with Big Ed Simpson's land grab. He wants all the land in this area."

"What about that, Ed?" Frank called. "What proof do you have this man stole cattle from you?"

"I don't need no damn proof!" Little Ed said. "He was seen on our land. That's good enough for me."

"I was hunting for game," the farmer said. "Nothing more than that. Up until a few weeks ago, the land I was on belonged to Paul Hansen. Big Ed's hands run him and his family off and took the land. And that's the truth. Are you really Frank Morgan?"

"Yes."

"Heard you was in town. Couldn't believe it."

"You want to press charges?" Frank asked.

"Would it do any good?"

"Sure, it would."

"Then I'll press charges."

"Ed, you and your hands drop your guns on the ground. Do it carefully."

"Hell with you, Morgan!" a Simpson hand yelled, and grabbed for his pistol.

Frank blew him out of the saddle. The big .44-40 slug hit the man in the chest and lifted him out of the saddle. He flopped on the ground a couple of times, then lay still.

"Anyone else want to get antsy?" Frank asked.

No one did.

"Drop your guns on the ground," Frank ordered. "Do it right now and do it slowly."

Pistols were carefully pulled from leather and tossed to the ground.

"Now what, Morgan?" Little Ed asked.

"Gather up their guns, farmer," Frank said. "Carefully. Including the rifles."

When that was done, Frank told Ed, "You dismount and tie that dead man across his saddle. Snug him down good and tight." He looked at the farmer, who still had a rather bewildered expression on his face. "What's your name, mister?"

"Asher. George Asher."

"Well, George. You keep that rifle on those ol' boys while I do something. If they try anything funny, shoot to kill. Can you do that?"

"With a great deal of pleasure, Mr. Morgan."

Frank stared at him. "I bet that's the truth, for sure." Frank wrapped up the guns in a blanket and tied that behind his saddle. Once more mounted, he waited until the body of the dead man was secure, then said, "Now we go to town. Lead off, boys."

"What about my wife, Morgan?" George asked. "She thinks I been hung."

"Your place far from here?"

" 'Bout two miles."

"We'll swing by there and get her. Kids?"

"Four. Two boys and two girls."

"We'll take them to town too. I'll treat them to some peppermint candy."

"Kind of you."

"Move out, boys," Frank told the Simpson crew. "You all have a date with a jail cell."

"You got to get us there first, Morgan," Little Ed said.

"I'll get you there, Ed," Frank told him. "Or I'll kill you. One or the other."

Little Ed shut his mouth and kept it shut.

Practically everyone in town turned out to see the sight, alerted by a group of boys who had been fishing in a creek just outside of town.

Mrs. Asher was driving the wagon, her two boys in the bed of the wagon, the two girls sitting on the seat with her. Following the wagon were Little Ed and his two live hands, the dead one belly-down across his saddle. Bringing up the rear of the parade were Frank and George.

"You going to jail again, Little Ed?" a local called.

"Go to hell!" Ed snapped.

"They tried to hang me," George called.

"Hang you?" a woman shouted. "Why, Mr. Asher?"

"They caught me hunting on Simpson land and said I was there to rustle cattle."

A low murmur of rage began from the crowd of locals, soon swelling into a roar of hate.

"Get a rope!" a man yelled. "Let's us have a hangin' of our own!"

"Good idea, Ralph!" a woman yelled.

"Get us into jail, Morgan," a Simpson hand said, twisting in the saddle and looking back at Frank "These people are crazy."

"Crazy?" Frank called. "Why? For wanting to hang you? Isn't that what you were planning to do with Mr. Asher?"

"You don't understand?" the cowboy said.

"I reckon not," Frank replied as he reined up at the

marshal's office. "But maybe a judge will. Get down and get into the jail, boys."

Marshal Wright had stepped outside when the crowds began to gather, a shotgun in his hands. He opened the office door. "Get them inside, Frank. The crowd is gettin' a mite ugly."

"Yeah," Frank replied. "We sure wouldn't want a lynching now, would we?"

"You got to protect us!" Little Ed said. "That's your sworn duty."

"Oh, shut up, Ed," Tom told him. "And get into jail."

"My pa will be here 'fore long," Little Ed said. "With our crew. By God, then he'll show you who's boss around here."

"Right, Ed," Frank said, pushing Ed into the office. "Keep hoping."

"He'll kill you, Morgan!"

"Is killing the only thing you ever think about?"

Little Ed cussed him.

Frank shoved him into a cell and clanged the barred door shut. "Relax, Ed. Take a nap. The rest will do you good."

"Hell with you, Morgan!"

The Simpson crew safely locked down, Frank closed the door to the cell block and walked into the office. The Asher family was telling Tom what had happened at their farm. Tom was taking notes. Frank poured a cup of coffee and sat down.

"Little Ed slapped you, Mrs. Asher?" Tom asked. "That's how you got that bruise on your face?"

"Yes, sir."

"Bastard!" Tom muttered under his breath.

"Beg pardon, Marshal?" George asked, leaning forward in his chair.

"Nothing, George," Tom said. "Just talkin' to myself."

"And the hands threatened to strip Amanda and . . . well . . . you know," Mrs. Asher said, her face reddening from embarrassment.

"They said that in front of the girl?" Frank asked.

"Yes, sir."

Frank and Tom exchanged glances. The threat of sexual assault on a good woman was grounds for a sure-enough hanging in the West. If word about that got out, no jail would be strong enough to hold back the folks with hanging on their minds.

"Keep that to yourselves," Tom told the Asher family. "How old is the girl now, George?"

"Thirteen last month."

Tom cut his eyes to Frank, and Frank nodded his head in understanding at the silent glance. Threatening to strip naked and assault a good woman was bad enough, but to threaten to do that to a young girl would be enough to cause the locals to riot and charge the jail.

Frank got a cup of coffee, sat down, and drank it while Tom wrote down the rest of Asher's story and the farmer and his wife both signed it.

"No bond for this, Frank," Tom said, closing the ledger and putting it away in the safe. "But you can bet broke ribs or not, Big Ed will be comin' into town, raisin' hell about his son."

"And Little Ed's mother?"

Tom grimaced. "Lord, I hope not. Not that foul-mouthed hellion."

Frank smiled at the marshal's expression. "I'm going over to O'Malley's and get some candy for the kids, Tom."

"Get some for me too while you're at it."

Frank bought a sack full of various types of hard candy for the kids and a big peppermint stick for Tom. The kids and Tom were delighted. Tom immediately started sucking on the peppermint stick.

"You folks hungry?" Frank asked the Ashers.

"I could eat," George said. "How about you, Mother?"

"Tom?" Frank asked.

The marshal waved the peppermint stick. "This'll do me till my noonin'."

While the Ashers ate an early lunch, Frank had coffee. "How many of the farmers will stand up against the Simpson crew?" he asked.

"Near 'bout all that's left will, I reckon," George answered. "Them that didn't have the stomach for it have already been buffaloed and pulled out."

"Stock up on ammo and watch for night riders," Frank warned them. "And I'll have a chat with Big Ed about any more rough stuff." Frank finished his coffee and pushed back his chair. "Your meal's on me. See you later."

"Much obliged, Mr. Morgan," George said, and his wife smiled her thanks at Frank.

Walking along the boardwalk, Frank noticed a man wearing a very natty suit and bowler hat putting up posters. He stopped to read one. An opera company was coming to town. They would be performing arias from operas whose names Frank could not pronounce and wouldn't even try.

"You have to see this show, Deputy," the fancy-dressed man said, observing Frank's interest. "It's a good one. We just finished two sellout weeks in San Francisco."

"Is that right?"

"Certainly is. I'm proud and happy to say that we're bringing sophistication to the once-wild West."

"Do tell?"

"Absolutely. Do you like opera music?"

"I can't say one way or the other. Never been to an opera concert."

"You'll enjoy it. I guarantee it. Here, let me give you these.'' The man reached into his suit pocket and handed Frank a couple of tickets. "You and a friend come to the show on us. Is that fair, Deputy?''

"Sounds fair to me. Thanks.''

"Don't mention it. Just enjoy the music and singing.''

"I'm sure I will.'' Frank walked on, cutting across to the hotel. He saw Lara sitting in the lobby, reading the local newspaper. He took a seat beside her and she smiled at him. The smile brightened his entire day.

"Morning, Frank.''

"Lara.''

"I saw you bringing in Little Ed and some of his hands. One across his saddle.''

"Yes.'' He told Lara about the incident.

"How horrible for the Asher girl!''

"Keep what I said to yourself, please. I don't want a lynching in town.''

"I won't say a word.'' She smiled again. "Who would I say it to? Most women in this town won't even speak to me.''

"Their loss, Lara.'' He told her about the opera company coming to town and showed her the tickets. "Would you like to attend?''

"With you, Frank?''

"Why . . . ah, sure.''

"I would love it.'' Again, she smiled. "That will really set tongues wagging.''

"Let them wag. We haven't done anything wrong.''

"Yet,'' she said, and this time she wasn't smiling.

"Yes. Yet.'' Frank looked up the street at the sound of many horses. A dozen Simpson riders were riding into town, a half dozen in front of a buggy, a half dozen behind. Big Ed Simpson and a woman were in the buggy.

"Stay in the hotel, Lara. Big trouble just rode in." Frank stepped out onto the boardwalk.

"You!" Big Ed yelled, pointing at Frank. "I want to talk to *you!"*

SIXTEEN

With Lara safely out of danger, Frank stepped to the edge of the boardwalk and said, "I'm right here, Simpson."

"You get my son out of jail!"

"You go straight to hell, Ed."

Big Ed immediately puffed up like a big ugly bullfrog and started yelling and cussing and waving his arms.

"Oh, shut up, Ed," Frank called. "You're making a fool of yourself."

"Are you going to let him get away with that, Ed?" the woman beside him shrieked. "Tell him to kiss your . . ." She launched into a string of profanities that were as filthy as any Frank had ever heard coming from a female mouth. She finished with: "And tell him to go get our son out of that damned jail."

"Elsie Simpson," a man standing in the doorway behind

Frank said. "She'd be a really pretty woman if it wasn't for that chamber pot of a mouth."

Frank nodded his head in agreement, keeping his eyes not on Big Ed, but on his hands, who had all lined up abreast in the street, six on each side of the buggy, all facing Frank. They were all hardcases, all of them, and Frank knew many of them. They had all been staying in town when Frank had arrived. Now he knew where they'd gone. And many of them were tough and hard as nails, with no backup in them. They were gunslingers, but Frank knew that once they signed on, they by God rode for the brand.

"Your boy tried to hang a man, Ed," Frank called, watching Marshal Wright quietly ease up the boardwalk on the other side of the street. He carried a Greener in his hands. "And assault a young girl."

"That's a damn dirty lie!" Elsie squalled, her voice carrying all over the main street, from one end to the other. "My son's a good boy!"

"Well, your good boy is in jail," Frank told her. "And he's going to stay in jail."

"The hell he will," Elsie hollered. "You two-bit piece of coyote crap!"

"I turn my boys loose on you, Morgan," Big Ed said, "and you'll be shot to bloody bits. I'd think about that were I you."

"And when your boys drag iron," Marshal Wright said from behind Big Ed, "I'll blow you and your bad-mouthed wife all to hell and gone."

The gunhands all stiffened in their saddles at the cold sound of Tom's voice. Big Ed and Elsie slowly turned their heads to look at him. Elsie said, "Aw, hell, that fat ass ain't gonna do a damn thing. He's a big-mouthed tub of guts, that's all."

Tom eared back the hammers on the Greener. "Try me, Elsie," he told the woman. "Just try me."

"Shut your damn flappin' mouth, woman," Big Ed tersely told his wife. "And keep that trap closed tight."

"Don't talk to me like that!" Elsie yelled.

"Shut up, goddamnit!" Big Ed said. "Before you get us all killed."

"And when your boys pull iron," Frank said, "I'll kill at least two and maybe three of them before they get me. You, Idaho, I'll kill you first, then Handy, then Curly. So if you boys are ready, make your play."

"Now wait just a damn minute, Morgan," Big Ed quickly said.

"No, *you* wait just a damn minute, Ed," Elsie yelled. "I got me a gun too. And I, by God, know how to use it."

Big Ed appeared just about ready to belt the woman out of the buggy. "All right, Morgan," he said, looking at Frank. "What's next?"

"You and your wife go on back home and take your hands with you. It's just that simple, Ed."

"And what about my son?"

"He stays in jail until a judge can set a bond for him."

"The hell he will!" Elsie yelled.

Big Ed shoved her out of the buggy. Elsie landed on her butt in the dirt of the street, right in the middle of a pile of horse crap. She jumped up, cussing and slapping at her denim-covered butt. "You rotten lousy, no-good son of a ..." She let her husband verbally have it, calling him every obscene name she could think of.

"Shut up, you whoor!" Big Ed hollered at her.

"Whoor!" Elsie squalled, horse droppings sticking to her jeans. "You callin' me a whoor, you pile of pig crap!"

Big Ed stepped down from the buggy and slapped his wife.

She balled a hand into a fist, rared back, and busted her husband in the mouth, snapping his head back and bloodying his lips.

Big Ed roared his anger. He wiped his suddenly bloody lips and slapped her, knocking his wife down into the street.

Elsie jumped up and tried to kick her husband in the groin.

Ed sidestepped the boot, grabbed her foot, and gave a heave. Elsie sailed backward a few feet and again landed on her butt in the dirt. She jumped up, yelling and cussing.

The boardwalks on both sides of the street had filled with locals, all watching and enjoying the show between Big Ed and Elsie.

"You son of a bitch!" Elsie cussed her husband.

"Whoor!" Big Ed yelled at her.

"What the hell is goin' on out there?" Little Ed yelled from the jail.

"Shut you, you ignoramus!" Elsie yelled at her son.

"Is that you, Mama?" Little Ed hollered.

"It ain't your local preacher's wife, you ninny!" Elsie shouted back.

"Shut up, boy!" Big Ed yelled. "We've come to take you home."

"Don't count on that, Ed," Tom yelled. "You're stayin' put till the judge sets your bond . . . if he sets one, that is."

"You ain't keepin' my baby in that damn stinkin' jail, you lard-ass!" Elsie yelled at the marshal. "I'll kill you first."

"That does it," Frank said, stepping off the boardwalk and walking toward the center of the street.

"Tom," Frank said, "if any one of those hands makes a move, kill Big Ed."

"I'll sure do it, Frank."

"Now wait just a damn minute!" Big Ed hollered.

Frank grabbed Elsie by the shirt collar and the back of her belt and shoved her toward the jail, hard. She was propelled across the street, stumbled, and fell flat on her face in the dirt, eating about a peck of dirt as she slid.

Elsie came up spitting and coughing and hollering and cussing. Frank grabbed her again and again gave her a hard shove. She went stumbling and staggering and cussing to the edge of the boardwalk, spitting out dirt as she went.

"You son of a bitch!" Elsie yelled. "I'll kill you, you bastard!"

"That's two counts of threatening the life of a peace officer," Frank said. "One count of disturbing the peace, and one count of disorderly conduct. Keep trying, Elsie. We'll see how long we can keep you in jail."

"You're going to put *me* in jail?" Elsie screamed. *"Me?"*

"You," Frank told her, picking her up bodily and tossing her onto the boardwalk. "Now get your butt in that jail."

"You go to hell, bastard!"

"Another count of disorderly conduct and another count of disturbing the peace."

"You sorry piece of . . ." Elsie really let the profanities fly, practically turning the air blue.

"For God's sake, shut the hell up, Elsie!" Big Ed yelled. "He means it."

Frank jerked the woman into the office, shoved her into the cell block, and tossed her into a cell, slamming the door.

"Mama!" Little Ed said.

"Hell yes, it's your mama, you nincompoop!" Elsie squalled. "It ain't Christopher Columbus!"

"Morgan, you can't arrest my mama!" Little Ed said.

"I just did, boy."

"But that ain't fittin' a-tall."

"Shore ain't, Morgan," one of the other jailed men said.

"This ain't decent. Supposin' one of us . . . or *her,* has to use the facilities."

"I'm 'bout to bust now," the other one said. "I was just reachin' for the pot when you brung her in."

"Oh, hell," Elsie said. "You ain't got nothin' I ain't seen plenty of before, Lonesome."

"Well, I ain't haulin' nothin' out of my britches and doin' it 'fore her!" Lonesome said. "My mama taught me better than that."

"Hell with your mama too," Elsie said.

Frank walked out of the cell block, struggling to keep a smile from his lips.

"Morgan!" Big Ed yelled as soon as Frank appeared on the boardwalk. "You can't lock up my wife!"

"I just did."

Before Big Ed could respond, a local called, "Oh, Lord! Here comes that crazy woman again." He pointed.

Alberta was loping her mule right down the middle of the road, coming directly for Main Street, and she was carrying her shotgun.

"Who the hell is *that?*" Big Ed hollered.

"You better get out of the way," Frank called. "Everybody, take cover. Quick. Here comes Alberta and her shotgun."

"What's the matter with that woman?" Idaho Red called. "She acts like she's crazy in the head."

"She is!" the barber yelled.

Alberta's shotgun boomed and the front window of a dress shop was shattered. Locals began to scatter in all directions. Horses tied at hitch rails bolted loose and began galloping up the street, wild-eyed from fear. The horse hitched to the Simpson buggy reared up in panic, and the reins hit the ground. The horse took off running.

"Whoa!" Big Ed yelled. "Whoa, goddamnit!"

Frank jumped behind a water trough and bellied down.

"Val Dooley!" Alberta shouted. "Where are you, Val? You double-crossing piece of crap. You better show yourself, Val."

The revolving shotgun boomed twice more, and the horses carrying the riders from the Simpson ranch went into a panic as the buckshot hummed and whistled all around them. Several gunhands were tossed from their saddles and landed on the dirt of the street.

One wheel of the buggy with Big Ed in it hit the side of the boardwalk and Big Ed was tossed out, landing on his butt in the street. He rolled a couple of times and got to his knees just as Alberta leveled her shotgun at him.

"Oh, hell!" Big Ed hollered and grabbed for his six-gun. It was gone. He had lost it when he fell out of the buggy.

Alberta let out some sort of war cry and pulled the trigger just as Big Ed managed to scramble out of the way. The buckshot tore up the street, sending a cloud of dust that completely covered Big Ed. Big Ed crawled under the raised boardwalk.

"Damn you, Val!" Alberta yelled. "Where are you?"

One of the Simpson hands tried to rush Alberta and jerk her off the mule. The woman leveled her shotgun at him and pulled the trigger just as the hand abruptly changed tactics. Most of the buckshot missed him, but a couple of pellets caught the gun hand in the butt. He squalled and jumped about two feet off the ground, grabbing at his suddenly pain-filled rear end.

"Oh, hell!" the gunslick yelled. "I been wounded in the ass!"

Alberta hit the trail, putting her heels to the mule's sides. A few seconds later, the woman had galloped away out of sight.

Frank crawled out from behind the water trough and took

a long look around him. No one appeared to have been seriously injured. The horses were settling down.

Big Ed crawled out from under the boardwalk. He had a dazed look on his battered face. "What the hell happened?"

"Alberta Davis struck again," Frank said just as the barber pole, which had taken a blast from Alberta's shotgun, gave up the ghost and fell to the boardwalk. The striped pole rolled off the boardwalk and fell to the street.

"My ass is a burnin' like far!" the butt-shot gunhand complained.

Frank sat down on the edge of the boardwalk, took off his hat, and started laughing.

"You think this is funny?" Big Ed hollered. "I lost my pistol, my buggy's a damn wreck, I look like I just survived a dust storm, my wife and my son are both in jail, and you think it's funny? I think you're crazy as a road lizard, Morgan!"

"Get a doctor!" the ass-shot Simpson hand said. "My butt's on far!"

"Look at it this way, Ed," Frank said. "With your wife in jail, you just might be able to have a few peaceful days at home."

Big Ed paused and gave that some thought as he stood in the street. "You know, Morgan, sometimes you do make a little sense."

Marshal Wright and half-a-dozen men he had hurriedly rounded up for a posse rode by. "We'll get her this time, Frank!" Tom hollered. "Be back when you see us. Take care of things."

Frank waved his hat at the marshal.

"Here comes the doc," someone yelled. "Is anybody hurt?"

"I am!" the gunslick standing in the street holding his butt hollered.

"Are you hurt bad?"

"I'm shot in the ass!"

Doc Evans stopped. "Any one else hurt?"

"No one else that I know of, Doc," Frank called.

"Come on to my office," the doctor told the gunhand. "I'll take a look at you."

"It hurts to move, Doc!"

"You want me to pull down your trousers right there in the middle of the street and take a look at your bare butt?"

"Hell, no! I'm comin'."

"Well, come on."

"Couple of you boys get him to the doc's office," Big Ed told his crew.

Frank stood up and put on his hat. "You need some help getting into your buggy, Ed?"

"I got out of it, didn't I?"

"Yes, you did. And none too gracefully, I might add."

"Hell with you, Morgan." Big Ed turned away and stalked off toward his buggy.

Lara walked to Frank's side and touched his arm. "How about a cup of coffee, Frank?"

"Sounds good to me."

"Let me out of this damn stinkin' crap hole of a jail!" Elsie Simpson squalled.

"Somebody do somethin' with her," Lonesome hollered. "I'm 'bout to bust I got to go so bad."

SEVENTEEN

Frank was standing on the boardwalk in front of the jail when Marshal Wright and his posse returned. They were a tired and dejected-looking bunch.

"No good, huh?" Frank asked.

"That woman is as wily as a fox," Tom said, sitting down at his desk with a sigh of relief. "You seen her brother?"

"No. They provisioned up for several days before they left."

Back in the cell block, Elsie started cussing.

"My God, that woman has a foul mouth on her," Tom remarked. "I honestly don't know what's kept Big Ed from shootin' her."

"Or her from shooting him," Frank said with a smile.

"There is that to consider," Tom agreed.

"I rigged up some blankets to give everyone some privacy," Frank told the marshal.

"I'm sure the men appreciated that more than Elsie did," Tom said, the sarcasm thick in his tone. "But you know we're not going to be able to hold her. The charges aren't strong enough for that."

"I know. I don't know if there is anything that would embarrass or shock that woman. How about their other kids? No one ever says anything about them."

"They were sent back East to school. I think the kids were really glad to leave."

"Younger or older than Little Ed?"

"Younger. Boy and a girl."

"Do they ever come home for a visit?"

Tom shook his head "Not to my knowledge."

Both men looked up as the front door opened and John Whitter stepped into the office. The lawyer got right to the point. "Let's dispense with the greetings and salutations, men, and get right to it. I've been retained to represent Mrs. Simpson and her son."

"All right," Tom said. "Duly noted."

"Has their bond been set?"

"Oh . . . you can have Elsie Simpson now, if you want her," Tom added dryly. "Little Ed's bond is going to have to be set by a judge."

"Very well," the lawyer said. "Will you release her now?"

"Sure," Tom said, glancing at Frank. "You want to do the honors, Frank?"

"Gladly."

Elsie was jumping up and down angry and cussing when Frank unlocked her cell door and motioned her out into the runaround.

"It's about damn time, you crap head." She glared at Frank. "I'm going to get you for this. Believe it."

"Yeah, yeah," Frank said. "Go on, get out of here."

"Bastard!" In the main office, she faced John Whitter and said, "I want to sue these two and this damn town, Whitter."

"We'll talk about that later, Mrs. Simpson. Right now it's important for you to join your husband. He's waiting for you at the hotel."

"What's he doing over there. Slobbering over your wife?"

John shook his head and sighed. "He's waiting for you, Elsie."

"Yeah. Right. I'm sure he can't live without me."

"Elsie!" John said, exasperation in his tone.

"All right, all right, John. I'm leaving." She looked at Frank. "You and me, gunslinger, we'll meet again."

"I can hardly wait."

Elsie stomped out, slamming the door behind her.

"What a delightful woman," Tom remarked.

"She has her finer points," John said.

"Name one," Tom challenged.

John turned away without replying and walked out of the office.

"Nice fellow," Frank said.

"Salt of the earth, for a fact."

"Hey!" Little Ed called from his cell, his voice carrying clearly through the open door of the runaround. "What about me?"

"Relax, boy," Tom yelled. "You're in here for a spell."

"I want to go home, fatso!"

Tom wearily got up and closed the door, muffling the voice. He glanced at Frank. "You'll see to their supper?"

"I'll take care of it. After I feed Dog."

Tom smiled at that, nodded his agreement, and walked out the door.

"I'm hungry!" Little Ed yelled. "When do we get something to eat around here?"

Frank fed Dog and then walked back to the hotel. Lara was waiting for him in the lobby. She took his arm and together they went strolling.

"I'm so excited about that opera company coming to town, Frank. I saw the poster on it a few minutes ago. Do you know the arias they'll be performing?"

"Ah, no, I don't."

Lara rattled off a whole bunch of foreign words that sounded to Frank as if she'd just cleared a frog out of her throat.

"I beg your pardon?" he asked.

"You're funny, Frank," she said with a laugh, touching his arm.

"I don't know about that. I've been called lots of things in my life, but never funny. I've been told I don't even have a sense of humor."

"Oh, but you do, Frank. You just hide it very well, that's all."

Mrs. Hockstedler lumbered past them, rattling the boardwalk with each footfall, refusing to speak to the couple. She instead averted her eyes, turned up her nose.

"I tell you what, if anyone ever told that woman to haul her butt, she'd have to make two trips," Frank said.

That broke Lara up. She started giggling, and continued laughing until they reached the end of the block. Wiping her eyes with a dainty handkerchief, she said, "You see what I mean about your sense of humor, Frank?"

"I was just stating a fact, Lara. Let's go over to O'Malley's. He has a suit I want to get."

At O'Malley's, Lara fingered the material for a moment. "Yes. This is quality, Frank. I bet you'll look nice in it."

Several woman shoppers in the general store were eyeing Frank and Lara, but not doing so in an unfriendly or malicious manner.

"I'll need a couple of shirts," Frank told Jack O'Malley. "One white and one black. And a couple of bandannas."

"Make one of them red," Lara told the store owner. "And you'll be dressed to the nines, Frank."

"Of course, Miss Lara." Jack said. "No problem at all." He moved away with Frank's purchases.

"The fashionable gunfighter," Frank said with a smile. "That's me."

Lara's smile faded. "If I have anything to say about it, Frank, "your gunfighter days will soon be a thing of the past."

"That would truly be a wonderful thing, Lara. But don't count on it."

"Why not? Wouldn't you like that?"

"Of course I'd like it. I've thought about it many times. But a man can't run away from his past. Not ever. Not really. It will almost always rear up and slap him in the face at the most unexpected of times."

"You've seen that happen before?"

"Several times. To friends of mine who tried to quit the business. Two of them were killed because they refused to wear a gun anymore. That won't ever happen to me, Lara. I won't let it happen."

She studied his face for a few seconds, then smiled. "Don't ever say never, Frank. Besides, I have time to work on you."

Frank returned the smile, then together they walked to the store counter, where Frank paid for his purchases.

Outside on the boardwalk, Frank said, "Did I forget to

tell you that your husband is representing Elsie Simpson? He got her out of jail about an hour ago.''

"That doesn't surprise me one little bit. They've been, ah, seeing each other for several years. *Seeing* each other is, of course, the nice way of putting it." She said it all as unemotionally as if asking someone to pass the salt.

"John and Elsie?"

"Oh, yes. And any other female he could lure into bed. Elsie, so I'm told, likes to be roughed up. And I can assure you, she gives about as well as she gets. I've seen the bruises on John. John and Elsie are a perfect match. Both of them are twisted."

"Good Lord!"

She touched his arm. "Poor Frank. As worldly as you are, things can still shock you, can't they?"

"I reckon so. I'm a simple man, Lara. I don't like complicated things. I guess I see most things in black and white."

"But most matters aren't in black and white."

"Unfortunately, that's true." He smiled. "I guess that's why I keep getting into trouble."

Frank was eating supper at the Blue Bird Café when the single shot echoed up and down Main Street. He stepped out onto the boardwalk and stood for a moment, listening. No more shots came and no one came running up the street. Frank had no idea where the single shot had originated. He went back inside and finished his slab of apple pie and coffee.

Just as he was rolling a cigarette, someone shouted, "It's Marshal Tom. Come quick, somebody. He's been shot."

Frank ran to the office and shoved his way through the crowd into the office. Doc Evans was kneeling down, bent over Tom, who was sprawled on the floor, the side of his head covered in blood. The doctor looked up at Frank. "He'll be all right, Frank. The bullet just grazed his head and took off a tiny bit of one ear. But he'll have a whopping big headache when he wakes up."

Frank looked into the runaround. Little Ed and the other ES hands were gone. Frank muttered a few very profane words.

"I figure someone slipped Ed a gun," Doc Evans said. "From the blood trail, Tom was shot in the cell area, then managed to crawl out here before he collapsed." He looked up at the crowd that had pushed into the office. "Some of you men get Tom over to my office. I've got to clean up this head wound."

"I'm heading out after Little Ed," Frank said. He looked at Jack O'Malley. "Jack, you pick a few good men and take care of things here in town while I'm gone. I'll be over at your store as soon as I get saddled up for a couple days' provisions."

"I'll have them ready for you, Frank. Including a little coffeepot. Don't worry about the town."

"Thanks."

In the livery, as soon as Frank lifted his saddle, Dog began running in circles, barking. He was ready to hit the trail.

Frank reined up in front of the general store and Jack handed him a burlap bag. "Bacon and fresh-baked bread and some beans and a skillet and small pot, Frank. Good hunting."

Frank headed out of town, toward the Simpson spread. Little Ed would head for home range, he was sure of that . . . if for no other reason than to pick up some money and supplies and a fresh horse. Frank did not bother to check for any sign behind the jail. He had no way of knowing where the horses used in the break had been tied, and even should he pick up any usable sign, he had no way of knowing what rider was on any given horse.

He headed straight for the Simpson range.

It was an easy hour's ride to the Simpsons' main house. Frank paid very little attention to the startled looks he received from the hands lounging about. He swung down from the saddle, walked onto the front porch, and knocked on the front door. The ES hands began gathering around behind him, in the front yard.

Big Ed himself jerked open the door, and for a few seconds the two men stood glaring at one another. Big Ed found his voice. "What do you want, Morgan?"

"Your son, Simpson, Little Ed. Where is he?"

"He's in your jail, you bastard! What are you talkin' about?"

Frank told him, sparing no detail. Elsie had walked up, to stand behind her husband.

"Shot Tom?" Big Ed finally said. "Little Ed shot Tom? No way, Morgan! He's dumb, but he's not that dumb!"

"Yes, he is," Elsie declared. "He can be as dumb as a sack of rocks. He takes after you in that respect."

"Shut up!" Ed told her.

Frank raised his voice. "Where is he?"

"We don't know, Morgan," Big Ed said. "And that's the truth. He didn't come here." He paused and looked out at his hands in the front yard. "At least I don't think he did. Come on, Morgan. Walk with me."

The two men, Elsie trailing along, walked to the barn. There, the trio looked at three hard-ridden and put-up wet horses in stalls.

"Goddamnit!" Big Ed said. "Miller, Bradey! Get in here and rub these horses down. Come on, Morgan."

Outside, Big Ed faced his hands. "When was my son and Vic and Jud here? Answer me, goddamnit!"

"Thirty, forty-five minutes ago, Big Ed," an ES hand said. "They swapped horses and told us not to say nothin' to you about it. So we didn't."

"Did they tell you what had happened in town?"

"Just that they broke jail and was on the run."

"One of them shot Marshal Tom," Big Ed said tersely.

"Oh, hell," a hand muttered.

"Which way'd they head out?" Ed asked. "And I want the truth."

"South," the hand said. "Little Ed said they was gonna try to make the Wilderness and hold up there till you could get them out of this mess."

"Dumb," Big Ed muttered. "Just plain stupid."

"Just like you," Elsie said.

With a visible effort, Big Ed ignored his wife's comments. "They get in the Wilderness, Morgan, you won't get them out."

"Oh, I'll bring them back, Ed," Frank assured him. "Sitting a saddle or belly-down across it. But I'll bring them back."

Elsie and Big Ed exchanged worried looks, Elsie saying, "We could have bought off that damn judge. But shooting Marshal Tom"—she shook her head—"that's bad news." She looked at Frank. "I got a big mouth, Morgan, and a dirty one, I know. But I wouldn't have really put lead in you or Marshal Tom. I might have *wanted* to . . . but I wouldn't have. On the other hand"—she jerked a thumb toward her husband—"stupid here, well, that's another story. He probably would have shot you."

"Oh, shut the hell up, Elsie!" Big Ed hollered.

Elsie proceeded to tell him what part of her anatomy her husband could kiss.

Big Ed gritted his teeth and faced Frank. "Don't kill my son, Morgan. I mean that. You don't have to. I mean, he'll be back here when he runs out of grub and money. I'll turn him in then. You have my word.''

"Ed," Frank said, "I believe you would. But before I left town, word of the shooting was already out on the wires. How many enemies do you have that would enjoy gunning down your son?"

Big Ed nodded his head. "All right, Morgan. Point taken. Every two-bit street trash in three states will be comin' in here lookin' for Ed. All right. Go do your duty as you see it, Morgan. I won't interfere."

"I appreciate that, Ed." Frank stepped back into the saddle and pointed Stormy's head south, toward the area known as the Wilderness.

EIGHTEEN

The area known as the Wilderness was a hard three days' ride south. Frank figured he'd make it in maybe five days, taking it slow and steady. He circled around the edges of the Simpson main house until he picked up the trail of three horses, heading south. From the bite the horses' hooves were making in the earth, Frank could tell the three were pushing hard.

"Keep it up, boys," Frank said, "and you'll kill those horses."

Frank lay back, not pushing Stormy, just following the trail. On a sunny midmorning, he found where the trio had made camp and cooked a meal. He pressed on, not hurrying, just riding at the same steady pace, stopping often to rest Stormy and give Dog a chance to catch his breath and rest his paws.

On the third day out, Frank studied the sign carefully. One of the horses had a loose shoe, and if the rider didn't catch it soon and fix it, that horse was going to pull up lame. A mile farther on, Frank came up on a man afoot, and the man was plenty mad.

"Your horse go lame on you, partner?" Frank asked.

"Bastards stole my horse!" the man said. " 'Bout two, three hours ago. Come up on me all nice and polite and then one of them stuck a pistol in my face and took my horse. Took my whole damn rig!"

"Did they leave you a lamed-up horse?"

"They didn't leave me nothin'!"

"You live far from here?"

"No," the man said, calming down a bit. "Couple of miles is all. What they done just made me mad as hell, that's all."

"They're a bad crew. Shot the marshal over at Chance."

"Tom?"

"Yes."

"I been knowin' Tom for years. Is he all right?"

"Yes. Lost part of one ear. But he's all right."

"You catch them outlaws, Deputy. But you watch that young one. He's a bad one. I can tell he is."

"I'll catch them. See you." Frank lifted a hand and rode on.

So they were about three hours ahead of him. The lamed-up horse had really slowed them down. Maybe the trio wouldn't make the Wilderness area. That would make Frank's job much simpler. He pushed on.

An hour later he came to a crossroads and a general store. He could tell by the remnants of the original log building it had once been a trading post . . . dating back many, many years. Frank reined up by the side of the building, waited while Dog and Stormy drank from the trough, then told the big cur to stay put. He took off his badge, stuck it in his pocket, and walked inside.

It was a combination store and saloon; no customers were in the general store part, but half a dozen rough-dressed men were lounging at the long bar. They all wore pistols, and Frank got the impression they knew how to use them . . . and would. Frank ordered a beer.

The men all gave him a long, careful once-over, then returned to their drinking and talking in low tones.

"Come far?" the barkeep asked, placing a mug of beer in front of Frank.

"Long ways," Frank said. "Crossed over into California from Nevada and just seeing the country."

"There's a lot of it to see, all right. Say, mister, you remind me a lot of somebody, you know that?"

"Oh?"

"Yeah. By God! You sure do resemble Val Dooley."

"What's a Val Dooley?" Frank asked.

One of the men at the bar laughed at that. "You shore ain't from around here, cowboy, or you wouldn't be askin' that."

"No, I'm not from around here. What's a Val Dooley?"

"An outlaw and fast gun."

"And ladies' man," another said.

"Well, I'm no ladies' man, for a fact," Frank said after taking a swig of the cool beer and carefully placing the mug on the bar.

"Does that mean you're a fast gun?" another man at the bar asked.

"I know how to use one."

"You ever been in this part of the country before?"

"Can't say I have."

"I think you have."

"Think whatever the hell you want to think," Frank replied easily. "It's a free country. But don't ever call me a liar again."

"Or you'll do what?" the man asked, stepping away from the bar and facing Frank, his right hand hovering over the butt of his six-gun.

"Why, I might take offense," Frank said with a smile. "And I'm thinking you wouldn't like that. Not a bit."

All the men at the bar laughed. One said, "You bes' be careful, Zeke. This ol' boy thinks he's a bad one."

"He just might be at that," another said softly. "I got me a bad feelin' about this cowboy. Let it drop, Zeke."

"The hell I will!"

The man who cautioned Zeke took his beer and moved to a table in the rear. "I'm out of it, mister. You hear me?"

"I hear you," Frank said.

"Maybe he wouldn't be so brave and all facin' two of us?" a man said, stepping away from the bar to stand beside Zeke.

Frank smiled.

"Somethin' funny, mister?" Zeke asked in a hard voice.

"Yeah, Zeke, you. Your kind never changes. I've been running into your kind ever since Luther Biggs braced me when I was about fifteen years old."

"What happened to him?"

"I killed him," Frank said very softly. "Then his brothers came after me."

"What happened to them?"

"I killed them. All of them."

Zeke swallowed hard. Something about Frank worried him, nagged at him. The man was just too damn calm. "You *say* you done that!" Zeke sneered.

"That's right, Zeke, I say."

"You got a name, mister?" the man who had moved to a table asked.

"Frank Morgan."

All the air seemed to go out of the man who had thrown in with Zeke. He held up a hand. "I'm out of this, Morgan. Leave me be."

"All right. Stay out of it."

Zeke cussed the man, all without taking his eyes from Frank. After the cussing, he said, "Morgan's a has-been, Tom. Look at him, he's got to be forty-five if he's a day— probably older than that. He's an old man; got gray in his hair."

"Then you take him, Zeke," Tom said. "I don't want no part of him."

"I'm with Zeke," another said, stepping away from the bar. "All them songs and sich about Frank Morgan is so much folderol. I never did believe none of it."

"You're a fool, Billy," the man who had seated himself at a table said.

"Hell with it!" a man standing at the bar shouted. "Die, Morgan!" he screamed, and dragged iron.

Frank shot him, the bullet striking the man just below the throat, shattering the bones there and blowing out the back of his neck. The man fell face-first on the bar and remained in that position while he died.

Zeke pulled his pistol, and Frank's second bullet hit Zeke in the belly. Zeke screamed and doubled over, dropping his pistol on the floor. The six-gun discharged and the bullet hit Tom in the ankle just as he was fumbling for his pistol. Tom hollered and fell to the dirty floor, his shattered ankle unable to support his weight. Frank quickly stepped to the man and kicked his pistol away, out of reach.

"Anybody else?" Frank asked.

None of the remaining three said a word.

The man who had died doubled over on the bar suddenly broke wind and fell slowly to the floor, falling right on Tom's broken ankle.

"Owwww!" Tom squalled. "Git him offen me."

"Git me to a doctor," Zeke moaned. "I'm hard hit, boys."

Frank waited, his Peacemaker in his hand.

"We're done with this, Morgan," another of the men at the bar said. "Drink your beer and relax whilst we look after them still alive."

Frank backed up, around the end of the bar, still holding his .45. He picked up his mug of beer and drained it, then signaled the barkeep for another.

"I'm crippled for life," Tom yelled as the corpse was lifted off his broken ankle. "The doc will probably have to cut off my leg. Damn you, Morgan. Damn you to the fires of hell for doin' this to me!"

"You brung it on yourself, Tom," the seated man said. "Don't blame Morgan."

"By God, I blame him," the man called Billy said. "Farley was a pal of mine."

"Is Farley the dead man?" Frank asked.

"Yes. And he was a good man."

"He wasn't good enough," Frank said, a matter-of-fact tone to his words.

"Damn you!"

Frank minutely shrugged his muscular shoulders, dismissing the man's comments without words.

"Shut up, Billy," the seated man told him. "Before you get turned into a corpse."

"You're a bastard, Morgan!" Billy yelled, his face reddening with anger. "You're a no-good bastard, that's what you are."

Frank had two rounds left in his Peacemaker. He had

left his short-barreled Peacemaker, his belly gun, in his saddlebags. He waited, saying nothing.

The bartender ended the standoff. He reached under the bar and came up with a Greener, pointed at Billy. "That's it, Billy. It's over. They's been enough killin'. Now stand easy and keep your hand away from your gun."

Billy immediately relaxed. No one in their right mind wants to mess with a ten-gauge sawed-off shotgun at close range. Frank took that time to quickly reload.

"You want to leave now, Morgan?" the barkeep asked.

"After I finish my beer and get me something to eat."

"You're cold, Morgan," the seated man said. "Too damn cold."

"I didn't start this trouble," Frank said.

"That's a fact. But Billy's a hothead. He won't forget this."

"That's his problem." Frank looked at the barkeep. "You got any hot food?"

"Got some good-tastin' stew and it's fresh. With some hot baked bread to go with it. I might have some puddin' left too."

"Sounds good to me. Put that Greener away and fix me some of it, please. I'm a hungry man."

"You the coldest son of a bitch I ever seen in my life," Billy said.

"I'm hurtin' something awful," Zeke hollered. "And y'all talkin' 'bout stew and puddin' and sich. Don't nobody give a damn 'bout me?"

"Nearest doc is miles away, Zeke," the one man at the bar who had, up to that point, not spoken finally said.

"My belly's on far, Able!" Zeke shouted.

Frank moved to a table across the room and sat down, his back to a wall.

"Ain't you got nothin' to say, Morgan?" Able asked, just as the barkeep brought out Frank's food.

"Yes," Frank said. "I'm fixing to eat now. Leave me the hell alone."

NINETEEN

Zeke died just as Frank was finishing eating. He had the barkeep put together a sack of scraps for Dog, then paid his bill as the others watched him.

"You just gonna ride away and leave Zeke dead on the floor and Tom with half his ankle blowed off?" Billy asked.

"What do you want me to do about them?" Frank asked.

"Well ... I don't rightly know. But you ought to do something. You're the cause of it all, ain't you?"

Frank shook his head in disbelief. "You boys are the dampest bunch I've run into in many a moon. I have to say that."

"What do you mean, Morgan?" Billy asked.

"Good Lord," Frank said, then turned and walked out the door without looking back.

"I'll see you, Morgan!" Billy shouted. "You can count

on that. You and me, Morgan. Then we'll settle up for Zeke and Tom. Count on it, Morgan.''

Frank stowed the food for Dog in his saddlebags and stepped into the saddle. He angled back and forth for a time, until once again picking up the trail of Little Ed and his men. He stayed with the trail until about an hour before sunset, then made camp for the night, not far from a small fast-running creek.

Frank fed Dog, then fried some bacon and made some pan bread for his supper. Just as the sun was slowly sinking over the horizon, Frank rolled a smoke and settled back with a cup of coffee. The nights were cool in this high country, but Frank had decided to let his fire burn down into coals before he rolled up in his blankets. Just as he was finishing his second cup of coffee, when the small fire had burned down to only a few coals, he heard the sounds of slow-walking horses.

''I tell you, Rich, I smell smoke,'' a voice drifted faintly to him.

''I never said you didn't, Bob,'' a second voice replied. ''But it was faint and probably drifted in from a long ways off.''

''And I smell coffee too.''

Rich laughed. ''That's your belly takin' over from your nose's business. There ain't nobody within ten miles of here.''

''That's a town, Rich. I ain't talkin' 'bout no town. I'm talkin' 'bout somethin' real close by. And my smeller don't lie.''

A town ten miles away, Frank thought. A good bet Little Ed and his hands had headed there for supplies before riding into the Wilderness.

''Well, we got to fight shy of town anyways,'' Rich said. ''Val'd have our butts if we got caught.''

"Providin' the law didn't hang us first," Bob said with a laugh.

The two men drifted on until Frank could no longer hear even a whisper of conversation from them. He would have liked to follow them to Val Dooley's hideout, but, he thought with a sigh, Little Ed and his two hands came first. Val Dooley would have to wait.

Frank rolled up in his blankets and went to sleep.

At midmorning of the fifth day out, Frank sat his saddle and stared at the trail he'd been following. Two riders had turned due east, one rider continuing on south.

"Now what?" Frank asked the air softly.

Frank mentally flipped a coin and decided to trail the lone rider, having a hunch that was Little Ed.

Frank came up on the lone rider while he was watering his horse. Stopping about a hundred yards back, Frank ground-reined Stormy and cautioned Dog to be quiet and stay put. Then, after removing his spurs, he eased up behind Little Ed.

"Stay easy, Ed," Frank cautioned the young man. "I don't want to have to shoot you."

"You're gonna have to, Morgan 'cause I ain't goin' back to stand trial for killin' that fat tub of guts."

"You didn't kill him, Ed. You just grazed his head. Tom is very much alive. But you did shoot off a piece of his ear."

"I still ain't gonna go to prison."

"Stand still, Ed. I'm taking your pistols. Don't try anything. I will shoot you."

Ed made no funny moves while Frank disarmed him, stowing the guns in his saddlebags. "Turn around, Ed."

The young man faced him and Frank tossed him handcuffs. "Put those on, boy. Let's do this legal."

"Hell with you, Morgan. I ain't gettin' myself chained up like a damn animal."

Frank took one step forward and busted Little Ed with a right to the jaw. The young man dropped like a rock, stunned but not completely unconscious. Frank locked the cuffs around his wrists and hauled him to his feet.

"Now get on your horse, boy. We have a long way to go."

Little Ed cussed him.

A crowd gathered along both sides of the street as Frank brought Little Ed Simpson back to town.

"Get a rope!" someone shouted.

"Yeah!" another yelled. "Let's hang the bastard."

"Settle down!" Marshal Wright shouted, stepping out of his office, a Greener in his hands. There was a big bandage covering one side of his head. "They'll be no lynching in this town. Ed Simpson will get a fair trial."

"That's a better chance than you gave *him,* Ed," Frank said.

"He's a fool. My pa won't let no one try me."

"I think you're wrong about your pa, boy."

"Him and Ma won't let me go to prison," Little Ed said confidently.

"I guess we'll see, won't we?" Frank said, reining up in front of the office. Dog immediately plopped down in the shade of the raised boardwalk, a tired canine.

"Welcome home, Frank," Marshal Wright said.

The warmth behind that greeting and the words themself hit Frank hard. *Home* had a real nice ring to it.

"Good to be back, Tom. Mighty good."

"Welcome home, Frank," Lara said, walking up to stand beside Tom.

Frank smiled at her. "Hi, Lara. You look mighty pretty today."

"Kind words, Frank. I know I look a fright. It's this heat." She fanned herself.

Lara couldn't look a fright if she went to a costume party wearing a worn-out flour sack.

Frank helped Little Ed down from his horse and led him into the jail, shoving him into a cell. Only then did he remove the cuffs, while Tom stood careful watch in the runaround, the Greener at the ready.

"You'll get word to my pa?" Little Ed asked after Frank had slammed the door and locked it.

"We'll make sure he knows you're back, boy," Tom told him. "But I can tell you this. There will be no bail for you. You're locked down until your trial."

"We'll see about that, fatso!"

Tom smiled. "Or maybe I'll get lucky and you'll run."

"Lucky?" Little Ed asked. "What do you mean by that?"

Tom lifted the Greener.

Little Ed got the message. "You'd like to shoot me, wouldn't you, tubby?"

"It would be the high point of my year, punk."

Little Ed walked over to a bunk, sat down, and stared at the wall.

Out in the office, Frank poured a cup of coffee and sat down. "I imagine someone in town will get word to the Simpsons."

"Oh, you can be sure a rider is already on the way. There were ES hands in town when you brought in Little Ed."

Frank brought the marshal up to date on all that had happened since he had ridden out after Little Ed and his hands.

"And Big Ed said he wouldn't interfere?" Tom asked.

"Really? The man just may have a decent streak in him after all."

"I think he and his wife both do," Frank said, further startling the marshal.

"Well, they've damn sure managed to hide it right well for years," Tom replied.

"No doubt about that," Frank said, standing up and stretching. "I'm going to stable the horses and feed Dog, then go get me a long hot bath, a shave and a haircut, and a change of clothes. My horse and dog smell better than I do."

Tom laughed. "Well . . . now that you mention it!"

On his walk back from the livery, after stabling Stormy and feeding Dog, Frank paused in front of the offices of the local paper to read a notice on the bulletin board. The opera company was coming to town that weekend. Frank made a mental note to have his new suit ready for that event, and to get his boots cleaned and polished. He went on to the barbershop and bathhouse and made arrangements to get cleaned up, then went to the hotel to pick up a few things.

An hour later, with two weeks of trail dust scrubbed off him, and sporting a fresh shave and haircut, Frank walked over to the Blue Bird for something to eat. Doc Evans was there, having a piece of pie and a cup of coffee. He waved Frank over to his table by the window.

"I just saw Ed and Elsie come into town," the doctor said. "They went straight to John Whitter's office."

"I knew something would come along to spoil my good mood," Frank said, sitting down.

Doc Evans laughed at Frank's expression. "Well, they weren't cussing or fighting with each other."

The waitress walked over and Frank ordered coffee and a meal. "John will probably try to get bail set for Little Ed."

"Any chance of that?"

"I don't think so. Although they might try to buy off the judge."

"That won't happen," the doctor said firmly. "Not with Judge Bledsoe. That judge can't be bought."

"I hope not."

"Tom's been looking around, trying to learn who slipped that gun to Little Ed."

"Any luck?"

The doctor shook his head. "No. He figures it was an ES hand. You noticed the fence by the side of the jail?"

Frank nodded his head.

"Town ordered that built. Makes it harder for anyone to get to the cell windows. Tom scattered tin cans and bottles on the ground in the area. Anyone gets over the fence now, they'll make a racket trying to walk."

"Good thinking on his part. I'm going to bunk at the jail until the trial is over. I'll move some of my gear over this afternoon."

Doc Evans smiled. "Good idea. That should definitely make it more diffficult for anyone to break jail."

"When is the judge due here?"

"I think Tom sent a wire today. Soon as you brought Little Ed in. Judge should be here in a few days."

Frank ate his meal and chatted with Doc Evans, occasionally glancing out the window. He was waiting for Big Ed and Elsie to make an appearance. He was just finishing his pie and coffee when the couple came walking up the boardwalk.

Doc Evans spotted them at the same time. "Here they come," he said. "Just in time to aid indigestion."

"That's one way of putting it."

Big Ed walked up to the table, Elsie trailing along behind

him. Both of them greeted Frank and the doctor very respect-fully.

"Can I see my son, Morgan?" Ed asked politely.

"Sure, Ed," Frank replied. "I was just finishing up. But I'm sure Tom is in the office."

"Well ..." Big Ed hesitated. "Tell you the truth, I'm sort of ashamed to face Old Tom. Ashamed of what my son did."

Frank stood up, reached for his hat, and dropped some money on the table. "Come on, we'll go see your son."

"Is he hurt at all?" Doc Evans asked. "Do you need me to look at him?"

"He isn't hurt," Frank said. "I, ah, persuaded him to come along peacefully."

Doc Evans raised an eyebrow at that, but said nothing.

"Thanks for that, Morgan," Ed said. "We both appreciate it. Me and the wife."

"You feel all right, Ed?" Doc Evans blurted out, sure there had to be something wrong with the man since he was behaving in such a civil manner.

"I feel all right, Doc. Just sort of down about my son's situation, that's all."

"That's understandable," Doc Evans said. He looked at Elsie. "Elsie?"

"I'm all right, Doc. Like Ed, I'm sorta down in the mouth about Little Ed, for actin' so damn stupid."

"Me and Elsie talked it over on the way into town," Ed said. "We both know Little Ed is goin' to do hard time for his crime. Don't neither one of us like that, but it's fittin' for what he done. And ..." He paused, "it's mainly my fault for not bein' a better father. I failed bad with Little Ed. Now he's gonna have to pay for my failure."

"And mine," Elsie said.

Both husband and wife were well aware that the café had fallen silent, every patron listening to them.

"Thank God," Elsie said, "we have two good kids back East."

"And we have some apologizin' to do to them," Ed said. "A lot of apologizin'. And we plan to do it real soon."

"Glad to hear it, Ed," Doc Evans said. "Congratulations on you both rejoining the human race."

"I reckon we deserved that, Doc. Hell, I know I did," Big Ed said.

"Me too," Elsie said. Then she smiled and jabbed her husband with a thumb. But not too hard. "But him, more than me."

Ed laughed. "She's right about that."

Doc Evans shook his head at the change in the two. A very welcome change.

"Come on," Frank said. "I'll let you in to see Ed."

"Mind if I tag along?" Doc Evans asked.

"Not at all," Frank told him.

Tom was just walking out of the office onto the boardwalk when they arrived. Tom hesitated for just a second, then stuck out his hand to Big Ed. Ed immediately took the peace offering and shook it.

"I can't tell you how sorry and ashamed I am, Tom," Ed said after staring at Tom for a few seconds.

"That goes for both of us," Elsie said.

"It's all right, Ed, Elsie," Tom said. "It's behind us and it's a brand-new day. Oh, Little Ed is anxious to see you both. I was just on my way to get you."

The elder Simpson grimaced. "I reckon we have to see him. But I'm not looking forward to it. I've arranged for John Whitter to represent him." Again he grimaced. "For all the good it will do."

"Go on in, Ed," Tom said. "The cell block door is open.

We'll wait out here. Help yourselves to coffee. It's fresh. I just made it.''

"Thanks," Big Ed said. He took a deep breath and pushed open the office door. He and his wife stepped inside, closing the door behind them.

"What a change in those two," Tom said, sitting down on the bench.

"I couldn't believe it myself," Doc Evans said. "But sometimes, a family tragedy will do that to people."

"I think it's a miracle," the marshal said.

"How's your head feeling?" Doc Evans asked.

"Just fine, Doc. When can you take off this big bandage?"

"Today, if you like. I want to look at the wound anyway."

"Suits me. I been missin' wearin' my hat."

A single shot cracked from inside the jail.

"Oh, hell!" Tom yelled, jumping up just as Elsie screamed.

TWENTY

Precious seconds were lost as the three men jammed each other up trying to get inside the office. When they did manage to get in, they ran into Elsie, almost knocking her down.

"Big Ed's been shot!" Elsie squalled. "Little Ed grabbed his gun and shot him. He run out the back door. The little shit shot his own father! I can't believe it!"

Frank ran around to the side of the jail and cussed. The new fence blocked him, and of course there was no gate. He ran back around to the front and down the small alleyway, finally reaching the rear of the jail. Little Ed had vanished into the thick timber that lay only a hundred or so yards all around the town. In many places that timber and its underbrush were very nearly impenetrable.

"I'll get a posse together," Tom said, walking up behind Frank. "For all the good it will do. That timber is thick.

With dozens of places to hide. A mile further on they's caves. Doc's with Big Ed. I'll see you, Frank. Take care of things."

Frank met Doc coming out of the office. "He's hard hit, Frank. I don't want to move him just yet. Stay with him. I've got to get some things from my office."

Big Ed motioned for Frank to kneel down beside him. "You're gonna have to kill him, Frank. I see that now."

"Don't talk, Ed. Save your strength."

"No. Listen to me. The boy's half crazy. He's kill-crazy. I've seen it in other men, and so have you. I should have seen it sooner. But he was my son. You understand, don't you, Frank? Don't you?" he pleaded.

"I understand, Ed. I really do."

Elsie was sitting on the floor next to her husband, weeping into her hands.

"Don't give him no chance at all, Frank," said Ed, "If you do, he'll kill you. He can't be trusted. Boy that would shoot his own father . . ." He coughed and grimaced in pain. "I never dreamed he'd try to grab my gun."

Elsie turned to her husband just as Doc Evans entered the office. "Don't you die on me, you big bastard!" she sobbed. "I love you, and you know I do."

"I know, baby," Ed whispered. "I know you do, and I love you." He tried to laugh. "We sure picked some funny ways to show it, didn't we?"

"All that is gonna change, Ed. I promise you, it will. I need you, Ed. We need each other. Don't we?"

"We sure do, baby."

"Elsie," Doc Evans urged, "get out of the way. I've got to work on Ed. Go make me a pot of hot water for these instruments."

Elsie got up and sniffed a couple of times. She wiped her

eyes and her nose with the back of her hand. "Right away, Doc."

"Get me some blankets, Frank. I've got to work on him right where he is. I don't want to move him. I've got to probe for that bullet." He looked at Frank. "And you've got to hold him down while I do so."

Frank nodded his head. "I've seen it done before."

"I imagine you have."

It was a nerve-racking and very painful next few minutes. Big Ed finally, mercifully, passed out from the pain. Doc Evans located the bullet and extracted it from Ed's chest, then leaned back and wiped his sweaty face, laying aside his bloody instruments.

"Will he live, Doc?" Elsie asked.

"He's got a chance, Elsie. A small one. I won't lie to you about that. But Ed is strong as a mule, and that will work in his favor. In a few minutes, we'll get some men in here and move Ed to a bunk here in this building. I don't want to move him around any more than is absolutely necessary. Not for the next twenty-four hours, at least."

"I'll stay right with him all the time," Elsie said. "I promise you I will not leave his side."

"I know you won't, Elsie."

"How about some coffee, Doc?" Frank asked.

"Sounds good. I think I could drink a whole pot."

Big Ed was moved into the small room where Frank was going to sleep, and made as comfortable as possible in the bunk. A rocking chair was brought over by Jack O'Malley for Elsie. Frank made another pot of coffee and, while the grounds were settling, stepped outside to sit on the bench and roll a cigarette.

Lara walked over from the hotel to sit beside him. "Is Big Ed going to make it?" she asked.

"It's touch and go right now."

"Very difficult for me to believe his very own son shot him."

"Ed admitted to me that Little Ed is crazy. Told me I'd have to kill him. And don't give him any chance at all."

"How awful!"

"Yes. Especially about your own son." Frank shrugged his shoulders. "But this mess has sure brought Ed and Elsie close together."

"I heard. And that is also hard to believe."

Frank smiled. "It was a shock to me and Tom too."

"It'll be dark soon. Tom and the posse should be riding in any time now. I hope they found Little Ed."

"I'd bet they didn't. That's rough country Ed took off in. Lots of places for a lone man to hide."

"That means you'll have to go after him, doesn't it?"

"Probably."

She touched his arm with her small hand. "I hate that. I worried about you every day you were gone."

"It's good to know somebody worried about me. It's a good feeling, but not a feeling I'm accustomed to."

"Get used to it."

"Yes, ma'am," Frank replied with a laugh.

The two of them sat close together on the bench in silence for a few moments, enjoying the coolness of twilight time. The town was closing up and settling down for the evening. Over at the Purple Lily, a woman laughed at something, the shrill sound drifting to the couple seated on the bench.

"I don't think that was a very happy laugh," Lara said. "It sounded . . . well . . . rather sad to me, I suppose."

"Paid laughter, Lara. A drink of bad whiskey. A silver dollar given for a few moments of company."

"That makes it even sadder." She looked at him in the waning light. "Have you ever paid a woman for company?"

"No. I always figured that would be very questionable company at best."

"I'm glad" was her only reply.

Frank looked up the street. "Here comes Tom and the posse. I don't believe they found Little Ed."

"That means you'll go after him. When will you leave?"

"If I go, probably in the morning."

"*If* you go?"

"I'll tell Tom my thoughts on it. And they are that it will be useless to go after him. Little Ed will show up around here. I don't think it will be long either. He'll come back for clothes and food and money. But he'd better not count on his mother giving it to him."

"What do you mean? You think she'll turn him in?"

Frank shook his head. "I think she'll shoot him."

Big Ed rallied early the next morning and opened his eyes. Elsie called for Frank to please go get Doc Evans. She didn't want to leave her husband's side.

"How do you feel, you big ox?" Doc Evans asked, sitting down on the side of the bunk.

"Like a man who's been shot, you old quack," Ed replied, his voice low.

Doc Evans smiled at that. "Now that sounds like the Big Ed I know. Let me take a look at that wound."

Doc Evans looked at the wound and clucked his approval. "No signs of infection. I think you're going to be all right, Ed."

"Oh, I'm going to make it, Doc. I want to kick the snot out of that worthless son of mine and then turn him over to Tom."

"After I get done kickin' his ass," Elsie said.

"Now, now, Elsie," Big Ed told her. He looked at Frank.

"Morgan, I want you to know I never sanctioned no hangin'. That was all Little Ed's doin's. I run off some nesters, yeah. I admit that. But I never shot none, and I damn sure never hanged none."

"Both of us talk big, Morgan," Elsie added. "But mainly it's just talk. There's been a lot of rumor about us, and that's mostly all it is, rumor." She shook her head. "Except for our runnin' around on each other. I got to admit, that's pretty much true."

"Done out of spite," Big Ed said. "Pure stupid spite against each other." His voice was getting weaker. "I got to rest some. Don't leave me, Elsie."

"I won't, Ed. I promise you I'll be right here when you wake up."

Frank walked outside with Doc Evans. "Really baring their souls in there, aren't they, Doc?"

"Sometimes getting real close to death will do that, Frank. I've seen it happen more than once. Whether it'll stay with them after Ed gets on his feet is another matter."

"You know, Doc, I think it will."

"You just might be right, Frank."

"Here comes Tom. You want to have some coffee?"

"Sure. More than that. I haven't had breakfast yet."

"I'm sure Tom will join you in a snack."

"If I pay for it, yes."

"And you will."

"Of course. I always end up doing that."

In the café over breakfast, Doc Evans looked at Frank and said, "Mind if I ask you a personal question, Frank?"

"Go right ahead."

"Are the rumors true that you're a wealthy man?"

"Moderately so, yes."

"Yet . . . you still drift aimlessly around the West."

"Doing what I want to do, Doc."

"Are you? Really?"

"For the most part, yes."

"Why don't you go abroad, Frank?" Tom asked. "Like maybe, oh, I don't know. France. See the country."

"I don't speak the language."

"How about Italy?"

"I don't speak that language either."

Both Tom and Doc Evans laughed at Frank's replies. Doc Evans said, "You don't have to speak the language to enjoy the country, Frank."

"I reckon they've got grass and trees and valleys and mountains and hills, Doc. So do we right here. They've got rivers and creeks. So do we. They got fancy food in the cities of France and Italy, so I've heard tell. But I bet none of them has ever sat down to a buffalo steak cooked over a campfire while the wolves sang in the background. I bet none of those fancy city folks over there has ever camped in the mountains and cooked and eaten a fresh-caught trout and been entertained by camp-robber birds and squirrels or watched an eagle soar high in the sky. None of those folks ever sat out a bad storm in an Indian village, talking sign while eating Injun stew, then rolled up in a buffler robe and slept while the storm blew itself out. They got old buildings over there, so I'm told. So what? Who the hell wants to sail across the ocean to look at an old building? Boys, I've seen canyons down in Northwest Arizona Territory that will take your breath away. They're damn near unbelievable. And the redwood trees you've got right here in California are a sight to behold. Beautiful. Almost spiritual. And I'm not a religious man. But I'm told some of those trees have been here for a couple of thousand years. That'll make a man start thinking about God. At least it did this man. I'd go visit New York City maybe, 'cepting those folks have had their freedoms took from them by all the rules and regulations and laws. Man can't be a man back there. Hell, you can't even carry a gun back there. You get in trouble, you have to call for a police officer to settle it for you. That's nonsense. I'll saddle my own horses and kill my own snakes. I don't need nobody else to do that for me. I don't *want* nobody else to do that for me."

"That's the longest comment I have ever heard you make, Frank," Doc Evans said. "In its own way, it was quite eloquent."

"Wasn't meant to be, Doc. I was just stating a fact."

"But are you happy, Frank?" the doctor asked.

"I've been asked that before, Doc. Happy? I don't know. But I do know I'm content."

"The contented wanderer," Doc Evans mused. "Sounds like the title of a book."

"Or a song," Tom added.

"Let's get off the subject of me," Frank suggested. "And get on to more important things. Tom, have you heard anything else about Val Dooley?"

"Not a word, Frank. And that sort of worries me. But there was a wire delivered to my house early this morning. Sheriff Davis and those deputies of his give up looking for his sister. They headed on back home. Said to tell you thanks for your help."

"She's close by," Frank said. "I'd take a bet on that. And she's not done with me or this town yet."

"That thought doesn't make me very happy," Tom said sadly. " 'Cause if she comes back here again, shootin' up the place, somebody is gonna put lead in her."

"I hope not, Tom," Doc Evans said. "The woman is obviously deranged."

"I don't know about deranged, Doc," Tom said. "But I do know she's actin' as crazy as a preacher in a whorehouse."

Both Frank and Doc Evans had a laugh at that, Frank

saying, "Tom, did you wire the judge about Little Ed's breaking jail?"

"Yes. He put off his trip here. Readin' between the lines of his wire, I got the notion the judge would be happy if we'd just shoot Little Ed and be done with the matter."

"The judge doesn't like to travel," Doc Evans said. "He has gout. And when it flares up, he can be very testy."

"I don't believe we'll take Little Ed alive," Frank said. "Not again. I think he'll go down shooting."

"Be good for all concerned if he does just that," Tom said. "Put an end to the matter." He drained his coffee cup and stood up. "I'll be at the office. I want to get some food to take to Elsie. I don't think she's eaten since Big Ed got plugged."

A local came into the café and walked over to Frank. "Mr. Morgan? There's a man over to the Purple Lily. Says he's come to kill you."

TWENTY-ONE

"Did he tell you his name?" Tom asked.

"No, Marshal. He just said for me to go fetch Frank Morgan. Said he come to town to kill him. He's all dressed in black, from his boots to his hat. Even his bandanna is black. Real fancy gunbelt. Got silver dollars on it."

Tom looked at Frank, who was leisurely finishing his coffee. "Sound familiar to you, Frank?"

"No. How old is this man?"

"He ain't neither real young nor real old, Mr. Morgan. If I was to guess, I'd say 'bout thirty."

Frank stood up and slipped the hammer thong off his Peacemaker. "Tom, I'll keep him talking long enough for you and Doc to get the people off the street. If that isn't possible, get them out of the line of fire."

"We'll do it, Frank. Give us a couple of minutes."

A moment later, Frank stepped out of the café and slowly rolled a cigarette. Then he looked up and down the street, his eyes finally settling on a man dressed in black standing on the boardwalk in front of the Purple Lily. Frank could see he wore two guns, both of them tied low. Frank walked slowly down the boardwalk until he was directly across the street from the man who wanted to kill him. He did not recognize the man. He looked up and down the street. The boardwalks were devoid of people.

"You looking for me?" Frank called.

"If you're Frank Morgan."

"That's me. Who are you?"

"Warner. Jack Warner."

Frank had heard of him. Warner had made a reputation down along the Mexican border and he was supposed to be fast and accurate. "What's your quarrel with me, Jack?"

"You're you, and I'm me."

"That might make some sense to you, but it doesn't make a lick of sense to me. What's the matter, don't you like my name?"

"I don't like hearin' your damn name everywhere I go. Frank Morgan this and Frank Morgan that. I'm so sick of hearin' about Frank Morgan I feel like pukin' every time I hear it. But after today, I won't be hearin' it no more."

"That's right, Jack. Because after today, you're going to be in the ground."

"That's something else I don't like about you, Morgan. You're just too damn cocky to suit me."

"I've faced dozens of two-bit gunslicks like you, Jack. They're all dead and I'm still walking around. I'd think about that were I you."

Jack Warner laughed. "You got a will all made out, Morgan?"

"Sure, Jack. But you're not in it. You have a burying place all picked out?"

The smile faded from Jack's face. "I plan to live a long time, Morgan."

"Not if you continue playing this deadly game with me, Jack."

"This ain't no game, Morgan. And I ain't no two-bit gunslick. I made my rep on the up and up."

"As far as I'm concerned, Jack, you're just another two-bit trouble-hunter. Too damn stupid to work and too damn lazy to steal."

"You better be ready to back up those words, Morgan!"

"Jack, I've been ready. I'm just waiting on you. It's your play, so make it."

"Step out here in the street, Morgan!"

"My pleasure, Jack." Frank stepped off the boardwalk and into the street. "Can you see me now, Jack?"

"Yeah, I can see you, Morgan."

"That's good, Jack. For a time there I was thinking you might be in need of spectacles."

"I see plenty good, Morgan!"

"Then get on with it, Jack," Frank said, throwing down the challenge. "The time for talking is over."

That remark visibly shook Jack. That and Frank's calmness. If he was expecting Frank to show fear at facing him, he was both disappointed and shaken. "Are you in that much of a hurry to die, Drifter?"

"Dying is not in my plans for today, Jack. Make your play."

"Damn you, Morgan!"

Frank stood calmly and faced the younger man. "Does cussing me make you feel better, Jack?"

Jack hesitated, then started his hook and draw. His eyes, the mirror to a man's inner feelings, gave him away. Just as his hand closed around the butt of his six-gun, Frank's Peacemaker cracked. The bullet slammed into Jack's chest and spun him around. He cussed Frank, and managed to clear leather and cock his pistol.

Frank shot him again, the slug hitting him in the belly and doubling him over. Jack sat down in the dirt of the street. He dropped his right-hand pistol and tried to pull his second gun. He fumbled for the weapon, but could not manage to pull it from leather.

"Give it up, Jack." Frank's voice came to the gunman. "It's over."

"Damn you, Drifter!" Jack said.

Jack was conscious of Frank walking toward him. He tried again to pull and cock his second gun. He simply did not have the strength to complete the task. Jack Warner fell over on his side in the street.

Frank's shadow covered him.

"I can't see so good," Jack said.

"You want me to move so the sun can touch you?" Frank asked.

"Yeah. It's too damn dark."

Frank stepped to one side.

"That's better," Jack said.

Doc Evans walked over and knelt down beside Jack. "I'm a doctor," he said. "You want me to take a look at you?"

"What's the point?" Jack asked. "I'm hard hit and I know it."

Dr. Evans noticed a pink froth forming on Jack's lips, and knew that meant he was lung-shot.

"I come to kill you, Morgan," Jack said.

"You should have stayed home."

"Somebody will get the job done someday. I'm gonna laugh when it happens. I'll know it and I'll laugh."

Preacher Bankston walked out into the street. "You want me to say a prayer for you, son?" he asked.

"Yeah. I reckon that would be nice. Tell the angels to come fetch me and carry me to heaven."

Bankston began softly praying.

Warner started hollering and jerking as the pain hit him savagely. He began coughing up blood.

"Won't be long," Doc Evans said softly, more to himself than to those around him. "Have you ever seen him before, Frank?" he asked.

"Never. But I have heard of him. He had his rep down along the border. He was supposed to be pretty fast."

"He wasn't as fast as us, Frank," Johnny Vargas said from the edge of the boardwalk.

"Hello, Johnny. I thought you'd pulled out."

"I came back."

"I see. Did you know this Warner fellow?"

"Not personal. But I do know he thought he was better than he really was."

"He must have been very lucky."

"His luck just ran out, Frank."

"Seems like it."

"Both of you go to hell!" Jack said as his coughing eased and he caught his breath.

"Now, now, son," Preacher Bankston said. "That is no way to talk. You're going to meet the angels soon."

"They can go to hell too!"

"Here now, son! Stop that kind of talk. Keep that up and you're sure to head straight into the embrace of Satan."

"Can't you do somethin', Doc?" Warner asked.

"I'm sorry, but no."

"Well, you can go to hell too then!"

Doc Evans shrugged his shoulders, then asked, "You have anyone you want us to notify?"

"My mother, back in Mississippi. If she's still alive."

"Where 'bouts in Mississippi, son?" Bankston asked.

"Hell, I don't know. Last I heard she was livin' outside of Jackson." He began coughing and spitting up blood again.

"What a disgusting sight!" Mrs. Hockstedler declared from the boardwalk. "Get out of my way, you hoodlum!" she said to Johnny Vargas.

"Excuse me, lady," Johnny said, removing his hat.

Mrs. Hockstedler harrumphed her displeasure and lumbered on up the boardwalk, rattling the store windows as she marched away.

"What the hell did I do to her?" Johnny asked.

"You're here, I'm here," Frank said. "That's enough for her."

"Old bat," Johnny muttered.

"Help!" Jack hollered. "Help me. I can't see no more."

"Steady, son," Bankston said.

"I shore would like to have me them guns of his'n," a rough-looking man said, walking up to stand beside Johnny.

"They didn't do him much good, Tucker," Johnny replied.

"That there's a natural fact, Johnny. But I'd still like to have 'um. Warner?" he called. "Can I have them guns of yourn when you expire?"

Jack told him in no uncertain terms where he could shove his guns . . . both of them.

"Well, that's downright unfriendly," Tucker said.

Jack Warner took a deep breath and died in the dirt of the street.

"I'll bury him for what's in his pockets," Undertaker Pennybaker said.

* * *

"The men just appear and challenge you to a gunfight," Lara said. She and Frank were eating supper in the Blue Bird Café. "A life-and-death confrontation. I don't understand the reasons why. It must be some sort of man thing."

Frank buttered a biscuit and said nothing.

Few people paid any attention to Frank and Lara now. Their being together was accepted by the majority of the locals. Many secretly hoped the two would eventually marry and settle down in the community.

"Did you have your new suit pressed for this weekend's opera event?" she asked.

"All ready to go."

"You're going to look very dashing, Frank."

"You're very good for my ego, Lara. I don't believe anyone has ever referred to me as dashing."

Tom stepped into the café and walked to Frank's table.

"Tom," Lara said, "won't you sit down and have something to eat?"

"No, thanks, Miss Lara. This is business. But thank you. Frank, Val Dooley and his gang just hit a town south of us. They robbed the bank and took some women hostage. Two girls in their teens and a grown woman. The woman was a customer in the bank making a deposit. The gang was headin' north, straight toward us."

"You want me to get a posse together?"

"No, I want you to stay here and look after things. At the marshal's request, I'm gettin' together some men and headin' out in a few minutes. I'd feel a lot better if you were stayin' here in town. And Frank? The marshal down at Dixsville said in the wire the Dooley gang killed two citizens."

"That doesn't surprise me at all, Tom. All right, I'll look after things here in town. Don't worry about that."

"Thanks, Frank. I'll see you."

As soon as the door closed behind Tom, Lara said, "Tom is getting entirely too old for this sort of thing."

"It's his job, Lara. And he takes it seriously."

She reached across the table and touched his hand. "But I'm glad you're staying here in town, Frank."

"Finish your meal, Lara. I'll walk you back to the hotel. Then I want to read that wire Tom received."

"He just told you what it said."

"I know. But I want to read it personal."

"Whatever on earth for?"

Frank smiled. "I'm nosy."

With Lara safely back at the hotel, Frank read the wire and then walked over to the telegraph office and spoke to the agent.

"Did you copy this wire?" Frank asked.

"Sure did, Mr. Morgan. Something wrong with it?"

"Did it seem right to you?"

"What do you mean?"

"The telegrapher's touch on the key."

The agent was thoughtful for a moment, then said, "Say! Now that you mention it, it wasn't Nick's touch. No, sir, it sure wasn't. I just figured he was training a new person, that's all. Why do you ask?"

"Can you send a wire to Dixsville?"

The agent shook his head. "No, sorry. I can't send or receive anything to or from south of here. Wires are down, I reckon."

"Thanks." Frank walked out of the office, thinking: *Pretty damn slick on your part, Val. Hit the town down there, then send a wire up here to pull the marshal and a posse out of this town, then cut the wires heading south. Only one thing wrong with your plan, Dooley.*

I'll be waiting for you.

TWENTY-TWO

Frank went over to O'Malley's General Store and told Jack of his suspicions. Jack listened and then said, "But Frank, Dixsville is a half day's ride from here. If the robbery just occurred, we have hours to get ready."

Frank shook his head. "No, no. Listen to me. There was no robbery, Jack. I'll make you a wager the Dooley gang wasn't five miles from here when they tapped into the wire and sent that message."

Jack blinked and then paled just a bit. "I'll alert the men, Frank. If you're right, and I'll bet you are, we don't have much time."

"Move, Jack. Get the men into position."

On the boardwalk, Frank ran down to the Purple Lily and looked inside. The saloon was deserted, with not a single patron. That cinched it in Frank's mind. A raid on the town was imminent. Many of the ne'er-do-wells who had drifted into town had joined up with Val Dooley.

Frank ran over to the office and grabbed a rifle from the rack, then stuffed his pockets with cartridges. He stuck a pistol behind his gunbelt and stepped outside. The long main street was deserted, devoid of foot traffic. Horses had been ridden or led away from the hitch rails. Most of the businesses had closed their doors.

Frank looked up to the rooftops of the businesses. Men were lined up all along Main Street, on both sides, with rifles and shotguns. The Dooley gang was going to be in for a bloody surprise when they hit this town, for many of the men were veterans of numerous battles—outlaws, rustlers, Indian wars, the War of Northern Aggression, or a combination of all of them. These men couldn't be frightened off and they wouldn't quit. They would go down fighting. Frank had no doubts at all about that.

Frank looked up at the sound of a galloping horse. It was the old wrangler from the livery. "They're on their way," he shouted, reining up and dismounting. "About a mile out of town now. 'Bout thirty or forty of them, looked to me. They'll be here shortly. I'll be in the loft of the livery. Good luck to us all. We're damn sure going to need it against that gang." He led his horse into the livery and closed the big doors behind him.

The Dooley gang had waited, Frank was sure, until Tom and the posse had passed their hiding place, heading south, before they rode out to the north, to the town.

"We're ready as we can be, Frank," Doc Evans called from the door of his office. "I'm ready to receive wounded. I know there will be some."

"Ready over here, Frank," Jack O'Malley called.

All along both sides of the street, men began calling in.

The town was ready for the gang. There would be gunsmoke in the air and blood in the dirt before this day was over.

"They're coming in from both ends of the street!" a man called. "Some of them must have circled around. Good God, there's gotta be fifty of them."

"Damn," Frank muttered through gritted teeth. He levered a round into the rifle and stepped into the mouth of an alley.

Dooley's men dismounted and Val split his gang up into small teams of three to five men, sending them all over town. Gunfire and the screaming of women echoed throughout the town as outlaws kicked in the doors to private homes, terrorizing the residents.

A bullet dug a furrow in the wood of the building, just inches from Frank's head, sending tiny splinters into his face and neck. Frank dropped to one knee and leveled his rifle. He pulled the trigger just as his assailant fired again. The gang member missed. Frank didn't. The bullet from Frank's rifle slammed into the man's chest and knocked him to the ground. Frank turned his attention back to the street just in time to see a local take a round in the head and fall from the rooftop of the bank, crashing through the awning of the boardwalk. He bounced on the boardwalk and slowly rolled into the dirt.

One of the men Frank had seen loafing in the Purple Lily came running up the boardwalk, a pistol in each hand, firing indiscriminately. Frank sighted him in and squeezed the trigger. The outlaw stopped abruptly and fell like a rag doll as the bullet ripped into his belly. He jerked once and then lay still.

Frank heard a woman screaming in one of the houses just behind the main street, but could not tell for sure which house it came from. He turned his attention back to the main street as a man carrying a bundle of something tried to make it into the bank. Frank could not tell what was in the bundle. A shotgun roared from inside the bank building, and the man was lifted off his feet and flung out into the street. A second later the bundle exploded, sending bits and pieces of the dead man flying all over Main Street. Windows on both sides of the street were blown out from the concussion of the blast.

"Nitro," Frank muttered. "Dangerous stuff to handle." He wondered why the Dooley gang would choose to use the highly volatile liquid rather than the easier-to-handle and much more stable dynamite.

"Go in the back of the bank," someone shouted from the other side of the street. "Blow the safe."

"You'll never make it," Frank muttered. Seconds later, heavy gunfire erupted from the bank building. The banker and his tellers were all heavily armed and making a fight of it.

Frank watched an outlaw stagger out of the leather shop, both hands holding his lead-perforated belly. The man stumbled on the boardwalk and fell into the street. He kicked and jerked for a moment and then was still.

The Dooley gang was taking a real beating from the residents of the town. Val should have known better than to attack a town, for it was extremely rare for a Western town to be treed by a gang.

During a momentary lull in the gunfire, Frank heard the unmistakable bellow of Mrs. Hockstedler coming from a row of houses directly behind Main Street.

"Get away from me, you hoodlum!"

Frank turned his head to see if he could spot Mrs. Hockstedler. He turned just in time to see an outlaw come stumbling out of the front door of a house, Mrs. Hockstedler in pursuit, wielding a large broom.

"Take that, you ruffian!" she hollered, and whacked the

outlaw on the back of the head, sending him rolling ass-over-elbows off the porch and into the yard.

"I'll kill you, you fat pig!" the outlaw yelled.

Mrs. Hockstedler let out a squall and came charging off the porch, swinging the broom. "You filth!" she bellered. "How dare you call me names, you, you . . . white trash!" She swung the broom.

The broom connected with the back of the man's head and knocked him flat on the ground. Mrs. Hockstedler jumped on him just as he was getting to his feet, all her considerable weight landing on the man, once again knocking the outlaw to the ground.

He hollered and made a grab for his six-gun. Mrs. Hockstedler balled a hand into a fist and belted the man, her fist connecting with the man's jaw and flattening him. "Take that, you ne'er-do-well!" she yelled. "How dare you assault a helpless woman."

"Helpless, my foot," Frank muttered as Mrs. Hockstedler commenced to pound the outlaw with the business end of the heavy broom.

The gunfire picked up, and Frank left the outlaw in the very capable hands of Mrs. Hockstedler.

"This ain't workin' out!" a man yelled. "We done lost too many men. Let's get the hell out of here."

"Let's go," another man yelled. "Back to your horses. It's over."

Frank waited, counting as many of the dead and the wounded as he could. Eight outlaws and two local men were dead in the street. He had no way of knowing how many outlaws and locals had been killed or wounded in private homes.

Frank looked behind him. The outlaw Mrs. Hockstedler had been pummeling with the broom had gotten to his feet and taken off running, leaving his pistol behind him on the ground. Frank figured the outlaw was very fortunate Mrs. Hockstedler didn't pick up the six-gun and shoot the man with his own pistol.

"They're gone!" a man yelled from a rooftop. "Riding out, heading toward the west."

Frank stepped out of the alley and walked across the street to the hotel. As soon as he stepped into the lobby, waves of panic hit him. He fought them down and walked swiftly to the desk clerk, who was sprawled in a pool of blood. The man was dead.

Frank took the steps two at a time, heading for Lara's room. The door had been smashed open. Lara was gone.

"My daughter's gone," a man yelled from the street. "Them outlaws took my girl."

"Doc Evans, come quick," another man yelled. "My wife's been hit on the head and is bleeding real bad."

The bank was secondary, Frank thought. The bastards were after women.

"They've done this before," a citizen said, as if reading Frank's thoughts. "They hit a town and kidnap half a dozen women. They rape them and when they're finished with them, they sometimes turn them loose."

"Sometimes? Or they kill them?" Frank asked.

"Only if they've caused them a lot of trouble. More often than not, they sell them into whorehouses along the old Barbary Coast. Sometimes the women escape and make it back home. But not many of them."

"Maybe they're shipped out to Mexico or other places?"

"Could be. I've heard of that happening."

Frank walked over to Doc Evans's office. The doctor was busy patching up a local, and he worked while Frank told him what had happened to some of the town's women. "I'm heading out, Doc. I'd appreciate if you'd take care of Dog while I'm gone. I'm going to be moving fast and Dog just couldn't keep up."

'I'll do it, Frank. I like Dog and he likes me. He can sleep right here."

"Thanks. I'll bring him by right now."

Frank went to the livery and got Dog, taking him to Doc's office and telling him to stay. Dog would obey him. He might not like it, but he would stay. Frank then provisioned up and put several boxes of rifle and pistol cartridges in his saddlebags.

Jack O'Malley and several other local men came to see him in the livery.

"You going after them, Frank?" Jack asked. "Alone?"

"I operate better when I'm alone, Jack," Frank replied. "I can move faster too."

The owner of the Blue Bird Café handed Frank a sack. "Fresh-baked bread in there. I baked it this morning."

"Thanks, Paul. Would you save some scraps for Dog? He's staying over at Doc Evans's while I'm gone."

"I'll take some over to him personal every day, Frank. I'll feed him well. You have my word on that."

"I appreciate it."

"We'll look after the town, Frank. And we're riding with you, in a manner of speaking," the man from the saddle shop said.

Frank nodded his head. "I know."

"They got my daughter, Frank," the owner of the Gold Nugget Saloon said. "Nellie. She's only fifteen. You bring her back to me and the Missus, Frank. Please?"

"I'll do my best, George."

"Half a dozen women was taken, Frank," Jack said. "Lara, Nellie, Dixie Malone, Harriet Baker, Lydia Wilson—she's only fourteen—and Penny Tucker. Half a dozen that we know of, that is. There might well be more from this town or the surrounding area. Probably are.''

"Probably," Frank said, tightening the cinch on Stormy.

"Frank," Jack said, putting a hand on Frank's shoulder. Frank turned to look at the man.

"You be careful, Frank."

Frank nodded his head and swung into the saddle. He looked down at the men. "I'll bring those women back if at all possible." He lifted the reins and rode out.

TWENTY-THREE

Frank picked up the trail of the gang and began following it, heading south. He felt without any doubt that the gang would soon split up into smaller groups; he also felt they would eventually wind up in the same spot: Val Dooley's hideout in the area known as the Wilderness.

A few hours after the abortive raid against the town, the gang split up into half a dozen smaller groups. Frank kept on the trail of the larger group heading straight south; that was the group he was sure had the women. He felt that Val Dooley would not let any of the others have their way with the women until he personally had raped them. Being the leader of a gang does have its privileges.

Judging from the imprint the horses' hooves made in soft earth, none of the women were doubled up on a single horse. As near as Frank could figure it, he was following sixteen people. Six women and ten of the Dooley gang, including Val.

Then the gang went into a shallow river in an effort to lose any pursuers by hiding their tracks. It's a good trick, and it will throw off dogs and inexperienced trackers, but it seldom works with any experienced tracker.

It didn't with Frank, and he only lost about an hour before he was once more on the trail of the Dooley gang.

Approaching darkness forced Frank to call a halt and to make camp. It was just as well, for Stormy was getting tired.

Frank built a hat-sized fire, and while water for coffee was boiling, he fried some bacon and then thin-sliced a potato into the bacon grease, and had that and some of Paul's fresh-baked bread for his supper. He used another hunk of bread to sop up the grease left in the pan and ate that. Then, over the first cup of coffee and several cigarettes, Frank allowed his mind to think more deeply on the fate of the hostages. The images he conjured up were not pleasant.

He was sure that some, if not all, of the hostages had been assaulted by now. All of them had probably been beaten into submission.

Frank got killing mad at the thought. And he knew in his mind right then, at that quiet thoughtful moment by the campfire, there would be damn little mercy shown to any member of the Val Dooley gang . . . not by him. And he was going to get those women back home. He couldn't guarantee what shape they would be in, but if there was any way short of making a deal with the devil, he would get them back home.

Then he let the golden image of Lara slip into his mind.

Bad mistake. For that only served to make Frank even angrier. He felt his blood run hotter and his emotions get all choked up.

If anything were to happen to her . . .

If she were to be killed . . .

He fought those thoughts away and tried to roll another cigarette. His suddenly trembling fingers made a mess of the first attempt. He angrily threw the wadded-up papers and what remained of the tobacco into the fire and fought back his hot anger.

This won't do, he thought, steadying his raging mind and calming his white-hot musings.

This won't do at all.

He sat still for a moment, calming his inner emotions, then, with steady fingers, rolled a cigarette and poured another cup of coffee. He had successfully mentally banked his fires of rage. But he could and would allow the flames to roar into an inferno when the time was right. And God help any Dooley gang member who was in the way when that happened.

God would have to help the outlaw . . . Frank Morgan sure as hell wouldn't.

Frank doggedly followed the trail of the Dooley gang. At midmorning of the second day out, he found where the gang had camped the night before. He found a piece of torn dress and the remnants of a woman's undergarments.

Frank squatted by the rags of clothing and softly cursed. The attacks on the kidnapped women had begun.

And there wasn't a damn thing he could do about it. At least, not yet, he thought. Frank put the torn rags in his saddlebags, to keep as evidence, and swung back into the saddle. Three or four hours behind them, he told himself. Only three or four hours. But he knew better than to push Stormy any harder than he already was. The big Appaloosa was as game as any horse on the trail, but he had his limits.

Frank maintained a steady pace, stopping often to let

Stormy rest. He nooned by a little creek, taking time to brew a pot of coffee and eat some bread, then was back in the saddle. And he was closing the distance between him and the gang. He could tell by the freshness of the horse droppings. And their horses were getting tired; the gang had been pushing them hard and it was telling on the animals. He was now maybe two hours behind the gang, at most.

A hour later, Frank caught a faint whiff of smoke. A few minutes later, the smell of smoke was mixed in with the odor of bacon frying. He had found somebody. Whether it was the gang or some traveler, he would soon know.

He left Stormy ground-reined and taking his rifle, Frank began cautiously working his way through the timber, following the scent of smoke and bacon frying.

He froze still when he heard someone say, "I don't like this a-tall, Danny. I just don't like sittin' here like a dummy waitin' for Morgan to show up."

"Relax, Shorty," Danny told him. "Morgan's half a day behind us. We'll eat and then we'll get in place to kill the bastard."

"And what if he's only half a hour behind us?"

Danny laughed and Frank worked closer. He could see the two outlaws.

"Huh?" Shorty laughed. "Don't laugh at me, Danny. What if he's closer?"

"He ain't that close, Shorty. I can feel it."

"You're right about that," Frank said, stepping into the clearing. "I'm right here."

Shorty grabbed for his six-gun and Frank put a .44-40 slug in his chest. The bullet knocked Shorty back, shattered his heart. The outlaw was dead before he hit the ground. "Don't kill me, Morgan!" Danny yelled, fear making his eyes wide.

"Oh, I'm not going to kill you," Frank assured him. "We're going to have a nice long talk, you and me."

"Huh? What are we gonna talk about?"

"You're going to tell me everything about Val Dooley."

"No, I ain't, Morgan. I'm more feared of Val than I am of you. I ain't gonna tell you a damn thing."

Frank walked to the man and gave him the butt of his rifle on the side of his jaw. Danny hit the ground out cold.

When he woke up, he was stripped naked and tied to a tree. He could see Frank squatting by the fire, doing something. "This ain't decent!" Danny hollered.

Frank turned his head to look at the man, contempt in his eyes. "You kidnap and rape women, some of them no more than children, and you talk to me about decency?"

"What are you doin' with that fire, Morgan?"

Frank stood up, a running iron in his gloved right hand. The tip of the running iron was glowing red hot.

"What the hell are you gonna do with that, Morgan?" There was a slight hint of hysteria in the man's voice.

"I told you, Danny. We're going to have a long talk."

"You ain't gonna burn me, Morgan. You a lawman, you can't do nothin' like that. It ain't legal."

"Neither is kidnapping and rape, Danny." Frank took a step toward the naked, trussed-up outlaw.

Danny's eyes bugged out in fear and Frank came closer. Danny's eyes were on the glowing tip of the running iron. He shook his head. "I don't know nothin', Morgan. I swear to you, I don't."

"You're a liar, Danny. You better talk to me and you better start right now."

Danny shook his head. "I won't! I won't!"

* * *

Actually, Danny had quite a lot to say to Frank about Val Dooley and his gang and his hideout and how to get there.

Frank touched Danny only once with the hot tip of the running iron, on the leg. After that, the words fairly flew from the outlaw's mouth. He began talking so fast, Frank had to slow him down a couple of times.

All the women had been assaulted, Danny said. But he, of course, denied having touched any of them. It was all the others, but not him.

Frank took Danny to the nearest town, which was a half day's ride away, and told the marshal to lock him up and keep him locked up.

"What happens if you don't come back for him?" the marshal asked nervously.

"Then you can shoot him," Frank said.

"Oh, hell!" Danny said. "I'll tell you everything, Marshal. You can write it down and I'll sign it. Just get me away from Morgan. That's all I ask."

"That's good enough for me," the marshal said. He looked at Danny. "You goin' to prison for a long time, mister."

"Long as Morgan leaves me alone," Danny said. "That man's as mean as a damn rattlesnake."

Frank provisioned up—including a sack full of dynamite—and rode out. He didn't need to pick up the trail; he knew exactly where the hideout was. He knew how many men were in Val Dooley's gang.

What he didn't know was how he was going to rescue the women. He'd work on that little problem once he reached the hideout in the Wilderness . . . and managed to get in alive. And that was something that might prove to be no small feat.

He came up on the remains of a woman. She was lying by the side of the trail, naked, the side of her head bashed in. Rigor mortis had not yet set in, and the buzzards and ground varmits had not yet found her, so Frank figured the body had been dumped no more than an hour or so before. Frank did not recognize the woman, so he could only assume she had been taken on another raid by the gang. Frank had no shovel, so he piled rocks on top of the body, said a few quiet words to the Lord, and resumed trailing the gang.

As soon as he forded a small river, Frank knew he was in the Wilderness, for the country abruptly turned decidedly wild and rough. He also lost the trail he had picked up shortly before finding the body of the woman.

No matter, he thought, taking off his hat and wiping his forehead. *I know where I'm going and how to get there. But caution is going to have to be the key word from this moment on. The gang knows I'm following them, and since Shorty and Danny did not rejoin them, they'll be waiting for me.*

Frank deliberately left the trail Danny had outlined for him, and began a wide circle, planning to come up at the rear of the outlaw encampment. He doubted they would be expecting that. At least that was his fervent hope.

This was, so Frank had learned, California's haven for criminals. The Wilderness boasted a little outlaw town consisting of, Danny had been very eager to point out, a saloon, a store, a café, and a hotel where the more affluent outlaws could stay, for a price. If they didn't have the money for a hotel room, they stayed in tents or in one of the many shacks that dotted the "town."

Danny had also told him that many of the West's most notorious gunslicks, killers, and outlaws called the place home, sometimes for months at a time. When they ran low on money, they would leave to pull a job, then return. Lawmen who had gone into the Wilderness after various desperadoes had never come out.

This was very rugged country, with mountains ranging

from six thousand to ten thousand feet, with winding canyons—many of them dead ends—and hundreds of places ideal for a deadly ambush. But that would work both ways, Frank thought with a small smile.

When he drew a few miles closer to the outlaw town, Frank would go in on foot. He could move a lot faster through the rough country that way, and duck into any of hundreds of nature's hidey-holes very easily.

That evening, Frank built a small fire and fixed the last hot meal he would probably have for several days. He fixed bacon and potatoes and made some pan bread and coffee, and then doused the fire. With a pot of hot coffee at the ready, Frank rolled a smoke and leaned back against his saddle. He allowed hard thoughts to once more creep into his mind: thoughts of what had happened and was surely still happening to the kidnapped women. He could but guess at the sheer terror the women must be experiencing. Over his second cup of coffee, Frank made up his mind. Once the women were safe, he was going to destroy the outlaw town.

Blow it up, burn it down, and kill any woman-abusing bastard that got in his way.

Frank rolled another cigarette and took a sip of hot coffee. He felt a lot better now. Now that he had a firm plan in his mind.

He was looking forward to the dawning.

TWENTY-FOUR

Frank found a dandy spot to leave Stormy: a shady little cul-de-sac with graze and water that was spring-fed. Stormy would have plenty to eat and drink and a good place to roll when he felt like it. Frank rigged some fresh-cut brush in front of the opening, loose enough so Stormy could break out if Frank didn't return. Frank stashed his spurs in his saddlebags, and slung his bedroll and saddlebag and took off walking toward the outlaw town, carrying his rifle in his left hand and the sack of dynamite and caps in the other hand.

Frank enjoyed walking—unlike many Western men of his time—and he was in excellent physical shape. He hadn't walked long, maybe an hour, when he began to smell wood smoke. Another fifteen minutes and he topped a rise and looked down on the outlaw town, and it was a crummy-looking place. Frank softly whistled at the size of it—there must be fifty or sixty men inhabiting the place.

More than Frank had counted on.

He studied the layout of the town for several minutes, then eased off the ridge and into some thick brush to do some thinking. He had not seen any sign of the kidnapped women, and had no idea where they might be held, or even if they were still alive.

He made his way out of the brush and cautiously worked his way around to the rear of the outlaw town, staying on the ridge, which ringed about half of the town, then gently tapered down into flats. He saw no sign of any guards, except on the main road leading into the town. The outlaws were either supremely confident of their inaccessibility from outside forces, or a pack of fools. Frank figured a combination of both.

He began working his way around to the other side of the town, which would put him off the ridge and into brush and timber on the flats. It was dangerous, but he had to learn everything he could about the town before making any plans concerning an attack.

That thought brought a smile to Frank's lips. One man attacking fifty or sixty. Talk about supremely confident!

Frank heard voices and immediately slipped into some underbrush, slithering on his belly like a big snake. Roaming guards, he thought. Good thinking on someone's part, and that someone was probably Val Dooley.

"I wants me some of that young gal," a man said. "She's prime."

"Val gonna put them up for bids, I hear tell," the second man said. "Ain't nobody outside of his personal gang touchin' them women till then."

"That ain't fair, you ax me."

"Nobody did."

"For a fact."

"You reckon Morgan's gonna show up?"

"I 'spect he will. One of them young gals said him and that good-lookin' blonde got something goin' 'tween them."

"Morgan's got good tastes."

"For a fact."

"I'd ride into hell for that one."

"Well, you can forget that. Val's got his eyes fixed on keepin' her for his private use. Ain't nobody else touchin' her."

"Not even that squirt Little Ed Simpson?"

"Nope. Not even him."

So Little Ed had linked up with Val Dooley, Frank mused while the two guards stopped a few yards away to have a smoke. *Why doesn't that surprise me?*

"Way I heard it," one of the outlaws said, "Little Ed's been talkin' with Val for a few months, somethin' about the town and his pa's ranch. I don't know all the particulars 'bout that. Sounds interestin', though."

"Shore does."

"Well, let's make one more pass and then hand this job over to someone else. I'm gettin' hongry."

"I'm gettin' itchy for them women."

"Well, you can just put some horse salve on that itch. You ain't gonna be liftin' no petticoats on none of them gals."

"Not yet anyways, I reckon."

"Maybe not never, 'lessen you got the money when the biddin' starts."

"We'll see 'bout that."

The men moved on, and Frank crawled out of his hidey-hole and stood up. That was too close. He would have to be much more careful, and would be, now that he knew there were roaming guards.

Frank stayed in the deep timber and brush until he came to a spot where he either had to go back to remain in the timber, or step out into an exposed area. He bellied down, took off his hat, and got his field glasses. Frank adjusted them for range, and began studying the town and its inhabitants more closely.

He spotted half a dozen outlaws that he knew. There was Goody Nolan, a killer from down Arizona way. Big Thumbs Parker, from West Texas. Freckles Burton from Missouri; he was wanted for the brutal killing of an entire family. Breed Vaca, a half-breed from New Mexico. Sam Semple, from Colorado. Finally, Frank spotted a man walking along the side of the road, picking his nose. Booger Bob.

Frank laid the field glasses down and shook his head. "Good God," he muttered. "Booger Bob. I might have known it."

If there was a gathering of outlaws anywhere in the far reaches of the West, Booger Bob would surely be among them. Booger was a back-shooter from Kansas who had drifted into California, liked the climate, and stayed. A very dangerous man with a rifle, but only a fair hand with a pistol. He had never been known to stand up and face a man he had been hired to kill. Booger wasn't a coward, he just knew his limitations.

There were rewards out for the men Frank had spotted and knew, and probably rewards out for all the men in the outlaw town. Dead or alive. If he could do it, he'd take as many bodies as he could to the nearest town and make sure the women got the reward money to split among them . . . if he could get them out, he added. And himself, he also added.

Frank again lifted the field glasses and studied the town. He found one of the nicer shacks—this one had a full roof and most of the windows—with alert guards both front and back. "That's where the women are being held," he muttered. "I'd bet on that."

The horses of the outlaws were held in a huge corral, which was attached to a very nice barn. The horses got good treatment; better than the men afforded themselves. For a very good reason. The outlaws' lives depended on their horses and they received the best of care.

Then Frank saw Little Ed come swaggering down the street with a man that had to be Val Dooley. Both Ed and Val wore two guns, tied down, and their clothing was nice, their shirts and britches clean. Frank studied Val closely. He did strongly resemble Frank, and Frank could understand how people could get them confused.

"You're a dead man, Val Dooley," Frank whispered.

Frank slipped back into the timber and waited for nightfall.

Most of the outlaws were in the town's saloon, talking, drinking, playing cards, or being otherwise entertained—for a nominal fee—by one of the town's half a dozen weary whores. Frank had slipped into town and was crouched by the side of the saloon, listening to the men inside talk. He had already identified half a dozen more outlaws, and two of the West's most notorious women outlaws: Sadie Saunders and Bloody Mama Colson. Both of those women were killers, with at least half a dozen kills each behind them . . . those were the known kills. Rumor had it that Sadie and Bloody Mama had many, many more dead bodies behind them. And both women practiced, so the rumors went, some very strange sexual habits. Frank felt squeamish just thinking about that.

There was nearly a constant stream of men coming and

going to and from the outhouse in the rear of the saloon, some barely able to walk as they staggered about.

"One of the pack trains due in tomorrow with supplies," one of the more sober men remarked on his way to the crapper.

"I'll be glad to see it," another said. "I'm shore gettin' tarred of beans."

"I'm a-gittin' tarred of thinkin' 'bout them fresh women here in camp. Val's gittin' plumb hoggish 'bout them fillies."

"You want to tell him that, Andy?"

"Nope. I reckon I'll pass on that, Claude."

"Thought you would. Proves you ain't en-tarly stupid."

The men laughed and walked, or staggered, on.

Frank waited until the privy was clear and a lone man came staggering out of the rear of the saloon. Frank popped him on the back of the head with a piece of broken board, and dragged the man some distance away from the town. Using the man's belt and bandanna, Frank tied him to a tree and slapped him awake.

"Who the hell are you?" the outlaw demanded. "I cain't see you a-tall. It's so damn dark out here."

"I'm an avenging angel."

"Huh?"

"And you're on your way to hell."

"Say what?"

"I'm one of God's mercenaries."

"You ain't neither. You're Frank Morgan."

"Then why did you ask?"

"Seemed the thing to do at the time. What do you want with me?"

"I want to kill you."

The man's eyes bugged out and he struggled against his

bonds. "Whoa now, Morgan! Why would you want to do that? I ain't done nothin' to you."

"It's what you've done to those kidnapped women in town."

"I ain't personal done nothin' to none of them women. At least, not *them* women."

"But you have raped other women taken in raids."

"Well ... shore," the man admitted. "So what?" he asked belligerently. "All they had to do was give it up without fightin' and there wouldn't have been no rape. Givin' what they got to a man don't hurt 'em none. They're all built for it, ain't they? Hale-fire, Morgan! That's why they was put on this here earth. To pleasure a man and to cook and clean and have kids."

"Is that a fact?"

"Shore is."

"You are a pitiful excuse for a man."

"Maybe you see it that way. That don't make no nevermind to me. Not a whit, it don't. But you gonna be no kind of man in a few minutes. 'Cause I'm a-fixin' to start hollerin'. And you gonna be dead."

Frank slipped a long-bladed knife from its sheath on his gunbelt and pressed it against the outlaw's neck. "Go ahead. Open your mouth to yell. Let's see how fast I can cut your throat. You want to see if you can yell before I do that?"

"I didn't say when I was gonna holler, Morgan," the outlaw whispered. "Be careful with that blade. It feels sharp."

"Oh, it is. Very sharp." He reached around and cut the man's bonds. "See how sharp it is? Now get up and start walking."

"Where to?"

"I'll tell you when we get there. Get in front of me and

start walking." As they walked away from the outlaw town, Frank said, "I've decided not to kill you right now."

"I shore appreciate that, Morgan. I shorely do."

"Shut up and listen."

"Yes, sir. Whatever you say, sir. But I'm a-havin' a hard time walkin' and holdin' my britches up."

"You'll manage. Now shut up and listen to me."

"Yes, sir. I'm a-shuttin' my mouth rat now."

"You go back to town and tell that pack of trash down there that exactly fifteen minutes after the dawning, I'm going to start killing every outlaw I see. You understand that?"

"Do I answer now?"

"Yes."

"I shore do understand it. I shorely do."

"If any want to ride out, be saddled up and ready to ride at dawn. At sixteen minutes after the dawning, the offer is null and void."

"It's what?"

"It's off."

"I know what that means. I will shore spread your message, Morgan. I shorely will do it."

"Fine. Now get the hell out of here."

"Does I get my pistol back?"

"What do you think?"

"I reckon not."

"You reckoned right. Move!"

The man went stumbling off into the night, toward the town. Frank went back and got his saddlebags and rifle and other gear, and moved to a place he had picked earlier: a spot that overlooked the town and gave him good cover. One thing Frank did not believe, and that was that the women had not been raped repeatedly. Probably only a few of Val's personal friends had raped them. That would stop in a few hours.

Either it would stop, or Frank would be dead.

Frank spread his groundsheet on the ground, rolled up in his blanket, and went to sleep.

TWENTY-FIVE

Frank longed for a cup of strong hot coffee as he waited for the sun to rise, but he dared not build even the smallest of fires for fear of giving away his location. So far, he had not heard any sounds of riders leaving the outlaw town. Less than a hundred yards below him, the town remained dark and very quiet. He wondered if the outlaw he had given the warning to had even passed the word to his cohorts. Frank also wondered if perhaps he had overplayed his hand by issuing his ultimatum.

But as he pondered that question, he again realized that he really didn't have much of a choice in the matter. He had to throw down some sort of challenge to Val and his people, and this seemed as good as any. At least it had at the moment.

Just as the sun began to shove rays of light over the

eastern slopes of the Wilderness, about a dozen men walked out of the barn, leading their horses. Their saddlebags were full and bedrolls were tied behind their saddles.

"We're pullin' out, Morgan!" one of the men yelled. "We don't want no trouble with you. You hear?"

Frank remained still and silent behind cover.

The men mounted up and rode out without looking back.

"Let them yeller-bellies go!" The shout came from somewhere in the town. "We're stayin' here and we're gonna kill you, Morgan! You hear that?"

Frank said nothing. He waited for those in the town to start the dance. It was not a long wait.

Half a dozen men ran from the rear of the town into the nearby timber. The search for Frank Morgan was on. The men would probably split up into three groups and begin their hunt. Frank stayed hidden and waited. It would take the men a good half hour of cautious, slow searching to reach his hiding place. Then it would get interesting.

Frank had his rifle fully loaded, and three pistols, all three fully loaded. His cartridge belt was full and he had a bandolier of cartridges slung across his chest bandit-style. And he had a sack of dynamite, about half of it capped and fused. Some of those sticks of explosives with very short fuses.

"What's the matter, Morgan?" The taunting shout came from the town. "You made your brag. Now why don't you come out and fight?"

Oh, sure, Frank thought. *Just step out so you boys can fill me with lead. That'd be real smart on my part. No, thanks. I'll wait.*

A man with more guts than sense jumped out from behind a building and made several obscene gestures to the ridge that ringed the town. When that drew no response from the hidden Frank, the man grew bolder, dropped his pants, and showed his bare butt to the ridges.

"I don't think he's up yonder, boys," the man hollered. "I think he's done gone yeller on us and pulled out."

Several more men stepped out into the open. That was all Frank had been waiting for. Two fast shots later and two of the outlaws lay dead on the ground. Frank had time to at least get lead in a third before the others hightailed it back behind cover, dragging the wounded and hollering man with them.

"You ambushin' bastard!" The shout echoed around the ridge. "You're a damn yeller coward, that's what you are, Morgan."

Frank smiled and waited.

"You boys heard the shots!" another man shouted. "He's up yonder on the ridge, in the rocks and brush, about a hundred yards from town. Get him!"

"Yeah," Frank muttered. "Come and get me, boys."

"He kilt Slim and Wally!" another man shouted. "And Nick's hard hit. Git that no-good bastard. Kill him."

"Good," Frank whispered as he shoved fresh cartridges in his .44-40. "Three less I have to deal with."

He laid his rifle aside for a moment and took out a couple of sticks of short-fused dynamite. Then he dug in his jacket pocket, making certain he had matches. This would be a hell of a time to run out of matches.

Frank carefully watched his flanks. It wouldn't be long before the two teams working the ridges would come into rifle range . . . or better yet, he thought, dynamite range.

He smiled at that thought.

"Y'all see him yet?" someone shouted from the town.

"No," someone from the team on Frank's left yelled. "I

think he's done shifted locations." The shouted reply was close; maybe thirty yards away from Frank.

Frank readied match and dynamite.

"We ain't spotted him neither," someone in the other team yelled. They were much farther away.

Frank centered his attention on the team coming up on his left. He had slipped out of thick cover to get a better throwing position.

He saw the three men just as one yelled, "We're here. But Morgan ain't. I think he's done moved on us."

Frank lit the short fuse and hurled it.

A few seconds later the dynamite exploded. The stick of dynamite landed directly in front of one man, killing him instantly. The concussion knocked the other two sprawling. One lay still on the rocky ground. The other one staggered to his feet, looking dazed.

Frank shot him.

"What in the hell was all that?" someone yelled from the town.

Silence greeted the question.

"Answer me!" the outlaw yelled from town.

"Morgan's usin' dynamite, Rich." The shout came from the second team, on Frank's right. And they were getting closer to Frank's position.

Frank slipped behind the brush he had been using and angled around, on a collision course with the second team.

"Can you see him?" The shout came from town.

"If I could see the bastard, I'd shoot him! No, I can't see him."

But Frank saw *him*. He lit and tossed the dynamite.

The stick of dynamite exploded right in front of a man, in midair, about chest high. The explosion took the man's head off and sent the headless man rolling down the hill. His friends took off running.

Frank dropped one with a leg shot. The third one made the timber, and Frank could hear him thrashing through the brush, hauling his butt down the hill.

Frank ran back to his gear, grabbed it up, and took off into the timber, heading for another location, on the far side of town.

"This ain't workin' out worth a damn," another outlaw shouted from the town. "We gonna have to rush him, boys."

Frank paused, checking to see if anyone took up the challenge and rushed the ridge.

No one did.

Frank moved on.

It's all been too easy, Frank thought as he ran to a different location. *It's all been just too damn easy. Why don't they all pour out of town, all heading in different directions, and blanket the ridges with men? That's the only way they're going to take me. Just hunt me down en masse. Are they so damn stupid they haven't realized that?*

Frank stopped to rest for a moment and looked down at the town. From this point, as it would be from his new vantage point, the town was only about seventy-five yards below him. There was no movement from the outlaws. "Incredible," Frank muttered. He shook his head in disbelief and continued on the last few yards.

He wormed his way into his new location, again in the rocks and brush, and took a sip of water from his canteen and ate a hunk of bread. He said to hell with caution—the outlaws weren't moving, so to hell with it—and rolled and smoked a cigarette. He longed for a cup of good hot, strong coffee, and with an effort, pushed that thought out of his mind.

Then he heard the pounding hooves of fast-running horses. Startled, Frank jerked up his rifle. Half a dozen riders were racing out of town. They had bedrolls behind their saddles and their saddlebags were bulging with gear.

"Well, I'll just be damned," Frank said. "Running out. This is incredible." Frank couldn't tell who the men were, not from this distance.

Frank figured there were probably less than thirty outlaws left in the ramshackle town. And he had no idea where the women were now being held. They might have been moved during the night. He couldn't start firing into the buildings hoping to hit an outlaw for fear of one of his bullets striking a hostage.

So it was back to cat and mouse. But whether the outlaws realized it or not—and obviously they didn't—theirs was a mighty big cat against a lone mouse.

"If'n you don't get the hell gone from here and leave us alone, Morgan," someone called from the town, "we'll start killin' the women."

Frank had wondered when that threat would be tossed out. And there it was.

"You hear me, Morgan? And afore we do that, we'll hurt these women. I promise you, we'll hurt them bad."

Frank had wondered when that too would be threatened.

He said nothing. He waited, but he had made up his mind about one thing. When night came, he was going into that town.

"We done kilt two women, Morgan. You prob'ly found one of them back yonder on the trail. We kilt the other one jist 'fore you got here. We double-teamed her, and she got to squallin' and carryin' on so bad we broke her neck. So don't think we won't kill these here. Don't you doubt that for a minute."

Frank didn't ponder long on the meaning of "double-teamed." He knew what it meant. He softly cursed.

"Go ahead and let them kill me, Mr. Morgan!" a girl's voice screamed. "I can't stand no more of this. They been hurtin' me real bad. They been makin' me do all sorts of things and they been usin' me in . . ."

Frank tried to block her descriptions from his ears. He could not. And the outlaws were letting her talk, letting her tell him every vile, perverted thing they had done to her. It was sickening. Disgusting. Frank could not imagine the type of men who would force a girl to do some of the acts the young lady was vividly describing.

When the girl began crying and sobbing hysterically, the outlaws began laughing, obscenely urging her on.

They're not men, Frank concluded. *And they're far worse than animals. To compare them to animals would be an insult to the animal world.*

Frank abruptly shifted locations, this time to a spot just above the one road leading out of the outlaw town.

"Hey, Morgan!" a man yelled. "While we's waitin' for you to make up your mind, we'll just have us another taste of this young gal. We want you to listen to her. You ready for this, Morgan? Listen to her now."

A girl suddenly began screaming in pain and humiliation and degradation. The outlaws were laughing.

There was nothing Frank could do. He waited in silence, letting his anger wash over him in invisible clouds of rage.

The day wore on, and the woman's screaming finally subsided into low moans, then into silence. Frank spent part of his time capping and fusing sticks of dynamite. At full dark, he was going to take the fight into the town.

"We're tarred now, Morgan," a man yelled from the town. "We done had our pleasures with the fillies. We're gonna take us a rest now while we're waitin' for you, Morgan."

"I'll be along, boys," Frank whispered. "Just as sure as the sun sets and the moon rises, I'll be along. And when I'm through, your town will be a ghost town. In more ways than one."

TWENTY-SIX

Frank left his rifle on the ridge and carried only his pistols and the sack of capped and fused dynamite. He had capped and fused *all* the dynamite. He was determined that once the women were safe, he was going to destroy the town. But getting the women to a secure place was his first priority.

Frank stepped around the corner of a building and came face-to-face face with an outlaw. The rapist reached for his gun and Frank laid his Peacemaker up alongside the man's head. The man dropped like a rock and did not move. Frank didn't bother trussing him up. He was about to make his presence known in a big way.

Frank looked through the cracks in a building and saw four men, all heavily armed, sitting at a table, playing cards with what looked like a very greasy deck. Frank slipped a stick of dynamite out of his pouch and took a match from his pocket.

"I want me some more of that kid," one of the men said. "I can't git me enough of that."

"Val said, 'fore he pulled out with them others this mornin', we could use 'em up and then kill 'em," another said. "So keep your britches on, Lars. She'll be here waitin' when we git shut of Frank Morgan."

So Val and probably Little Ed had pulled out and were long gone. Frank had suspected that would be the case. No matter. He would track them down one by one—all of them—and even the score as much as possible for what had happened to the women.

"I like the way that young'un hollers and squalls when I git with her," Lars said, his lips curving in an evil smile. "I like to slap her around and settle her down when I've had enough of her whimperin' and cryin'."

"You're a pig, Lars," another said.

"Maybe I am that, Waddy. But you poked your share of that other young gal as I recall—right?"

The man called Waddy laughed. "And I aim to git me some more of it too, Lars. But first we got to git ourselves rid of Morgan."

"That's right," the fourth man said. "What I want me is some more of that cold-lookin' blonde. She needs a good beatin' to show her who's boss. And I aim to give her another one."

"She shore ain't one to beg none, is she?" Waddy said. "I never seen a woman take on a whole line of men and not beg for mercy."

That did it for Frank. He popped the match head into flame, touched the flame to the fuse, jerked off one of the boards covering the broken window, and tossed the stick of dynamite into the room.

"Jesus Christ!" one of the men yelled just as Frank was leaping into a ditch behind the house.

That was all the rapist had time to utter before the dynamite blew. The heavy charge blew the walls out and collapsed the roof on top of the four men, crushing them, if any were still alive, that is.

"Good riddance," Frank whispered. There was no sound of moaning or yelling for help from the rubble.

Men began running out of a building close by, and Frank pulled out his Colts and started evening the score. Outlaws were hitting the ground, hollering in pain as their hands clutched at perforated chests and bellies.

Frank shifted positions, the darkness covering him as he ran, crouching low. He jumped into a ditch and quickly reloaded his guns. He had scouted out the town earlier and knew where the women were being held, so now there was no danger of his accidentally harming them. They were being guarded by four men. Those would be the last of the outlaw/rapists he would deal with.

"Somebody kill that son of a bitch!" a man shouted.

"Where is he?" The question was tossed out into the night just as Frank was lighting the fuse on a stick of dynamite, his body shielding the slight flicker of flame.

"Right here," Frank called, a second after he tossed the explosive into a knot of men standing outside the hotel.

The outlaws didn't even have time to scream out a warning or shout in fear before the charge blew. Bits and pieces of shattered bodies went flying in all directions. Several men ran out of an alley just as the enormous sound was fading into the night. They ran right into the guns of Frank Morgan. Frank blistered the night with .45-caliber death, firing until his guns were empty, and the men went down into the littered dirt.

Frank quickly reloaded and again shifted positions, this

time darting into an alley and running across the rutted street. He crouched beside a shack and waited.

"Cecil?" a man called from directly across the street. "Where you is, Cec?"

"I'm down here, Luke." The answer came from Frank's left.

Not more than a dozen yards away, Frank guessed. Probably on the other side of the building next to the one he was standing beside.

"How many boys you got with you, Cec?"

"Five, I think. You?"

"About that, I reckon. Got some hurt real bad. They ain't gonna make it neither. One of 'um's innards is all a-hangin' out. It's plumb sickenin'. That goddamn dynamite really screwed it all up."

"The last bunch got some lead in Morgan's direction. I seen it. Maybe he got hit, you think?"

"I hope. But I ain't countin' on it. Hell, didn't nobody figure the man would really come down into the town after us."

"We got to kill him, Luke. We're all gonna die if we don't. You know that, don't you?"

"I know." The reply was almost whispered. Frank had to strain to hear it.

"Or give it up."

"I thought 'bout that too. Believe me, I have."

"Reckon he'd let us?"

"Don't know. I ain't above axin' him. You?"

"Me neither."

"Y'all ax if you want to," another voice added. It came from across the street and a couple of shacks down from Luke. "I ain't givin' up. Not me. I aim to kill that bastard and take that cold-lookin' blond woman and have my way with her. And I know some ways that'll make her squall."

"You do what you want, Sam," Luke said. "We'll do what we want. Right, Cec?"

"Damn right."

"Y'all yeller, that's what you are," Sam called. "I got Kallen and Otis and Louie and Wilson with me. We're gonna kill that damn Morgan. You hear me, Morgan?" he shouted to the night. "You're a dead man."

"Yeah," yet another voice added. "And I'm gonna be the one who shoots your eyes out, Morgan. My name is Ham Nederland. I want you to 'member that name in the time you got left you. Ham Nederland."

Frank said nothing. He waited in silence. But his thinking was that this person called Ham was trying really hard to get his courage up and working.

"He's so damn yeller he won't even answer nobody," Ham called. "Hey! You reckon he took lead and is hurt bad?"

"I wouldn't count on that," Cec called. "He's just layin' low, bidin' his time. He's waitin' for the right moment to strike."

"I think you're yeller too," Cec called. "You and Luke. I think both of you done pissed your pants you're so a-feared of Morgan."

"Think what you want to think, Hambone."

"Don't you call me Hambone, Cec! Damn your scummy eyes. I'll kill you if you call me Hambone."

Both Cec and Luke laughed.

"Goddamn you!" Ham shouted. "Don't neither of you dare laugh at me. My God, I'll kill you both."

"Cec, Luke!" Frank called softly. "Get your gear together and clear out. Go far away. Don't ever let me see either of you again. If I do, I'll kill you. Now get out of here. I'll let you both ride out."

"We're gone, Morgan. You'll not see neither of us again. I promise you that."

"Good. Now clear out of here. If some of your own friends don't kill you when you try, that is."

"Let's go, Cec," Luke called. "Careful now."

"I'm goin' the back way to the livery. Meet you there."

"Well, I ain't skirred of you, Morgan!" a woman shouted.

"You tell 'im, Mama!" another man called.

"Go git him, Bloody Mama!" Ham shouted.

"You may be a stallion now, Morgan," another woman shouted. "But when I git done with you, you gonna be a geldin'. I'm gonna de-nut you, Morgan."

"You tell him, Sadie!"

Lovely ladies, Frank thought. On a sudden hunch, Frank decided to shift locations. He slipped away silently just as he spotted several dark shapes moving toward his old position.

Just in time, he thought. *Getting me to talk was a setup by Cec and Luke.*

Frank crawled under one building and as quietly as possible wriggled out the other side.

"The bastard's gone, Luke!"

In the very dim light, Frank could see the legs of the man. He sighted in on the man's knee and squeezed the trigger. Cec went down to ground, hollering in pain.

"I'm hit, Luke. He's on the other side of this building. Oh, God, it hurts somethin' awful. Git him for me."

"Hell with this," Luke called. "I'm gone. Good luck, Cec."

"Damn you!" Cec yelled. "You cain't leave me like this. I cain't walk, Luke. Come help me."

There was no reply from Luke. Luke was hauling his ashes.

"I thought you was my pard," Cec moaned.

Honor among thieves, Frank thought. Nonexistent.

Bloody Mama and Sadie began cussing Frank, filling the night air with the most vulgar of profanities. They used words and phrases Frank would not use. They suggested things they were going to do to the kidnapped women, once Frank was dead. And when he was killed, they said amid the vulgarity, they were going to dismember his body and make the women cook and eat various parts of him.

And they were going to pickle and preserve a certain part of him, to show to other outlaws in the West. Maybe charge admission to see it.

"What a couple of nice ladies," Frank whispered under his breath. Then he smiled at the thought: Come one, come all. Only twenty-five cents to see Frank Morgan's . . .

He shook his head at the absurdity of it.

"Hey, Morgan!" A new voice was added. "This here is Bob. Booger Bob. I got me a bullet with your name on it, Morgan."

Frank shifted locations again, this time moving to the far end of the street, behind the last building in the ramshackle town. The building was without most of its roof and minus a part of one wall.

"Hey, Morgan!" Booger shouted. "You know where I'm gonna shoot you? I'm gonna stick my rifle up your . . ."

Frank sighed as Booger finished the sentence. The outlaws were certainly getting quite inventive about what they were going to do with him.

Frank let them shout suggestions back and forth. He took that time to dart across the road and peek into the building where the women were being held. The four men guarding them were not taking part in the shouting of insults. They were tense and at the ready. Frank could see some of the women, all huddled together under blankets at the far end of the building. He could not see them very well, but well enough to know they were all in bad shape.

Time to bring this battle to a conclusion.

Frank moved cautiously behind the buildings. He could not understand why all the outlaws had taken refuge in buildings and were not out looking for him. It was one thing to be cautious, and quite another to be stupid.

Frank lit the fuse to a stick of dynamite and tossed it under a building, then ran two buildings up and squatted down just as the explosive blew.

The floor of the old building was shattered by the charge and the walls puffed out. The roof collapsed, falling on top of those trapped inside. One man staggered out. Frank shot him.

"He's behind us!" someone shouted. "Let's get him."

A knot of men came running through the darkness. Frank lit another stick and tossed it. The outlaws ran right into it. The explosion sent some of them spinning like tops, and sent bits and pieces of others hurtling into the night. It momentarily deafened several others, and Frank solved their discomfort with .45-caliber medicine, sending them forever to a place where the only sounds they would hear would be their own flesh sizzling from the flames, their own wailing in agony, and the laughter of Satan.

"Hey, Morgan?" a man shouted as Frank took that time to run back down the back of the shacks of the main street of the outlaw town. He wanted to be near the building where the women were being held. "Can we make some kind of a deal?"

Frank offered no reply. They knew he was listening.

"This is Goody Nolan, Morgan. We've run into each other a time or two."

Frank waited.

"I can only speak for myself and the two men I rode in here with. Shiv Lopez and Aaron Samuels. You know 'em both."

Frank did, and they were just as sorry and worthless as Goody.

"We're next to the livery, Morgan. We can ride and circle around, get clear of town and any of the others who might want to shoot us for pullin' out. If you don't say nothin', then I'll take that as a deal made, Morgan."

Frank remained still and silent.

"We're gone, Morgan."

Several minutes later, Frank heard the sounds of horses' hooves, the riders lying back as far as they could from the town.

"You yellow bastards!" Sadie screamed. "Ain't a one of you got no balls."

"Cowards!" Bloody Mama shrieked. "No-good pissants."

Frank had moved back to the building where the women were held. One of the men guarding the women said, "Goody's got him the right idea. Let's get the hell out of here, boys."

"What about the women?"

"Hell with them. Lookie here, gals," he said to the women. "Me and the boys are pullin' out. Y'all stay quiet and don't yell or nothin'. Your man's gonna luck up and win this fight and you'll be safe."

"If I ever see you," Lara said, her voice as cold as frost on a pump handle, "I'll kill you myself."

"You won't see me again, lady. Bet on that."

"Let's do it, Dag," another said. "Let's get gone."

Frank slipped under the old building and waited until the men had exited the building. He listened as they rode away, taking the same route as Goody and his pals.

Frank stood up, brushed off the dirt from his clothing, and stepped into the building, mentally preparing himself for the worst as he viewed the women close up.

It was even worse than he had imagined.

TWENTY-SEVEN

"Don't say a word," Frank urged the women in a whispered voice. He was trying to keep the shock he felt upon seeing them from his face. He wasn't at all sure he was succeeding.

"Frank," Lara said, standing up, holding a blanket around her to cover her nakedness. "I felt sure you'd come."

Lara's face was swollen and puffy from being beaten. Her lips were twice their normal size. Both her eyes were nearly closed from the swelling. All the women were in very bad shape. Two of them, Frank noted, could not even stand up.

The four men who had hastily pulled out had left behind two rifles, leaning in a corner of the building. Frank picked one up and checked it, then handed the weapon to Lara. "You know how to use this, Lara?"

"Oh, yes." She took the rifle.

"I've got to clean this place out," Frank said. "There are still some snakes that need to be stomped on. Lara, if I don't come back . . ."

"I know," she replied softly, then lifted the rifle. "They won't take any of us alive, Frank."

Frank took a deep breath, then nodded his head. "All right, Lara." His eyes touched the blanket-covered body of a woman lying on the floor. "Who is that?"

"One of the women they kidnapped earlier. She died about an hour ago. Val beat her with his fists yesterday. She never regained consciousness."

"I'll be back," Frank said.

"We're counting on it, Frank."

Frank slipped out of the building and stood for a moment, letting his eyes adjust once more to the night. He felt his emotions hardened and then turn mean. Mad-dog mean. He reached into the sack hanging from his gunbelt and pulled out a stick of dynamite. Then he walked to the next house and pressed his ear to the outside wall. He could hear the muffled sound of voices. He lit the dynamite and tossed the sputtering stick under the house, then ran for cover.

The dynamite blew and the old building completely collapsed; the walls blew out and the roof came crashing down. People might have survived that, but if they did, they were badly hurt.

Just then, Frank heard the sounds of galloping horses. He looked toward the road and could just make out the shapes of about a half dozen or so horses. The last of the outlaws were pulling out; they were calling it quits.

Frank began walking the town, looking for survivors. The first one he found was the outlaw with the busted knee, Cec.

Frank squatted down and looked at the man. Someone had bashed his head in and turned his pockets inside out, stealing whatever the man had. They had also taken his guns. "Nice friends you had, Cec," Frank muttered.

He walked on. He found several wounded outlaws and dragged them to a house. He put them inside and closed and locked the door.

"Are you gonna leave us in here to die, Morgan?" one called.

"Yes," Frank replied. "At least for tonight. I'll turn you loose in the morning and leave you horses to ride out on."

"This ain't Christian, Morgan."

"Take it up with God," Frank told him, and walked away.

Frank leveled a rifle at the driver of the heavily laden supply wagon, and the men lifted their hands. "I ain't nothin' but a delivery man, mister," the driver said. "But I know you. You're Frank Morgan. Booger Bob said you was here. I come with the supplies and for my money."

"I'll pay you. Go to the livery and saddle two horses. Get out. I ought to shoot both of you dead for consorting with the trash that lived here."

"How 'bout our money?" the other man asked.

Frank tossed him a wad of bills and a sack of gold coins he'd taken from the dead outlaws at first light. "There's your money. Now get the hell gone from here."

The pair were gone ten minutes later. They did not look back.

Frank drove the wagon down to the livery and unhooked the team. He rubbed them down and forked hay to them, then unloaded the wagon. Lara walked down to the barn and stood in silence for a moment, watching him.

"Is that how we're leaving, Frank, in that wagon?"

"Yes. I'll put hay in the bed to cushion the ride. We'll pull out in the morning."

"How far is the nearest town?"

"About four days, in this wagon. It isn't going to be a pleasant trip."

"Neither was the ride here or our stay."

Frank looked at the woman. "No, I'm sure it wasn't. But it's over now."

"It will never be over, Frank. Not in our minds, that is. Our bodies will heal. But not our minds."

"I reckon not, Lara." He continued forking hay into the bed of the wagon.

"Did you bury the dead men, Frank?"

"I put their bodies in a shack. I'll set it on fire in the morning. That'll have to do."

"It's more than they deserve."

"I'm sure of that."

Lara walked to the front of the livery. "I'll gather up as many blankets as I can, Frank. And those of us who are able will heat some water for a bath of sorts. We have to bathe, Frank. Do I have to explain that?"

"No. I understand."

"Good."

"As soon as I get done here, I'll fix us something to eat. A big pot of stew or something. Soup maybe."

"Whatever, Frank. I made some coffee. It's on the stove."

"Thanks. I could use some."

When Frank finished in the livery, he walked the town, making one last check to see if he'd missed any outlaws that might still be alive. He had not. Then he walked back to the building where the women were staying and poured a mug of coffee. He went outside, sat down, and rolled a cigarette. He drank his coffee slowly and smoked. He was tired, very tired. The events of the previous night were catching up to him. Frank was far from being an old man, but he sure as hell was no longer a young buck, full of piss and vinegar.

"Mr. Morgan?" The young girl's voice opened his eyes.

Frank looked into the battered face of young Lydia Wilson. All of fourteen . . . now going on forty, Frank thought. "Yes, honey?"

"What am I going to tell my mama and papa?"

"The truth, Lydia. As much of it as you think they can stand to bear."

"And how much is that?"

"I don't know, honey. Maybe you can talk to Doc Evans and he can help with that. You're going to have to see him."

"I know. But I don't know what to say to him. It's . . . well . . . so personal and awful." She ran back into the house, weeping uncontrollably.

Lara came out and sat down beside Frank. "I think," she said, "I will be heading back East, Frank. I still have some family back there."

"Might be a good idea." Frank knew right then and there that once he got Lara back to town, he would never see her again.

"I could never live in Chance again, Frank. I couldn't face the townspeople day after day. I just couldn't."

"It would be a hard thing, I'm sure."

"Would you come back East with me, Frank?"

Frank shook his head. "No, Lara. I couldn't live back yonder. Too damn many rules and regulations for me. I like my freedom."

"People are free back there."

Again, Frank shook his head. "No, they're not. They just think they are. We've had this discussion before. It wouldn't work for me."

Lara rose from the step and walked back into the building without saying another word to Frank. Frank experienced a very acute sense of loss for a moment, then sighed and stood up. He would have liked another cup of coffee, but didn't feel like facing the women again . . . not just yet. He was bone-tired, and he was dirty and would have liked a bath and a shave. He looked rough, and probably smelled that way. He just wanted to lie down and go to sleep. But he had promised the ladies he'd fix a pot of stew. Frank went back to the cache of supplies and rummaged through the pile. He decided to fix some bacon and fried potatoes. That would have to do.

Dixie Malone had walked down to the livery, and watched Frank for a moment. "Let me do that, Mr. Morgan," she said from the doorway.

"You sure?" Frank asked.

"It would help get my mind off . . . things."

"I reckon so. Sure. I'll get a fire going and we'll fix something to eat."

While the food was cooking, Dixie said, "Those among us who are married are wondering how much we should tell our husbands."

Frank looked at her. "I can't answer that, Dixie. How strong is your husband?"

"You don't mean physical strength, do you?"

"No."

"He's a mighty jealous man, I can tell you that."

Frank hesitated. How to answer her question? In the minds of many, once a good woman had been raped, she was soiled. The husbands—many of them anyway—would always wonder several things. One, could she have prevented it? Two, could she have found a way to kill herself? Death was better than rape. And three, did she secretly enjoy it?

"You tell him what you think he needs to know, Dixie. I'm going to talk to the men and tell them what I personally saw and heard . . . tell them up to a point, that is."

She smiled at that. "Thank you, Mr. Morgan."

"Frank. Just Frank. Mr. Morgan is going to get burdensome. We've got a long way to go."

Frank set fire to the outlaw town, torching every building. On the morning they pulled out, the outlaw town was blazing.

There were nine women to be transported back home. Six from the town of Chance, and three others from nearby farms. One of them, a woman called Pearl, had seemingly lost her mind. She never spoke a word. She just sat quite still in the bed of the wagon and slobbered down the front of her dress.

"Two outlaws at once took her several times," Dixie said. "It was awful to watch. Little Ed was among them."

"I intend to find them all, Dixie," Frank told her. "I'll see they get justice."

"After the last assault on her," Lydia said, "her eyes just sort of glazed over and she never said nothin' else to nobody."

Lydia and Nellie chose to ride horseback on the way back home . . . astride. Which was sort of embarrassing to Frank, but he declined to say anything about it. The girls had found some men's britches in the town, washed them proper, and put them on, using a bit of rope for belts to keep them up.

"Those two women, Sadie and Bloody Mama," Lara said, "they were worse than the men."

"Perverted bitches," Dixie said.

Then Lara proceeded to tell Frank some of the things the two outlaw women had done. Frank would have preferred she had kept that information to herself. When she finished her rather graphic retelling, Frank felt his ears burning.

"Thank you so much for that information, Lara," Frank

told her, trying without success to keep the sarcasm from his voice.

"You're certainly welcome, Frank," she replied with an equal amount of sarcasm.

With the burning town behind them, Frank and the women started the long trek home. Frank had no idea what had happened to the whores who lived and worked in the town. They'd either run off into the timber or ridden out with some of the outlaws. Really, he didn't much give a damn what had happened to them. He'd read a line once in a book about how people who lie down with dogs usually got up with fleas. Something like that. Couldn't remember who wrote it. Shakespeare maybe.

Frank had packed enough supplies to last the trip. The women would share the driving chores.

It was going to be a long trip.

The people of the town of Chance turned out en masse to watch as Frank escorted the women into the town. No one cheered. They all stood in silence and simply watched. Frank reined up in front of Doc Evans's office, and the women quickly got out of the wagon and went into the office. Frank had told a boy who had met the procession outside of town to get into town and make sure Doc Evans was in his office. None of the women said a word to any of the townspeople.

Frank stood outside the office to make sure no one else went in.

Lydia Wilson's father pushed his way through the crowd to face Frank. "Frank? My daughter?"

"She's alive, Will."

"Thank God! I got to get home and tell her mother."

"I saw them come in, Will," Mrs. Hockstedler said, a

very smug look on her face. "Lydia was riding a horse . . . astride."

"I don't give a damn if she was sittin' on the horse's nose," Will told the busybody. "She's *alive!*"

Mrs. Hockstedler sniffed her displeasure at Will's remark and turned away.

Lawyer Whitter walked up. "My estranged wife, Mr. Morgan?"

"She's alive, John. All the women who were taken from this town are alive."

"After being gone for several weeks and, ah, having been sexually, ah, shall we say, *entertained* numerous times by various men, the women being alive, as you put it, is purely a matter of opinion."

Frank knocked the lawyer off the boardwalk. John crawled to his knees, his mouth bloody, and then uttered the words that even back in the 1880s were on their way to the de-balling of America, "I'll sue you!"

Frank laughed at him just as Marshal Wright came walking up.

"Go home, John," Tom told him. "Before Frank tears your head off and hands it to you."

Doc Evans opened the office and motioned for Frank to step inside. "Go tell the barber to heat up all the water he can and lay out all the tubs, Frank. Then go over to O'Malley's and tell Mrs. O'Malley to give you some good-smelling women's soap."

"Will do, Doc."

Doc Evans sniffed a couple of times and frowned. "And you need to find yourself some good strong soap and a horse trough too."

"Thanks a lot, Doc."

Johnny Vargas stopped Frank before he got to the general store. "Lucked out again, hey, Drifter?"

"This time I'd have to agree with you about that, Johnny."

"Did you get Val?"

"No. Or Little Ed."

"Little Ed really hooked up with Val? That don't surprise me none. I heard they'd been plottin' something even before Little Ed got in trouble." Johnny stared at Frank for a moment, then smiled. "You look rough, Drifter. You better get some rest and get cleaned up. You and me are gonna settle something tomorrow."

"What?" Frank asked.

"Who's the fastest gun. I'll see you at noon tomorrow, Drifter." He pointed. "Right out there in that street."

TWENTY-EIGHT

"Can't you do something about this fight, Frank?" Doc Evans asked.

It was just after eleven o'clock. Frank and Doc Evans were sitting in the Blue Bird Café, having coffee. Doc Evans was watching the minutes tick away on the clock.

"I don't know what I could do, Doc. Johnny has been wanting a showdown for a long time. It had to happen."

"Tom can arrest him."

"On what charge? Johnny hasn't broken any laws that I know of."

"Threatening a peace officer."

Frank smiled. "This is still the West, Doc. A man gets called out, he either meets his challenger, or leaves town."

"And you're not planning on leaving town."

"Not because of Johnny Vargas."

"Can you beat him, Frank?"

"It'll be close, Doc. Johnny's real fast. Doc? How about those young girls who were raped?"

"What do you mean?"

"The chances of them being with child."

"I did what I could, Frank. Doctors, many of us, that is, keep a small amount of grain that has been contaminated by a certain fungus. It can induce labor. It doesn't always work, but . . ." He shrugged his shoulders. "It's the best I can do."

"And the woman who won't speak?"

"She's in shock, Frank. She might come out of it in the next five minutes, she might never come out of it. If you asked me to guess, I'd say she's heading for an asylum. And those are very grim places."

"So I've heard."

"Back to this Johnny Vargas . . ."

"He often misses his first shot."

Doc Evans frowned and shook his head. "Frank, why not just get a shotgun and blow him out of his boots?"

"Because we're gunfighters, Doc."

"What the hell has that got to do with the situation?"

"It's an unwritten code, Doc."

"Nonsense!"

Frank smiled at the expression on the doctor's face. "Lara called it a man thing."

"About you and Lara . . ."

"That's over, Doc. Before it even had a chance to properly begin."

"Give her some time, Frank."

"That won't solve a thing, Doc. She doesn't like the West. She wants to go back East where it's civilized."

"I'm from the East," Doc Evans said. "You couldn't get me back there with a sledgehammer and a pry bar."

Frank looked at the clock, then motioned for more coffee.

"You don't appear at all nervous, Frank," the doctor observed.

"I've done this many times, Doc. Nothing to get nervous about."

"It's life and death, man!"

Frank shrugged. "On another matter, the women gave me a list of names of the men who assaulted them."

"And you'll be going after them?"

"You bet I will."

"A personal vendetta, Frank?"

"You can call it that."

Doc Evans sighed. "Where is this Vargas person? Getting drunk in the Purple Lily?"

"No. I assure you, Johnny will be cold sober when we meet. He's a professional."

"The one thing I have never understood about the West: a *professional* gunfighter. How do you make a living doing that?"

That brought a quick laugh from Frank. Before he could reply to Doc Evans's question, he saw Johnny Vargas step out of the hotel and onto the boardwalk. Frank looked at the clock. It was not yet noon. "I guess Johnny got impatient. There he is."

Without looking around, Doc Evans said, "So now you walk out and soon one of you will be dead."

"That's the way it usually goes, Doc."

"You don't appear to be in any hurry."

"I'm going to finish my coffee. Let Johnny wait. He'll get a little jumpy when I don't immediately show."

"You've given these showdowns some thought, haven't you?"

Frank slowly nodded his head. "I've had plenty of practice."

Both men watched as the main street of town was quickly cleared of people and horses. Frank slowly drank his coffee. Doc Evans watched the man closely. The man known as the Drifter showed no emotion; no nervousness, nothing. His face was expressionless. His hands did not have the slightest tremor. But his eyes were like looking into the bony face of death. Doc Evans knew then why so many men were scared of Frank Morgan.

Frank drained his coffee cup and pushed back his chair.

"It isn't yet noon, Frank."

"Oh, we'll stand on opposite sides of the street and have a stare-down for a few minutes. That's the way it usually goes."

"One trying to intimidate the other?"

"Something like that."

"I don't like this, Frank. Not at all. The town has plans for you to stay and be a part of this community."

"I won't be staying, Doc. I'll be pulling out very soon. I've got some justice I've got to deliver."

"Maybe we can change your mind about that."

"Don't count on it." Frank walked out of the café, then strolled over to the edge of the boardwalk and leaned up against a support post. He slowly rolled a cigarette, lit it, then looked over at Johnny Vargas.

Johnny lifted his cigar in greeting.

The men stared at each other in silence across the wide street. The townspeople who had remained on the main street quickly stepped into stores. Dozens of faces began appearing in store windows along Main Street, everybody wanting to witness this shootout between two of the West's most famous and feared gunslingers. Tiny dust devils began whipping and circling madly in the street.

Johnny stepped off the boardwalk and walked to the center of the street. Frank tossed his cigarette away and stepped out in the street, walking to the center and turning slowly to face Johnny Vargas.

"This has to be, Drifter," Johnny said. "It just has to be. You know that, don't you?"

"No. But if that's what you think, so be it."

"One of us has to be top dog, Drifter. There isn't room at the top for both of us."

"If you say so, Johnny."

"You're gettin' old, Drifter. You should have hung up your guns a long time ago. It didn't have to end like this."

Frank smiled as he saw the fingers on Johnny Vargas's left hand twitch nervously. He knew then, sensed it, that he was going to beat Johnny. Knew because Johnny Vargas was scared.

"What are you smiling about, Drifter?" Johnny asked.

"What's the matter, Johnny?" Frank asked softly, in a voice so low that only Johnny could hear it.

"What do you mean, Drifter?"

"You're scared, Johnny. I can almost smell the fear on you."

"That's a damn lie, Drifter," Johnny whispered.

"No, Johnny. It's the truth. That's sweat running down your face. And it's a cool day. You don't see me sweating."

"Damn you to hell, Drifter!" Johnny hissed the words.

"Walk away, Johnny. Do it now and live."

Johnny hesitated, then whispered, "I can't, Drifter. I can't do it. I done made my brags and I've got to see it through."

"Don't be a fool. Man, you've got a chance to live. Don't force me to pull on you. Don't do it."

"No, Drifter. It has to be this way."

"What's wrong, Johnny? Tell me what's the matter."

"Nothin'."

"You're lying."

"I ain't lyin', Drifter. Don't push me on this."

"No, Johnny. Something is wrong with you. What is it?"

Johnny sighed so heavily, Frank could hear him thirty feet away.

"Tell me, Johnny."

"Damn you, Drifter. I got the cancer in my belly. The doctors say I'm dyin'. But I'm goin' out knowin' I got lead in you."

"Who in town knows about it?"

"No one. And I'd be obliged if it stayed that way. Providin', of course, you somehow luck up and beat me."

"I'll beat you, Johnny. I'll make my shot true and stop the pain."

"You bastard!" Johnny whispered. "You arrogant bastard. I've always admired and hated you at the same time."

"I never hated you, Johnny. Never had any reason to. Hate is a mighty strong word."

"Yeah, I reckon it is. You ready, Drifter?"

"Only if you are, Johnny."

There was thirty feet between them. The wind suddenly died away, the sighing ceased. No dogs barked. The town was very quiet.

"I'll see you in hell, Drifter."

"Drag iron, Johnny."

Both men grabbed for the deadly Big Iron.

TWENTY-NINE

Both guns spat fire and death, not an instant's difference in the speed of their draw. The bullet from Johnny's pistol nicked Frank on the arm. Frank's bullet hit Johnny Vargas in the center of the chest and knocked him down in the dirt.

Frank walked up to stand over the man. Johnny smiled at him and said, "Damn, you're good, Drifter. I thought sure I could take you."

"Sorry about this, Johnny."

"Least it was you who done me in. I'm glad about that. I'll see you, Frank Morgan." Johnny Vargas coughed, closed his eyes, and died in the street.

Doc Evans was the first to reach the men. "You're hurt, Frank!"

"Just a nick, Doc. A little bit of horse liniment and it'll be fine."

Doc Evans knelt down beside Johnny for a few seconds, then slowly rose to his feet. "He's dead, Frank. My God, I never even saw you men draw. I've never seen anything that fast."

"I damn shore never seen nothin' like it," a local stated.

"The telegrapher is right now wirin' up and down the line," a man said, walking up to stare down at the body of Johnny Vargas.

"What's he wiring?" Doc Evans asked.

"That Frank Morgan killed Johnny Vargas in a stand-up-and-hook-and-draw in the middle of the street."

Undertaker Pennybaker walked over and said, "You reckon he's got any money?"

"I'm sure he does," Frank said.

"Then I'll give him a right nice funeral. If he's got fifty extra dollars, I'll have a band and some moaners and wailers too."

"I think Johnny would have liked that," Frank said.

"Consider it done, Mr. Morgan."

"Come on over to my office, Frank," Doc Evans said. "I want to look at that arm."

Frank looked up at a hotel window. Lara was standing there. She frowned at him and turned away.

"So much for that," Frank muttered.

Doc Evans had seen Lara at the window. "Give her time, Frank. She's had quite a terrible experience."

The men began walking to Doc Evans's office. As they walked, Frank said, "I'd give her all the time in the world if I thought it would do any good. But it won't."

Doc Evans had nothing more to say on the subject.

The nick Frank had received was cleaned out and a small bandage put over it. "You'll live, Frank," the doctor said. "At least for now," he added dryly.

"I'll be pulling out in the morning, Doc."

"So soon?"

"Yes. With the news of my killing Johnny Vargas out over the wire, there'll be gunslingers heading this way to try their luck with me. It'll be better for the town if I ride out as quickly as possible."

The doctor slowly nodded his head. "Reluctantly, I have to agree with you."

"I'll go provision up now, Doc. Get the packsaddle ready to load. I'll catch you later at the café."

Frank went to O'Malley's and bought coffee, bacon, flour, sugar, beans, potatoes, and a dozen cans of bully beef for Dog. Jack O'Malley refused to let him pay for any of it.

"No way, Frank. This town owes you too much. I'll be sorry to see you go."

"Thanks, Jack. I'll see you again before I ride out."

"I'm counting on it."

Dog got all excited when he saw Frank start readying the packsaddle. He began running around in circles and barking.

"All right, all right, settle down," Frank told the big cur. "We need to get on the trail. You're getting fat."

Frank got his clothes from the laundry, then bought a bit of grain to take along for the horses. He was almost ready. He planned on going to sleep early and pulling out long before dawn. He walked the main street, stopping at various stores and shops to say his good-byes. Then he walked over to the marshal's office.

Tom had just made a fresh pot of coffee, and Frank poured a cup and sugared it, then sat down.

"I really hate to see you go, Frank. I was hopin' you might decide to settle down here with us."

"It's a nice town, Tom. But settling down is not in the cards for me. Not yet anyway."

"You told Lara you're leavin'?"

"She knows, in a way."

"Whatever the hell that means."

"I'll be pulling out before dawn."

"Going after the men who kidnapped and raped the women?"

"Yes."

"You know where I wish you'd shoot them?"

Frank smiled. "I can guess."

"I 'spect the women have the same wish."

"I imagine they would rather I'd use a knife on a certain part of their anatomy."

"You're probably right about that."

Frank drank his coffee, then stood up and stuck out his hand to Tom. "Good knowing you, Tom."

Tom stood up and gripped Frank's hand. "Good knowin' you, Frank. Thanks for all your help and Godspeed and good luck."

Frank walked out and closed the door behind him.

He had one more door to close.

Lara opened the door to her hotel room at Frank's knock. She stood for a moment, not speaking. Finally she said, "Good afternoon, Frank."

"Lara. I know it's not proper for a man to enter a lady's hotel room, but . . ."

"Oh, pish-posh, Frank," she said. "Come on in."

Frank removed his hat, and Lara waved him to a chair. "I'll be pulling out in the morning, Lara. I wanted to say good-bye."

"I'm glad you came by, Frank. I would have been hurt had you not done so."

"I really didn't know if you wanted to see me."

"I was hurt when you told me you would not come East with me. I'll admit that. But I see now that you would be terribly uncomfortable living back East. You're a man of the West; a man of direct action. You're a man's man, Frank.'' She allowed herself a small smile. ''And the perfect woman's man too, I must admit. Just not this woman, I'm sorry to say. I should have taken all those things into consideration before I asked you.''

''Will you be all right, Lara?''

''I have funds, Frank. But thank you for asking.''

''Do you know where you'll be staying back East?''

''Oh, yes. But I think that when we part today, this should be the end of whatever we were building between us.''

''If you say so.''

''You don't think so?''

''I really don't know, Lara. But you are probably right. I shall, of course, certainly respect your wishes.''

''I thank you for that, Frank. Will you be leaving early in the morning?''

''Very early, Lara.''

''Then I guess this is really good-bye.''

''I suppose so.''

''I enjoyed knowing you, Frank. However brief it was.''

''And I enjoyed our time together, Lara.''

''I shall miss you, Frank Morgan.''

''I'll think of you often, Lara.''

''And I you, Frank. But in time, all memories fade.''

''I suppose so. What about your son?''

''That is something that will have to be worked out before I leave.''

''Tom will help you, and so will Jack and Ginny O'Malley.''

''I'm sure they will.''

''Good-bye, Lara.''

''Good-bye, Frank.''

Frank turned and walked out of the hotel room, softly

closing the door behind him. Just as the door closed, he heard Lara sob. Frank walked away without looking back. He couldn't afford to look back; Lara's crying might have induced him into going back East with her, and that was something he knew would be a disaster for him.

He stood outside the hotel for a time, smoking and looking around the main street of the town. A nice town, full of good, friendly people. If Lara had not decided to go back East, Frank might have tried to make this town his home.

If, if. Always an *if*.

"Mighty fine shootin' this noon, Mr. Morgan," a local said as he passed by Frank.

Frank smiled and nodded his head. That remark brought him back to reality. *You're a gunfighter, Frank,* he reminded himself. *A fast gun. A pistolero. A professional. You won't settle down. Not now, not ever. You can't afford to even consider it . . . even if you wanted to. Which you really don't.*

Not really.

You are what you are, Frank. So just accept the cards and play them. For nobody forced this game on you. You shuffled the deck, you dealt the cards. No one made you sit at the table, buy the chips, and get in this game.

Frank's hand touched the butt of his Colt Peacemaker.

Time to move on, Drifter.

Drift.

THIRTY

Frank made a pot of coffee on the stove in the office of the livery and while the water boiled, he packed up and saddled up. It was four o'clock in the morning.

In the quiet of predawn, Frank drank coffee and smoked a couple of cigarettes. Dog lay by his boots, every few minutes getting up and padding to the door, then looking back at Frank. He was ready to hit the trail.

"In a little while, Dog," Frank told him. "I'm just about ready to head out."

In his stall, Stormy stamped his hooves impatiently. The big Appaloosa was anxious to get on the trail.

After a moment, Frank finished his coffee, made sure the butt of his cigarette was out, and turned down the lamp. He was ready to go.

Frank led Stormy out of his stall and swung into the

saddle. His packhorse was trained to follow; rarely did Frank have to use a lead rope.

Frank rode out of town, heading west. In a couple of days, he would cut due south. He would make inquiries at every town and country store along the way about the men he was hunting. He would find them, he had no doubts about that. The West was a big place, but most areas were still sparsely populated. He knew that some of the outlaw/rapists were from—or called home—parts of Arizona, New Mexico, and Texas. Others were from Southern and Central California. Jack Rice, one of Val's lieutenants, was from the Sierra Madre range. Jack was a bad one, an unusually cruel man who enjoyed inflicting a lot of pain on his victims. Jack was one of the men who had brutalized and helped drive mad the silent woman Frank had brought back.

At noon of the fourth day out, Frank reined up at a small settlement located at a crossroads. It was a two-store, four-house hamlet. The largest store was a combination general store/saloon. Frank looked at the four horses tied at the hitch rail in front, then dismounted, slipped the hammer thong from his Peacemaker, and entered the saloon.

"Howdy, stranger," the man behind the bar greeted him. "What'll it be?"

"Got any food?"

"You bet I do. Best stew you ever et, and got some fresh-baked bread to go with it."

"Any coffee?"

"All you can drink. And it's fresh. I just made it. I'm a coffee-drinkin' man myself."

"Something to eat and a pot of coffee."

"Comin' right up."

Frank took a table with his back to a wall, and glanced over at the four men sitting at the rear of the room. They were playing cards, drinking whiskey, and being very careful to avoid looking at him.

The barkeep brought the stew and bread and a pot of coffee, and leaned close to Frank. "Them ol' boys is bad ones, I'm thinkin'. They got that look about them."

Frank looked up at the man, and the man recognized him and almost recoiled in shock. "Not as bad as I am," Frank told him very softly.

"Oh, Lordy, Lordy," the barkeep whispered. "The Drifter. Frank Morgan. Good God A'mighty."

"You stay ready to hit the floor, partner."

"Thanks. I done made up my mind to do that." The man went back behind his bar and busied himself polishing glasses.

Frank ate his stew, and it was very good eating. It was made with beef and potatoes and onions. The bread was indeed fresh, and the coffee was hot and strong. When he had finished his second bowl of stew, Frank poured another cup of coffee and rolled a smoke.

"Good grub, mister," he called. "Best I've had in a while."

"Thankee. My wife is a good cook. Got some doughnuts too, if you'd like some."

"I'll take a sackful," Frank told him. "A big sackful. You got any scraps for my dog?"

"Shore do. I seen that big animal out there. Does he bite?"

"Sometimes."

"I'll fight shy of him then."

"Son of a bitch bites me, I'll kill him," one of the men at the table said.

"He won't bite until you mess with him," Frank said in a cold voice. "But you harm my dog, I'll kill you, you and anyone else who wants to buy into the hand."

"You talk big, mister."

"I can back it up."

"I think you gonna have to," another of the quartet said, pushing back his chair.

"Anytime you're ready."

"You're crazy!" another one said. "They's four of us and one of you."

"That's Frank Morgan," the barkeep said.

Frank picked up his coffee cup with his left hand and took a sip.

The four men were silent for a moment, then one said, "So what? I'm Ted Brown. These boys with me is Hal, Stony, and Slim. Now that we're all introduced, why don't you leave, Morgan? Or whatever your name is."

"I like it here. And my name *is* Frank Morgan."

"I don't believe you're Frank Morgan," Slim said. "I heard Morgan got killed over in Montana or Wyoming or some damn place."

"You heard wrong," Frank told him.

"I think you're a liar, mister," Stony said. "That's what I think."

"I think you're a fool," Frank said coldly.

"I've killed men for less than that."

"You won't kill this man."

"You 'bout a smart aleck, ain't you?"

Frank smiled and said nothing.

"He's skirrred," Slim said. "I can see it in his eyes. He's skirred of us."

"I wish you boys would take this outside," the barkeep said.

"Shut up!" Ted told him.

"Yes, sir."

Frank waited, seated in his chair, his right hand close to

the butt of his Peacemaker. It would be an awkward draw, but he had done it before.

"You're skirred of us, ain't you?" Slim said.

"No," Frank said softly.

"He is too," Slim insisted.

The sound of horses stilled the conversation. Two cowboys walked in and greeted the barkeep.

"Jimmy, Ross," the barkeep said.

"You heard the news?" Jimmy asked. Neither of them had paid any attention to the tension in the saloon.

"What news?"

"Frank Morgan killed Johnny Vargas 'bout four, five days ago. Little town north and some west of here."

The barkeep nodded his head and cut his eyes to Frank. Jimmy and Ross turned and looked.

"It's him!" Ross blurted. "That's Frank Morgan. Damned if it ain't him sittin' here drinkin' coffee."

Ted leaned forward and put both his hands on the tabletop, palms down, signaling he was out of this ... all the way out.

"He tried to tell you boys," the barkeep said to the quartet. "He shorely did."

"I'm listenin' now," Ted said.

"Well, Frank Morgan don't mean skunk piss to me," Slim said, standing up.

"Me neither," Hal said, standing up beside his partner.

"I'm out of this," Stony said. "I'm out of it."

Frank stood up.

Ross and Jimmy backed up, around the end of the bar. The barkeep made ready to duck down.

"This doesn't have to be, boys," Frank said. "Let's just call it a misunderstanding that got out of hand, how about it?"

"I told you all he's yeller," Slim said. "I told you. Now he's a-tryin' to crawfish on us. The yeller dog."

"Yeah, he's as sorry as that damn ugly dog of his'n outside," Hal said with a laugh.

Outside, Dog barked.

"I believe he heard you, Hal," Frank said.

"Huh?" Hal questioned. "You tryin' to tell me that damn dog of yourn can understand people talk? You're not only yeller, you're stupid."

Frank laughed at the pair.

"You think this is funny?" Slim yelled.

"Yes," Frank replied. "I think so. And I also think the two of you aren't worth wasting any more of my time. So I think I'll leave, after I pay for my meal."

"It's on the house, Mr. Morgan," the barkeep said.

"Don't you turn your ass to me, mister!" Hal said. "I'll plug you if you do. I swear I'll shoot you."

"So now you're telling me you're a back-shooter?" Frank asked.

"Let it drop, Hal," Stony urged. "The man is givin' you an out. Take it and let's get the hell out of here."

"I ain't runnin'!" Hal yelled. "Not from no old chicken fart like this one."

"You're a fool," the barkeep said.

"You shet your mouth!" Slim told him.

"No, sir, I won't do no such of a thing," the barkeep said. "Morgan give you all a way out. You won't take it. Now you're gonna keep pushin' him and he's gonna kill you. Then I'll have me a big mess to clean it. Now, Hal, Slim, you boys sit down and cool off."

"Shut your blow-hole!" Slim told him. "Draw, Morgan. Draw or I'll shoot you where you stand. You understand?"

"I understand," Frank said softly.

"Now!" Hal yelled.

Both Hal and Slim and grabbed for their pistols.

Frank's Peacemaker boomed twice, the shots so close together they were almost as one. Hal and Slim fell back, both of them shot in the chest. Without knowing he did it, and it was very seldom he did, Frank twirled his Peacemaker before settling it back into leather.

"Good God!" Ross blurted out in a whisper. "He's fast as lightnin'."

Hal groaned on the floor. Slim would never make another sound; he was stone dead and cooling.

"Can I see to my pard, Morgan?" Stony asked.

"Go ahead."

Stony knelt down on the floor and opened his friend's shirt. After a moment, he stood up and said, "He ain't a-gonna make it. He's hard hit."

"I don't want to die," Hal groaned.

"He shoulda thought of that 'fore he braced Frank Morgan," the barkeep said.

"It was the whiskey talkin' in all of us," Ted said. "It was the whiskey that killed him."

"It's gettin' mighty dark in here," Hal said. "Is the sun goin' down?"

No one replied.

Frank poured another cup of coffee and, using his left hand, lifted the cup and took a sip. "You want to fix that bag of scraps for my dog?" he asked the barkeep.

"I'll do that right now, Mr. Morgan. You fixin' to leave?"

"Soon."

"Oh, God!" Hal screamed as the first waves of pain struck him. "Where's Slim? Slim? Where you at, boy?"

"Slim didn't make it, partner," Stony told him.

"I ain't neither, am I?"

"I don't think so, partner."

"It's gettin' awful dark in here, Stony. I'm skirred."

"You want some whiskey for the pain?"

"The pain's done stopped, Stony. What does that mean?"

"I don't know, partner."

"It's real peaceful in the dark," Hal said. "Real . . . peaceful . . ." Hal closed his eyes and never opened them again.

"Me and Hal rode a lot of trails together," Stony said, standing up. "He really wasn't a bad feller. He just had more guts than sense." He looked at Frank. "I don't hold nothin' agin you, Mr. Morgan. You done what you had to do."

"Did he have any family?" Ted asked.

"Some back in Missouri, I think. But he ain't heard from them in years and years."

"How 'bout Slim?"

"I don't think so. None he ever talked about leastways."

"They's a small graveyard out back," the barkeep said, walking back in the room with a bag of scraps. "Right next to the woods. Y'all can plant them boys back yonder if you like."

"You know any words to say over them?" Stony asked.

"I reckon I could come up with a verse or three."

"You got any shovels?"

"Out back in the shed."

Frank walked to the bar and picked up the sack of scraps and the bag of bear sign. "Much obliged."

"My pleasure, Mr. Morgan."

Frank walked out, tightened Stormy's cinch and the harness to the packsaddle, and rode out, Dog trotting along beside.

He had no wish to stay for the funeral. He'd seen too many of them.

THIRTY-ONE

At a county sheriff's office two days after the shootout in the old country saloon, Frank introduced himself and was invited into the office for a cup of coffee and some conversation.

"Heard about your work in busting up the Dooley gang, Frank," the sheriff said. "Damn nice piece of work. What can I do for you?"

"Tell me where I can find the rest of the gang," Frank replied with a smile.

The sheriff laughed and slapped his leg. "Well, now, Frank, I can't do that, but I just might be able to put you on the track of Bloody Mama. And wherever you find her, you'll find Sadie. Interested?"

"They close by?"

"Couple of days' ride south of here. Way out of my jurisdiction."

"Killing a woman doesn't set well with me, Sheriff."

"Put that thought out of your mind, Frank. Those two ain't of the female species, you ask me. They're cold-blooded and brutal. Vicious as any man you ever heard of. You put one of them in a cage with a puma, you better bet against the cat."

"So I've heard."

"Besides, they aren't alone. They've got half a dozen men with them. I'll draw you a map. It's rough country and I sure can't guarantee you'll find them."

"I'll find them," Frank said coldly.

The sheriff caught the deadly quality in Frank's tone and looked hard at him, then nodded his head. "Yeah, I reckon you will, at that."

"What men? Do you know?"

The sheriff shook his head. "I don't have any idea, Frank. But if they're riding with Bloody Mama and Sadie, they're as worthless as a bucket of buzzard puke."

"You're probably right about that."

"You bet I am." The sheriff drew a rough map. "Their hideout is near an old army fort, right on the edge of this range here." He tapped the piece of paper. "Been deserted for, oh, near'bouts twenty years, I reckon. Maybe longer." He folded the map and handed it to Frank. "Good luck, Frank."

Frank stuck the map in his jacket pocket. "Thanks." He finished what remained of his coffee. "Good coffee."

"Stop by anytime."

"You mind if I grab a meal while I'm in town?"

The sheriff shrugged. "Why should I mind? Marshal Tom Wright has wired all over the southern part of the state about you."

"What about me?"

"You never *officially* resigned your deputy sheriff's commission, Frank. You're still a legal marshal's deputy tracking down criminals that committed a crime in your jurisdiction. You're just as legal as I am."

Frank smiled. "Well . . . he's right. I guess I didn't."

"Good luck, Deputy."

The sheriff was sure right about this being rough country, Frank thought as he stopped by a creek to water his horses and fill his canteen. Bloody Mama and Sadie picked a great spot for a hideout. Frank bellied down on the bank to get himself a drink, Dog beside him, lapping at the cool water. Refreshed, Frank squatted under the shade of a tree to escape the fierceness of the noonday sun, and rolled a cigarette. He figured he was only a couple of miles from the old abandoned army fort, and was on high alert for any signs of trouble.

Dog's ears suddenly perked up and he growled low in his throat.

"Easy now, boy," Frank whispered. "Be quiet."

Then Frank heard the sounds of walking horses, followed by a low murmur of voices.

"Damn, it's hot," a man said.

"Yeah," another replied. "Let's stop and get a drink and rest some."

"Good idea."

Frank laid his hand on Dog's head. Dog understood and was quiet, sensing the tenseness in Frank's touch.

"I been seein' Sadie givin' you the eye lately, Leo. I reckon she's got plans for you this evenin'."

"She can go to hell too, Tanner. I'd sooner bed down with a damn hog than with that woman."

Leo laughed. "Well, that leaves Bloody Mama."

"That's even worser. That woman makes me wanna puke. I think it's time we pulled another raid and got us some good-lookin' young stuff."

"Bloody Mama says we gonna do that next week sometime. Town about forty miles south of here."

"No foolin'?"

"No foolin'. We gonna hit a church whilst Sunday services is a-goin' on. The men won't be armed and the women will be aplenty."

"That there's a damn fine idee."

The men were silent for a couple of minutes. Frank could see them through the sparse brush along the creek bank. Stage a raid on a church, he thought. What a sorry, no-good, worthless pack of trash.

Frank took off his spurs and silently made his way toward the men. When he was about forty feet away, he stepped out into the clear. "Howdy, boys," he called.

Both men grabbed for iron, Tanner hollering, "Morgan!"

Frank drilled Tanner in the belly first, then shifted the muzzle of his Peacemaker toward Leo and put a .45 round into his belly. The entire matter took about two seconds. Leo and Tanner never got off a shot. The outlaws were stretched out on the ground, alive and moaning in pain. Frank walked over to them and kicked away their guns.

"You boys are a couple of sorry pieces of trash," Frank bluntly informed them.

"You ain't got no call to talk to us like that, Morgan," Tanner said. "Not after what you just done."

"I want a drink of water," Leo moaned.

"With a stomach wound?" Frank asked. "You know that's not good for you. That might make you worse and you'd end up dying."

"Your bullet tore up my innards, Morgan," Tanner said. "I'm hard hit and ain't gonna make it. They's some whiskey in my saddlebags. Would you fetch the bottle for me?"

"Why should I?" Frank asked coldly.

"Because it's the Christian thing to do."

Frank laughed at him. "You were looking forward to raiding a church on Sunday morning, killing some men, kidnapping women to rape them, and then possibly selling them into prostitution . . . and you dare to speak the word *Christian* to me?"

"You go to hell, Morgan!" Tanner told him.

Frank laughed at him.

"Damn you, Morgan!" Leo groaned. "You're just as bad as you claim we are."

"Maybe," Frank agreed. "But I'll make a deal with you."

"Deal?" Tanner moaned the words. "What kind of deal?"

"You tell me everything about your hideout, the people there, and I'll get you all the whiskey and water you want, string a groundsheet over you for shade, and then ride out and let you die in peace."

"And if we don't?" Leo asked.

"I'll leave you here and let the ants and snakes have you."

"You'd do it too, wouldn't you, Morgan?"

"Try me."

"I'll tell you, Morgan," Leo said. "And it'll be the truth too."

"I'm listening."

Two hours later, Frank was hidden in a jumble of boulders, studying the layout of the old army fort. The crumbling buildings were about seventy-five yards away. He could see no activity. Sadie and Bloody Mama and the others were staying inside, out of the heat of the early summer day. And Frank sure couldn't blame them for that.

After watering Stormy and Dog and the packhorse, Frank had left them a few hundred yards back. He had taken his rifle and a bandolier of cartridges and walked to his present position. Leo had died before Frank had left the creek, and Tanner had slipped into unconsciousness. Leo had told Frank that besides Bloody Mama and Sadie, there were six men hiding out in the crumbling buildings of the old fort. And only one had been a part of Val's gang . . . other than Bloody Mama and Sadie. A man called Wilder.

"Wilder?" Frank had mused aloud. "I know a Lou Wilder. A no-good from New Mexico. Has a knife scar on his cheek."

"That's him," Leo said. "He's a bad one. How's Tanner?"

"Still alive."

"I guess it won't be long for me."

"Probably not."

A few minutes later, Leo closed his eyes and did not open them again. At least not on this earth.

"Did Leo croak?" Tanner asked.

"Yes. Just then."

"I hope one of them boys at the fort gut-shoots you, Morgan. I hope you die hard, you sorry son of a bitch."

"So nice of you to care," Frank replied.

Tanner moaned a couple of times and then slipped into unconsciousness.

The corral where the outlaws' horses were being held was about fifty yards behind the only building where a very faint whisper of smoke was coming out of the stone chimney.

Probably used to keep the coffee hot, Frank thought. *If they try to run for their horses, I'll nail at least some of them.*

As that thought was fading from Frank's mind, a man stepped out of the large building and looked toward the north.

Probably looking for Leo and Tanner, Frank thought.

The man turned and said something to a person standing inside. A few seconds later, Bloody Mama stepped out, dressed in men's bib overalls. Frank recognized her by her big butt. As Frank had once heard a man say, "Bloody Mama do drag some ass behind her."

Frank lifted his rifle and started to sight her in, then shifted the muzzle. He just couldn't do it. Even though Bloody Mama was just as bad as, or worse than, any of the men who rode with her, shooting a woman just simply went against the grain for Frank.

Of course, if she ever started shooting at him, that was quite a different matter.

Frank shot the man standing next to the woman.

The man was knocked to the ground by the .44-40 slug, and Bloody Mama leaped for the open door, hollering at the top of her voice.

"It's a raid!" she squalled, her voice carrying clearly to Frank. "Lawmen have found us."

"Lawmen, your butt!" a man yelled. "I'll bet you that's Frank Morgan."

"Kill that bastard!" Bloody Mama yelled. "Kill him, I say!"

"You kill him, Mama!" another voice shouted from the other side of the building.

"Don't you argue with me, Willis!" she shouted. "Go get him. Avenge your partner, Jerry. He's layin' out yonder in the sun, dead and startin' to stink."

What a nice woman, Frank thought. *So ladylike.*

"You hear me, you turd?" Mama shrieked. "Go get him."

What Willis then said to Bloody Mama was something that could not be repeated in a San Francisco brothel.

Willis's comments didn't phase Bloody Mama. "Blow it out your ass, Willis," Mama retorted in a shout.

"And that goes double for me, Willis!" Sadie yelled. "You sorry piece of buffalo crap."

"Open fire on that shooter!" a man yelled.

Frank hunkered down in the boulders as the lead began howling all around him, hoping that no bullet would hit the rocks behind him, flatten out, and ricochet into him.

"Santos!" Sadie yelled. "You and Neal go left and right and get behind that shooter. Move it!"

"*You* go left or right, Sadie," Santos shouted. "Get your ass shot off."

Sadie cussed the outlaw, coloring the hot air with profanity, ending with, "Mama, we sure hooked up with some yeller-bellies this run."

"Damn straight we did," Bloody Mama yelled. "I reckon you and me are gonna have to handle this ourselves."

"I ain't never seen a man that was worth a crap for anything other than a good hump," Sadie hollered. "And most of them ain't even good for that."

Bloody Mama laughed at that, her shrill braying echoing out of the building.

Crazy, Frank thought. *Both of those women are crazy.*

"This gunfire will bring Tanner and Leo back here," a man said.

"Tanner and Leo are dead, you stupid bastard!" Bloody Mama yelled. "Morgan—and you can bet your stinkin' drawers that's Morgan out there—killed them both."

Frank fed a couple more cartridges into his rifle and waited.

"We'll wait him out," Sadie said. "Come dark, we'll get him."

Suits me, Frank thought. He settled into a more comfortable position in the boulders and waited.

THIRTY-TWO

If Sadie and Bloody Mama had counted on the night hiding them, they were sadly mistaken. The moon was full and bright and the heavens were sparkling with stars. Frank sat amid the jumble of rocks and boulders and smiled as he waited for the outlaws to make a move.

Then Frank rethought that and said to hell with it: *He'd* take the fight to *them*. They wouldn't be expecting that . . . he hoped.

Frank left the rocks and began crawling on his belly, slowly and carefully, toward the large building, hoping he would not run into a rattlesnake along the way.

When he reached the building, he paused beneath a broken window and listened.

"I ain't goin' out there," a man said. "Morgan's jist a-waitin' for one of us to make that stupid move."

"Me neither," another man replied. "We got food and water in here. I say we wait him out."

"Cowards!" Sadie said. "Craven cowards, all of you."

"Why don't you haul your ass out there then?" a third man suggested. "So far, all you've done is run that mouth of yours."

"By God, Vinnie, you can't talk to me like that!"

"I just did, Sadie."

Frank leaned his rifle against the building, pulled his Peacemaker and his spare Colt from leather, and cocked them. Then he rose to his feet and sprayed the inside with lead, cocking and firing as fast as he could. When he was empty, he grabbed his rifle and took off running, leaving the sounds of yelling and moaning behind him. He had sure hit somebody. By the sounds inside the building, more than one outlaw had soaked up lead.

Frank knelt by the side of a building and quickly reloaded. He watched as Bloody Mama came staggering out into the moon-bright night, a pistol in each hand.

"I'll kill you, Morgan," she shouted, and began firing wildly in all directions. "Goddamn you, Drifter. You've shot me, you . . ." Bloody Mama filled the night with the most vulgar of profanities.

She fell to her knees, remained that way for a moment, then toppled over on her face and was still.

"Penelope?" Sadie called.

Penelope? Frank thought. Her real name was Penelope?

"Are you all right, baby?" Sadie asked.

Bloody Mama lay motionless and silent on the ground. Sadie began cussing Frank, alternately cursing and screaming out her rage. She ran out of the building, a rifle in her hands. Frank could have easily shot her, but he held his fire.

"Damn you, Morgan!" Sadie screamed. "I'll see you in hell." She stuck the muzzle of the rifle in her mouth and pulled the trigger. She fell to the rocky ground, dead next to her friend in crime.

"That's it, Morgan," a man called from the building. "Me and Santos is all that's left in here. Neal and Jerry is hard hit, Willis is dead."

"Step out where I can see you," Frank called.

Two men stepped out of the building to stand in the moonlight, their hands raised. They carried no weapons that Frank could see.

"I'm Vinnie," one of the men said. "This here is Santos."

"You ride with Val Dooley?"

"I never met the man. Sadie and Mama rode with him. They told us all about the kidnappin' of them women and you comin' after them. I don't want no more trouble with you, Morgan. And that's the truth."

"Saddle your horses and ride out of here," Frank called. "Don't ever let me run into either of you again. If I do, I'll kill you. Understood?"

"Plain as day, Morgan," Santos said.

"Do you get to keep our guns?" Vinnie asked.

"What do you think?"

"I think I'd better shut my mouth and get gone."

"Wise decision. Get out of here."

Santos and Vinnie quickly saddled up, under Frank's watchful eye, and rode out, with a full canteen of water, the clothes on their back, and nothing else. Frank suspected they would ride for a few miles, then make a cold camp and come back to the old fort in the morning, to hunt around for clothes, guns, and food. Frank would leave them whatever food and clothing remained, but they would not find any guns.

When Frank was reasonably certain they were gone, at least for the night, he checked on those outlaws remaining in the building. They were dead. Frank's wild spraying of lead had done the job. Frank dragged the bodies out and into a shed on the edge of the old fort's perimeter. He did the same with the bodies of Bloody Mama and Sadie. He gathered up all the guns and tossed them into the building, then went about picking up old boards until he had enough to keep a blaze burning for a long time. He put them both inside and outside the shed, then saturated everything with kerosene he found in the outlaws' quarters.

While the kerosene soaked into the old boards, Frank made a pot of coffee and then settled down for a cup of hot coffee and a smoke. The coffee perked him up, for he was tired.

After another cup of coffee and the last of the pan bread he had brought with him, Frank set the building blazing; a funeral pyre for the already damned.

He knew where he was going next, for he had found a map with a note among the women's personal belongings. The note was from a man called Curly. Frank knew him from years back, and Curly Lewis was a bad one, cruel and mean. Bloody Mama and Sadie were going to hook up with Curly and his bunch in a few weeks.

"Well, now, Curly," Frank had said after reading the note and studying the map. "I've got a little surprise for you. Bloody Mama and Sadie will be unable to make it. But I'll come in their place. Count on it."

Frank did not shave for a week, and his naturally heavy beard proved to be a very effective disguise. He was able to ride into a town, provision up, have a meal in a café, and take a hot bath without being recognized. Then he was once more on his way. He did not tell the county sheriffs or the town marshals about the deaths of Bloody Mama and Sadie.

Frank was sure that Santos and Vinnie would spread the word.

In a café Frank overheard talk about the breakup of the Val Dooley gang and the shootout with Johnny Vargas.

"That Frank Morgan must be a ring-tailed-tooter," one local remarked. "I guess all them things that's written and said about him are true."

"I reckon so," another said. "I'd like to see that fellow just one time."

"What would you say to him?"

"I don't know. Howdy, I guess."

Frank smiled and continued enjoying his meal.

"I hear he's a big man," the first local said. "Six feet five or six. Two hundred and seventy-five pounds."

Frank again smiled. It would take a damn big horse to tote that big a man around.

"And he's killed men with just one blow with his big fist."

Frank laid down his knife and fork. The rumors were getting entirely out of hand.

"No, he's not none of them things," another local spoke up. "I seen pictures of him. He's about six feet tall and built up pretty good in the shoulders and arms. But he ain't no giant." The man glanced over at Frank and blinked a couple of times. "As a matter of fact, he sorta looks like that feller right there."

All eyes in the café turned to Frank.

A man seated to Frank's right said, "Don't Morgan carry a Peacemaker?"

"Yeah, he does," the local who was eyeing Frank said.

"So does this fellow. And it's tied down too."

"My God in Heaven," another man said in hushed tones. "That's the Drifter, Frank Morgan."

Here we go, Frank thought.

"Are you really Frank Morgan?" the waitress asked.

"Yes, ma'am, I am," Frank replied. "Could I have some more coffee, please?"

"Yes, sir, Mr. Morgan. You sure can. How about some apple pie to go with it?"

"That would be real nice," Frank said with a smile. He watched as a local beat it out of the café, grabbed the first person he came to, and began talking and pointing.

Within minutes, the boardwalk in front of the café was lined with people. A large man with a star on his vest pushed his way through and entered the café. "Frank Morgan?" he called.

"Right here, Sheriff."

"Coffee, Wilma," the sheriff called to the waitress as he walked to Frank's table and sat down. "Telegraph wires been hummin' with messages for you for near'bouts a week, Morgan."

"Oh?"

"Yeah. From a Dr. Evans and a Marshal Tom Wright. You know them?"

"I sure do. What's up?"

"You want to read them or you want me to just tell you?"

"Tell me. You can give me the wires later."

"You rescued some women that had been kidnapped, right?"

"Yes, that's right."

"One of 'em was in shock, couldn't speak?"

"Yes."

"She committed suicide. Hanged herself."

"Damn."

"Sheriff Davis over in Deweyville has a sister 'bout half crazy?"

"Yes, that pretty well describes Alberta."

"Yeah, that's her name. She's been placed in an asylum."

"That's no surprise."

"Couple more things. You familiar with somebody named Little Ed Simpson?"

"Yes. What about him?"

"His mother killed him. Shot him stone dead when the boy pulled a gun on his father. The father caught the boy trying to steal some horses." The sheriff shook his head. "That must have been a very strange family."

"Was and is, Sheriff."

"A woman named Lara Whitter. You familiar with her?"

"Yes."

"Her and her son, a boy named Johnny, were kidnapped by some remaining members of the Val Dooley gang. Word is they're heading for, or are already in, Southern California. Maybe right here in this area."

"Any word on who kidnapped them?"

"Goody Nolan is the leader of the gang."

"I know him. Was there any good news?"

"I'm afraid not. Marshal Wright says you're a deputy sheriff. Is that right?"

"Yes."

"Sorta out of your jurisdiction, aren't you?"

"You might say that."

"You gonna start trouble in this county?"

"I don't plan to."

The sheriff studied Frank as he sipped his coffee. "I don't know just how a gunfighter got to be a lawman, but ride on, Morgan. Get out of my county."

"You object if I finish my pie?"

The sheriff shook his head. "No. You can provision up, get a bath and a haircut and shave if you like. Then move on. 'Cause I think when you find the men who kidnapped the woman and her boy, they's gonna be a bloodbath. I'd rather not have that in my county."

"You think Goody is in your county?"

"No. I think he's southwest of here, in the desert. Maybe in the Sierra Madres."

"You trying to tell me something, Sheriff?"

"Could be." He pushed back his chair, then leaned over the table and whispered, "Good hunting, Morgan."

Frank found Art Butler two days later, at a combination general store/roadhouse. There were only four people in the place: Frank, Butler, the bartender/owner, and a sales clerk. Frank walked up to Butler and knocked him to the floor with one punch, then jerked the man's pistol from leather and tossed in on the bar. While Art was crawling around on the floor, trying to clear his head, Frank turned to the bartender.

"You and your clerk go outside and get some fresh air. I have some business to discuss with this man."

"You're Frank Morgan, ain't you?" the bartender asked.

"Yes."

"Take all the time you need, Mr. Morgan." The bartender left the saloon part of the building, closing the front door behind him.

"I know what you're gonna do, Morgan," Butler said. "Just make it quick, that's all I ask."

Frank slowly took a long-bladed knife from a sheath on his belt. "That all depends on you, Butler."

"What do you mean?" Butler asked, his eyes never leaving the big blade, fashioned after a bowie knife. He could tell it was very sharp.

"You were one of the men who went back to town and kidnapped Lara Whitter and her son. Where are they?"

"You gonna let me live if I tell you?"

"I'll give you a chance to live."

"They was alive when I left them, Morgan. I can tell you that much."

"Did you rape Lara?"

"Yeah, I did. We all did. And Freckles Burton, well, he took a shine to the boy . . . if you know what I mean."

"God*damn* you!" Frank raged at the man.

"I didn't do nothin' to the boy, Morgan. I ain't like that. But Freckles, he's, well, sorta strange that way . . ."

"But you let it happen, you son of a bitch!"

"I couldn't hep it!" Butler screamed. "You know Freckles is crazy and snake-quick with a Colt."

"Where are they, and don't lie to me, Butler, or I'll make this last a long time."

"Not far, Morgan. 'Bout an easy two-day ride to the south. We was goin' into the mountains, but Freckles was havin' himself a time with the boy and . . ."

"Shut up about your perversions with Johnny!"

"I didn't touch him, Morgan! I swear to God I didn't."

"Why did you leave the gang?"

"I . . . got tired of hearin' the boy whimper and the woman holler when the men . . ."

Frank blocked the rest of it out, as best he could. Butler suddenly jerked out a knife and lunged at Frank. Frank sidestepped and buried the big blade of his bowie into the man's stomach and twisted. Frank let the outlaw/rapist fall to the floor and die.

Frank wiped the bloody blade on Butler's shirt and walked to the front door, opening it. He motioned to the owner.

"Yes, sir?"

"You can have his horse and what's in his pockets if you'll bury that bastard in there."

"I can do that, Mr. Morgan. Say, that's a right unfriendly dog of yours."

"He takes after me," Frank told him, then swung into the saddle and rode away.

THIRTY-THREE

Frank made his way slowly toward the campfire, stopping about twenty-five feet away, just at the edge of the clearing. He had been tracking the lone rider for two days, ever since a man in a saloon had told him he recognized the outlaw.

But Frank wanted to be sure the man squatting over the fire was the right man. When the man stood up and half turned, Frank was sure.

"Vaca!" Frank called.

The outlaw known as Breed Vaca stiffened, but kept his hands away from his guns. "You goin' to back-shoot me, Morgan?"

"I'll give you a chance, Vaca. A better chance than you gave the woman and the boy."

"I never touched that boy, Morgan. I ain't that type. I done the woman some. But not the boy."

"Are they still alive?"

"They was when I pulled out three days ago."

"Why did you leave the gang?"

"Jack Rice rode into camp and joined up with Curly Lewis and Booger Bob and the others. Me and Jack don't get on a-tall."

"There's more, Vaca. Tell it all."

"Jack claimed the woman for hisself. Freckles give her up right off the bat. No argument. And you know what happens to a woman with Jack."

Frank felt sick to his stomach. He knew what Jack had done to a couple of women. The man was twisted in the head ... twisted about as bad as Frank had ever seen.

"Why didn't you kill him, Vaca? You know what he's going to do to her."

"Wasn't none of my affair, Morgan."

"You son of a bitch!"

Vaca shrugged his shoulders; did so very carefully.

"Name them all, Vaca."

"Goody, Big Thumbs, Sam. I told you the rest. Sonny Carter and Hibbs might have joined them by now. I ain't sure."

"My gun's in leather, Vaca. You want to try it now? It's going to be your only chance."

Breed Vaca turned and grabbed for his pistol. His hand closed around the butt, and that was as far as he got before Frank's bullet tore into his chest. Vaca stumbled backward and sat down hard on the ground. Then he toppled over and closed his eyes for the last time.

Frank had a cup of coffee and a smoke by the fire. His thoughts were dark and mean, raging through his head. Lara and her son were certainly dead by now ... and if Jack Rice had claimed Lara, she had died hard. And Frank hoped the boy had died swiftly; he also knew all about Freckles Burton's twisted nature with boys. Somebody should have put a rope around Freckles's neck a long time back.

Frank looked over at the body of Breed Vaca, no emotion in his gaze. One more piece of crap removed from society. Frank finished his coffee and carefully put out the fire. He swung into the saddle and rode away without looking back. The buzzards and varmints would take care of Breed.

Frank picked up the trail of Jack and the others and followed it southeast. Along the way, Frank found a bit of torn dress and torn pieces of undergarments. Then he found the body of Johnny Whitter. About twenty-five feet from the body of the tortured boy, he found the body of Lara. Both the boy and his mother were naked, and they had been used badly. He hoped Lara had died before somebody—and Frank had a good idea who it was—had used a skinning knife on her.

Frank buried the boy and his mother side by side and covered the graves with rocks. Then he stood over the graves, hat in hand, trying to think of some words to say. He finally remembered some lines about walking through the valley of death, and said them. Then he recalled some words about vengeance is mine, sayeth the Lord.

"Not this time," Frank murmured.

The outlaw/rapists knew they were being followed. When they did stop to rest their horses, they were making cold camps and trying to take routes over rocky ground, and when they could, they took to the water in a futile attempt to lose Frank. But steel-shod horses leave marks on rocks, and taking to creeks won't throw off an experienced tracker. Frank followed relentlessly, staying constantly alert for an ambush. Frank thought they might be heading for the Sierra Madre Mountains, Jack Rice's old stamping grounds, but then the men turned more east than south, as if they might be riding for the Mojave.

Then it dawned on Frank where the outlaws might be heading: an old ghost town east and some south of the town of Bakersfield. As a town it hadn't lasted long, maybe five or six years. But there was good water there, and Frank had been told that the buildings were still intact. He couldn't recall the name of the ghost town, not that it mattered. He was sure that was where Jack was leading the gang.

"All right, boys," Frank whispered to the hot winds. "I'll be there, just about the same time you are."

Frank rode up to a general store and swung down. He had to rest Stormy and the packhorse and he needed some food and rest himself. Dog got himself a good long drink of water from the horse trough, and then plopped down in the shade of the building. Frank didn't have to tell the big cur to stay put. Dog was tired; he wasn't going anywhere.

Frank stepped onto the porch and stood for a moment, enjoying the shade from the midday summer's sun. He turned and walked into the small saloon side, and came face-to-face with Sam Semple, standing at the bar.

Sam froze at the sighting. His elbows were on the bar and he knew if he moved an inch, Frank's Peacemaker would roar.

"Sam," Frank said softly.

"I broke with the gang, Morgan," Sam said. "I ain't lookin' for no trouble."

"But you were there when the boy and his mother were tortured and killed, Sam."

"Yeah, I was, Morgan, but I didn't have no hand in it."

"You could have stopped it."

"How, Morgan? One man agin half a dozen?"

"Did you even try to stop it?"

"Morgan . . . listen to me: I couldn't have stopped it."

"I could have, if I'd been in your boots."

"I ain't you, Morgan!" Sam screamed.

"Did you have a hand in raping the woman?"

"Yes, damn you. I did. It was . . . I had to. The others would have laughed at me if I didn't. You have to understand that."

"They would have laughed at you for being decent one time in your miserable life?" Frank asked softly.

"Yes! It was a man thing, Morgan."

"Men don't rape and torture women and little boys, Sam."

"Are you really Frank Morgan?" the store owner/barkeep asked. "In my store?"

Frank ignored him. His hard eyes never left Sam. "You believe in God, Sam?"

"You damn right I do. Why?"

" 'Cause you're about to meet him."

"Morgan . . ." There was an edge of panic in Sam's voice. "The others is goin' to that old ghost town south of Bakersfield. Don't me tellin' you that count for nothin'?"

"My Lord," the barkeep whispered. "Frank Morgan in my store."

"I'm fast, Morgan," Sam said. "I can take you. Don't force me to draw on you."

Frank smiled. "Consider yourself forced, Sam."

"I don't want to have to kill you, Morgan!"

"Oh, you won't, Sam."

"Damn you, Morgan! You just don't understand what happened. All them pressures that was on me."

"I could maybe get the county sheriff out here," the barkeep said. "But that'll take a couple of days."

"We don't need him," Frank said.

"Yeah, we do," Sam said. "Get him. I'll surrender to him."

Frank cussed Sam Semple, cussed him low and long and hard.

"I don't have to take that from you or no man, Morgan!"

"Then do something about it, Sam."

"Hell with you, Morgan!" Sam screamed. "You want to kill me? Go ahead. But I'll tell you somethin' 'fore you do. That woman was some kind of fine poke. I 'specially liked the way she begged and hollered. Then she got to prayin'. That was funny. She was on her knees. But not in the prayin' position, if you know what I mean. We all got some laughs out of that." Spittle was oozing out of Sam's mouth and his eyes were wild.

Frank waited, letting him rave and rant his obscenities. Then he began talking about the boy. Frank put an end to it.

He shot Sam.

Sam slammed back against the bar, pulling his pistol. Frank shot him again. Sam twisted, still against the bar. He refused to go down. Sam lifted his six-gun, and Frank put a third round in him. That one put Sam on the floor.

Frank walked through the gunsmoke to stand over Sam Semple.

"I hate your guts, Morgan!" Sam gasped.

"I can live with that, Sam."

Sam cussed Frank, blood spraying from his mouth. "You'll never git them other boys, Morgan. They'll kill you and I'm glad."

"Don't count on them doing that, Sam."

Sam didn't reply. He closed his eyes and died on the saloon floor.

Frank looked at the bartender, standing with wide eyes. "Where's his horse?"

"Out back, Mr. Morgan."

"You can have it and all his gear if you'll bury him."

"That sure sounds more than fair to me. I'll do it, sir. I promise I will."

"I'm going to provision up now. You want me to help you carry him out?"

"Oh, no, sir. I'll just drag him out back and plant him there."

"Fine. You do that." Frank stepped over Sam's body and went into the store section of the old place. He began picking up supplies and setting them on the counter. When the store owner returned, Frank paid for his goods and asked, "You have a place where a man can bathe?"

"Yes, sir. But I ain't got no water heated for it."

"I'll bathe in cold water then. Get some of this crud off me."

"Whatever, sir."

"Then I want something to eat."

"I got salt pork and taters."

"Coffee?"

"Oh, yes, sir. Lots of coffee. And I got some biscuits I made this morning."

"That'll do."

"I'll get started. Say, that dead man had some money on him, Mr. Morgan."

"Keep it. It's yours."

"That's right nice of you. What do I tell the sheriff or the deputies if they come by?"

"Tell them his name is Sam Semple. They'll know who he is . . . or was."

After a good night's sleep, Frank pressed on. He didn't bother trying to keep to the trail; he knew where he was going. And he damn sure knew what he was going to do when he got there. Frank knew he was riding a vengeance trail; knew that no matter what he did, it would not bring back Lara and Johnny, nor would it lessen the horrible pain of their dying. But he also knew the West was slowly changing in its treatment of criminals; knew that the evidence against these bags of crap was circumstantial, now that Lara and Johnny were dead and could not testify against them. No way they would get the rope. They might not even get prison time. Frank could not allow that to happen, so he would mete out the appropriate justice for the crimes committed.

And that penalty was death.

But for one of them, it was going to be a hard death. Frank would personally see to that. When Frank got through with him, the man would be begging to be released from life.

"Bet on that, Jack Rice," Frank muttered.

Frank made a lonely camp near a spring that night. After letting the horses roll and drink, Frank hobbled them on some graze and then fed Dog. He put on water to boil for coffee and fried some salt pork and potatoes, cutting up a bit of wild onions for added flavor.

Dog came to him and lay down by his side. Frank put a hand on the big cur's head. "Won't be long now, Dog. And I got me an idea about where to go next. I know of a valley down in New Mexico that is so pretty it'll take your breath away. It's in the mountains, and it's isolated. We just might be able to make that place a home. Would you like that?"

Dog growled softly.

Frank turned his head, and Dog grabbed a piece of bacon out of Frank's plate and ran off into the shadows.

THIRTY-FOUR

The wind shifted and Frank smelled the food cooking. He reined up, whispered to Dog to stay, and made his way on foot toward the smells of bacon frying and the aroma of fresh-made coffee. Two men were sitting with their backs to him. Frank didn't think he knew either of them. He stepped closer and said, "Take it easy, boys."

Both men turned around, still sitting on the ground. "Morgan!" one said.

"I knew he'd find us, Sonny," the other one said.

Sonny stood up. "Shut up, Hibbs," He looked back at Frank. "You ain't killin' me without a fight, Morgan."

The other one remained sitting on the ground.

"Why would I want to kill you?" Frank asked.

"I didn't kill that woman or that boy," Sonny said. "I done the woman some. But I didn't kill her."

"How about you, Hibbs?" Frank asked.

"I didn't touch neither one of them. I don't hold with rapin' women or abusin' children."

"That's the truth, Morgan," Sonny said. "He ain't lyin' 'bout that."

"You both were there when they were killed?"

"Yeah," Hibbs said softly. "And I ain't proud of that."

"I told you, Morgan," Sonny said. "We didn't kill neither of them. That was Freckles who done the boy and Jack Rice who done the woman. Not us."

Hibbs started crying softly.

"Shut up with that damn blubberin'!" Sonny told him. "It ain't manly."

"I'll never get that sight out of my mind," Hibbs said. "It was awful. I hope to God I never see nothin' like it again."

"Shut up, damn it!" Sonny yelled.

"Let him talk," Frank said.

Sonny stepped away from Hibbs. "I think I can take you, Morgan. But by God, at least I'm gonna try."

"Did I say anything about fighting you?" Frank asked.

"You ready, Morgan?" Sonny yelled.

"This doesn't have to be, Sonny. I . . ."

"Draw, goddamn you, *draw!*" Sonny grabbed for his gun.

Frank drilled him in the belly. Sonny's feet flew out from under him and he fell backward, losing his pistol when he hit the ground. He tried to grab his six-gun. Hibbs kicked it out of his reach.

"It's over, Sonny," Hibbs said.

Sonny cussed his riding pard.

Hibbs looked at Frank. "You goin' to kill me, Morgan?"

"No. See to your pardner. I'm riding on."

"Freckles Burton and Jack Rice are evil men, Morgan.

Made me sick to my soul what they done to the woman and the boy.''

Sonny groaned in pain, both hands holding his perforated belly. "I'm thirsty, Hibbs. Gimme a drink of water."

"You're belly-shot, Sonny," Hibbs told him. "You know it ain't right to drink no water."

"Gimmie some damn water, Hibbs!''

"Give him a drink," Frank said, squatting down and pouring a cup of coffee. "He's done for anyway."

"Damn you, Morgan!" Sonny hissed.

"Whatever," Frank replied, taking a sip of coffee.

"I'm gonna head on back to Nebraska," Hibbs said. "See if my pa needs some help on the farm."

Sonny cussed his riding pard, calling him all sorts of vile names.

"I think that's a good idea," Frank said.

"I'm done with this outlaw business. I was a fool to get mixed up in it."

"Least you're smart enough to realize that," Frank said.

"I'm dyin' and you two are talkin' 'bout farmin'," Sonny said. "Ain't you got no laudanum, Morgan?"

"No."

"I hope you burn in the hellfires forever, Morgan," Sonny said. "I hope Jack Rice and Freckles shoot you full of holes. I hope . . ." Sonny ranted and raved on until he was out of breath. He spat out a mouthful of blood and gasped for breath.

Hibbs began talking, telling Frank everything that had been done to Lara and her son. Frank listened and fought back waves of nausea. When Hibbs finished, the outlaw was crying, tears streaming down his face. "Goody Nolan held a gun on me toward the end," Hibbs said. "They all knew I wanted to kill those men. I rode out right after that. Sonny hooked up with me later."

"I wish they'd a-shot you, Hibbs," Sonny gasped. "You're nothin' but a yeller coward."

"Ride on, Hibbs," Frank told him. "Go on back to your pa's farm and live a decent life. I'll take care of Sonny."

"I don't need no second invite, Morgan. Thanks." A few minutes later, the Nebraska farm boy turned outlaw was riding north.

"You gonna sit there drinkin' coffee and watch me die, Morgan?" Sonny asked.

"I reckon so, Sonny."

"You gonna bury me?"

"I'll plant you."

"That's white of you, Morgan." Sonny closed his eyes and did not open them again.

Frank dug a shallow grave, wrapped Sonny in a blanket, and rolled him into the hole. After covering the body with dirt, he looked at Dog. "Let's get the hell gone from here, Dog."

From a ridge about three hundred yards away, Frank studied the ghost town through the lenses of his field glasses. It certainly looked deserted . . . except for a small finger of smoke coming from the chimney of a building in the center of the old town.

"We end this right here," Frank said. "Right now." He returned to his horse and stripped the saddle off him. Stormy could graze and would not go far. Not after Frank told Dog to stay put. Dog would keep the horse close to where Frank had made a cold camp. Dog might be a cur, but he was very smart and easy to train.

Frank got his rifle and a canteen of water, slung a bandolier of ammunition across his chest, and headed for the old town. He would circle the town and come in from the south, a

direction the outlaw scum he knew were waiting for him
would not expect. It would probably take him a good two
hours of careful going to reach the other end of town, for
there wasn't a lot of good cover.

Frank paused for a brief rest and counted nine horses in
the old livery corral. Figuring a couple of the animals were
packhorses, that meant he was up against seven guns. He'd
sure gone up against greater numbers in his time.

Frank began walking toward the front of the livery. He
got midway there, and a man he didn't know walked up.
The stranger's hand dropped to his pistol and he yelled,
"Morgan!"

Frank put a .44-40 slug into the man's chest. The bullet
turned the man around and sent him out into the weed-grown
and tumbleweed-littered street. He sat down hard, a dazed
look on his unshaven face. Then he toppled over and died.
Frank ran to the livery's front and waited.

Booger Bob stepped out of what used to be the saloon
and onto the warped boardwalk, a Colt in each hand. He
was yelling obscenities at Frank, about Frank. The Drifter
dropped him with one well-placed shot. Booger hit the
boards and rolled off into the street. He kicked and cussed
and then was still.

A man ran out of another building, both hands filled with
pistols. He was shooting as he ran, trying to run across the
wide street. He didn't make it. Frank's shot sent him tum-
bling to the dirt. The man lay still, his life's blood leaking
out of him.

"Hey, Morgan!" a man yelled. "It's me, Goody Nolan.
Can we make a deal?"

"Yeah, Goody, we can."

"We can?"

"You bet. You stick a pistol in your mouth and pull the
trigger. That way, I won't have to shoot you."

"That ain't a bit funny, Morgan."

"That's the only deal you'll get from me, Goody."

"Hey, Morgan!" another man yelled. "It's me, Big Thumbs Parker."

Frank located where the voice was coming from: the second floor of the old hotel. He wanted to keep Big Thumbs talking so he could pinpoint his location. "I hear you, Parker."

"You don't want me, Morgan. I didn't kill that woman or the kid."

"You were there and didn't stop it."

"Yeah ... I was. But I didn't kill neither of 'em. 'Sides, it wasn't none of my affair."

Frank put four fast rounds to the left of the second window. Big Thumbs screamed in pain. Frank heard a thump. No way of knowing if his shots were killing ones.

Goody Nolan decided to make a run for it. He didn't get far. Frank lined him up in the sights and dropped him.

"Dumb move, Goody," Frank yelled.

Goody struggled to get to his feet, flailing around in the street, kicking up dust. He cussed Frank until Frank fired again. The cussing stopped and the dust began to settle around Goody's still body.

"I'll kill you, Morgan!" The shout came from the second floor of the old hotel. Big Thumbs was still alive.

Frank shoved fresh rounds into his .44-40 while he waited.

Big Thumbs suddenly showed himself in the broken window. Frank drilled him. Big Thumbs seemed to rise up on tiptoes, and then did a header right out what was left of the window. He crashed through the old awning to the boardwalk and did not move.

"Just us left," Frank called.

"Hell with you, Morgan," a man called. "You're crazy.

That boy wasn't nothin' to get all excited about. Hell, he liked what I done."

"You're a damn liar, Freckles," Frank yelled.

"It's true, Morgan! I just got tarred of his whining and broke his damned neck."

"Hey, Morgan! It's me, Jack Rice. Your woman was a-prayin' and a-beggin' for you to come rescue her whilst I was pleasurin' myself. When I commenced to skinnin' her, she really got to carryin' on. That was fun."

Frank had left the livery and had run up behind the old stores to the saloon. That was where Freckles and Jack were. He slipped into the rear of the saloon and carefully made his way toward the front. The door from the rear was missing, and he could see Freckles and Jack near the front. Frank didn't hesitate. He lifted his rifle and shot Freckles Burton right in the center of his ass. Freckles dropped his rifle and began howling and thrashing around on the floor.

Jack spun around and Frank shot him in the shoulder. Jack's rifle hit the floor.

Frank stepped out of the darkness and smiled. "Now, Jack. I deal with you."

THIRTY-FIVE

When Jack Rice regained consciousness a couple of hours later, he was tied belly-down across a saddle. His shoulder throbbed from Frank's bullet, but Jack had a hunch his shoulder wound wasn't what he should be worried about.

"Morgan? Where the hell are we?"

"In the desert."

"I can see that! But why are we in the desert?"

"You'll find that out soon enough."

"It's real uncomfortable ridin' this way, Morgan."

"You're about to be a hell of a lot more uncomfortable, Jack."

Tiny fingers of fear touched Jack, overriding the pain in his shoulder. "What are you gonna do to me, Morgan?"

"Time to pay, Jack."

"What the hell does that mean?"

"You'll find out."

"Did you kill Freckles?"

"He was alive when I left him."

"I thought you shot him in the back."

"I guess my bullet went a little low, Jack. Hit him in the privates."

"You shot off his privates?" Jack yelled the question.

"Yeah. He was in a lot of pain when I left him."

"You're a cruel man, Morgan."

"You're a great one to talk about being cruel, Jack."

Jack said no more until Frank reined up and cut the ropes that held Jack belly-down across the saddle. He hit the sand hard and grunted in pain. "I'll walk out of here and hunt you down, Morgan."

"No, Jack. You're not going to walk anywhere. Not ever again."

Frank squatted down a few yards away from Jack, his Peacemaker in his hand. "Tell me about Lara, Jack."

"You'll let me live if I do?"

"You'll be alive when I ride out, Jack."

"You swear?"

"I swear."

"Me and the boys got all the good out of her we could and then I killed her."

"Tell it all, Jack."

"She had nice titties, so I decided to skin one and make me a pouch of some sort. But she was thrashin' around so much I messed it up. I got tired of hearin' her scream so I killed her."

Frank stood up and eared back the hammer of his Peacemaker.

"You said you'd let me live!" Jack squalled.

"I sure did, Jack." Frank shot Jack Rice in first one knee, then the other.

Jack screamed in pain and pounded the earth with his fists. "You blowed off my kneecaps, Morgan. I can't walk. You crippled me, you bastard! Oh, God, the pain is terrible!"

Frank walked to his horse and got his canteen, taking a long drink.

"Can I have a drink of water, Morgan?" Jack asked, his voice shaky through his pain.

"No."

"You're not a decent man, Morgan."

"Probably not, Jack."

"God'll get you for this."

"I'm sure you're right about that."

"I can't stand this pain, Morgan. I never hurt so bad in my life."

"Good, Jack. Pain is good for the soul."

"You're gonna leave me out here, ain't you, Morgan?"

"That's right, Jack."

"I'll die out here, Morgan. I can't walk! I can't use my legs."

"That's a real shame, Jack." Frank looked up into the cloudless blue of the sky. Black dots were circling. He smiled.

Jack followed his eyes. "Them's buzzards, Morgan!" he screamed. "You know what they do to a man."

"You're not a man, Jack."

"Them buzzards will tear my guts out whilst I'm still alive!"

"They sure will, Jack."

"You son of a bitch!"

Frank swung into the saddle. The carrion birds were slowly circling, growing ever closer.

"Don't leave me out here, Morgan! Give me a gun so's I can end it."

"Not a chance."

"Goddamn you!"

"He probably will, Jack." Frank lifted the reins.

"Take me into a town and have me arrested, Morgan. I'll confess to all I done. I swear to you I will."

'No way." Frank took the reins of Jack's horse.

"I don't want to die this way, Morgan."

"I'm sure you don't."

"Morgan!" Jack screamed, his eyes searching the sky frantically. "Them ugly bastards is gettin' closer."

"They sure are, Jack." Stormy began a slow walk away from Jack Rice. Dog padded along.

"You can't let me die thisaway, Morgan!"

"I'm sure Lara and the boy didn't want to die the way they did either."

"I'm sorry about them, Morgan. I truly am sorry."

"You're a damn liar."

"Morgan! Them stinkin' buzzards is so close I can hear 'em and smell 'em. You got to help me. Please, I'm beggin' you."

"Like Lara begged, Jack?"

"Morgan! For God's sake, *help me!* Oh, Jesus, get these stinkin' things off me. *Morgan!"*

Frank rode on.

Jack screamed in agony as the big carrion birds began ripping at his flesh.

"Morgan!"

Frank rode on. He did not look back.

For a sneak preview of William W. Johnstone's next

novel in the *Last Gunfighter* series,

coming from Pinnacle Books in March, 2003,

just turn the page . . .

ONE

Frank rode into Los Angeles and stabled his horses at the best livery in town, telling the stableman to rub them down, wash them, and feed them, hay and oats. Dog, the big cur, would stay in the stall with the Appaloosa, Stormy.

Frank walked to a nearby café and got a sack of scraps for Dog. That done, he checked into a nice hotel, then dropped off his suit and some shirts at Wo Fong's Laundry, then he headed for the nearest barbershop for a long, hot, soapy bath and then a haircut and shave.

A couple of hours later, feeling much better, and smelling a damn sight better, Frank, dressed in a black suit, white shirt, and red kerchief, with his boots polished, stepped out onto the boardwalk and looked around him at the rapidly growing town.

Frank had been told by a proud desk clerk that the population of the town was about fifteen thousand, and when the railroad arrived in a few years, that would more than double, maybe even triple.

Frank whistled and shook head. "That's too many folks for this cowboy," he told the clerk.

Frank was a cowboy, and a damn good one. He'd started off as a cowhand in Texas. Then, when he was just a boy, he'd been forced into a fight and killed a man. The dead man's brothers came after Frank. Frank killed them, all four of them. His reputation as a fast gun grew and spread rapidly. He was still in his teens when the Civil War split the country. Four years later, at war's end, Frank was a captain of the Confederate cavalry. Rather than turn in his weapons, he headed west to become a part of the untamed frontier. In Colorado, he married a beautiful young lady, but the girl's father broke up the marriage. It was years later that Frank learned he had a son. The boy didn't much care for his father, so Frank left it at that and drifted. That's how he got his nickname: the Drifter.

He became a legend: Frank Morgan, the fastest and deadliest gunfighter west of the Mississippi River.

Western Adventures
From F.M. Parker

___Blood Debt___

          0-7860-1093-2 $5.99US/$7.99CAN

They thundered across the Rio Grande as one of the most powerful fighting forces in the world. But disease, ambushes, and the relentless heat turned America's fighting forces into a wounded and desperate army. By the time General Winfield Scott reached Mexico City, some of his men had become heroes, others outlaws.

___Blood And Dust___

          0-7860-1152-1 $5.99US/$7.99CAN

Grant had smashed Vicksburg and cut open the heart of the Confederate States. Still, the war raged on. But the fighting was over for Captain Evan Payson, a wounded Union Army surgeon, and John Davis, a Confederate prisoner of the Union Army. Now, two desperate soldiers have struck a deal: in exchange for his freedom, Davis will carry Payson home to die in Texas.

Call toll free **1-888-345-BOOK** to order by phone or use this coupon to order by mail.

Name_____

Address_____

City_____ State _____ Zip _____

Please send me the books I have checked above.

I am enclosing $_____

Plus postage and handling* $_____

Sales tax (in NY and TN) $_____

Total amount enclosed $_____

*Add $2.50 for the first book and $.50 for each additional book.

Send check or money order (no cash or CODs) to: **Kensington Publishing Corp., Dept. C.O., 850 Third Avenue, 16th Floor, New York, NY 10022**

Prices and numbers subject to change without notice. All orders subject to availability.

Check out our website at **www.kensingtonbooks.com**.

Western Adventures
From Pinnacle